THE GIRL WHO TOOK
WHAT SHE WANTED

ALSO BY DAVID HANDLER

THE STEWART HOAG MYSTERIES

The Man Who Died Laughing
The Man Who Lived by Night
The Man Who Would Be F. Scott Fitzgerald
The Woman Who Fell from Grace
The Boy Who Never Grew Up
The Man Who Cancelled Himself
The Girl Who Ran Off with Daddy
The Man Who Loved Women to Death
The Girl With Kaleidoscope Eyes
The Man Who Couldn't Miss
The Man in the White Linen Suit
The Man Who Wasn't All There
The Lady in the Silver Cloud

THE BERGER AND MITRY MYSTERIES

The Cold Blue Blood
The Hot Pink Farmhouse
The Bright Silver Star
The Burnt Orange Sunrise
The Sweet Golden Parachute
The Sour Cherry Surprise
The Shimmering Blond Sister
The Blood Red Indian Summer
The Snow White Christmas Cookie
The Coal Black Asphalt Tomb
The Lavender Lane Lothario

THE BENJI GOLDEN MYSTERIES

Runaway Man
Phantom Angel

FEATURING HUNT LIEBLING

Click to Play

FEATURING DANNY LEVINE

Kiddo
Boss

THE GIRL WHO TOOK WHAT SHE WANTED

A STEWART HOAG MYSTERY

DAVID HANDLER

THE MYSTERIOUS PRESS
NEW YORK

THE GIRL WHO TOOK WHAT SHE WANTED

Mysterious Press
An Imprint of Penzler Publishers
58 Warren Street
New York, N.Y. 10007

First Mysterious Press edition

Interior design by Maria Fernandez

Library of Congress Control Number: 2022917524

ISBN: 978-1-61316-384-9
eBook ISBN: 978-1-61316-388-7

10 9 8 7 6 5 4 3 2 1

Printed in the United States of America
Distributed by W. W. Norton & Company

For Little Eva,

a genuine flapper who never gave up

on her dream of Hollywood stardom

THE GIRL WHO TOOK
WHAT SHE WANTED

CHAPTER ONE

I saw the Silver Fox drinking a piña colada at Trader Vic's, and her hair was perfect. Then again, my literary agent's helmet of silver hair was always perfect. Everyone in the publishing world called Alberta Pryce the Silver Fox partly because of her hair but mostly because she'd been the shrewdest literary agent in New York City for thirty-five years. Had represented the likes of John Cheever, Norman Mailer, Kurt Vonnegut, and that tall, dashing young superstar Stewart Hoag. That would be me.

And this would be a story from the earliest days of my non-chosen second career as a celebrity ghostwriter that I've never shared with you before. It began almost exactly five years ago in the frigid February of 1989, right there in Trader Vic's, and ended less than a week later on the shores of sunny Southern California. One of the reasons why I've never mentioned it is that the project never got off the ground. Real life got in the way, which it has a nasty habit of doing, and real life ended up costing four people their lives. The other reason why I've kept it to myself is that I promised someone I would. But for reasons that will eventually become clear to you I'm no longer bound by that promise. I should warn you that this isn't a pretty story. No story that involves rich, famous people is ever pretty. But I ghosted half a dozen best-selling celebrity memoirs before I at long last found my own voice again, and I must warn you that this particular misadventure stands out in my mind as the single most sordid.

The Silver Fox was wearing those oversized round glasses of hers that made her look like a devious owl, a burgundy shawl-collared cashmere cardigan, gray flannel slacks, and white silk blouse adorned with a silver brooch of a fox that had been given to her many years earlier by Daphne du Maurier. I wore the charcoal glen-plaid suit from Strickland & Sons, Savile Row, with a pale blue shirt and navy blue and pink polka-dot bow tie. I'd checked my trench coat and fedora along with Lulu's duck-billed rain hat at the coat rack when we'd arrived at Trader Vic's, the famously kitschy tiki bar that was down a flight of stairs in the basement of the Plaza Hotel on Fifth Avenue. An icy cold rain was falling that day and Lulu is susceptible to sinus infections. She snores when she gets them. I know this because she likes to sleep on my head.

For as long as I'd been an aspiring novelist, successful novelist, and stoned-out wreck of a novelist—which is to say for as long as I'd lived in New York City—Trader Vic's had been, by unwritten accord, the designated safe haven where literary and theatrical people could meet in public without meeting in public. If a major Broadway star was cheating on his wife, he could safely meet another woman, or man, for a discreet drink there. If a best-selling author was being lured to another house by its editor in chief, the luring took place there. Once you descended into that dimly lit basement grotto you became legally blind. If you saw someone you knew, you didn't see them and they didn't see you. Liz Smith, Cindy Adams and the other gossip columnists respected this unwritten accord and never so much as mentioned Trader Vic's. Sadly, an attention-starved real estate developer/ tabloid clown named Donald Trump had just bought the Plaza and would soon terminate Trader Vic's lease because he thought the place lacked class. But that winter, it was still the place to be.

Maybe my name is familiar to you. I was, for a brief, golden time in the early eighties, the Silver Fox's hottest client—as big a star as a first novelist could ever hope to be. Hell, the *New York Times Book Review* called me the first major new literary voice of the 1980s. My novel, *Our Family Enterprise,* sold so many copies that it made me rich and famous. I married Joe Papp's loveliest and most gifted young discovery, the Oscar and Tony Award–winning actress Merilee Nash, and for a while we were New York's *it* couple. We bought an apartment on Central Park West with eight windows overlooking the park. We zipped around town in a red 1958 Jaguar XK150 with wire spoke wheels. And we got a basset hound, Lulu, the only dog who's ever had her own inscribed water bowl at Elaine's. I'd kept my crappy, unheated fifth-floor walk-up apartment on West Ninety-Third to use as an office. And it turned out to be a good thing I did because it meant that I had somewhere to live after Merilee kicked me out. The pressure to produce an even bigger and better second novel was too much for me to handle. I got writer's block, snorted my career up my nose and ended up broke and alone, unless you count Lulu. Merilee had been very patient and understanding with me, right up until I started sleeping with her friends. That was when she filed for a divorce. She ended up with the apartment on Central Park West and the Jaguar. She also ended up married to that fabulously successful British playwright Zach somebody.

I read about it in Liz Smith's column.

By the summer of '87 I owed money all over town and was facing the prospect of Lulu and me living out of a shopping cart in Riverside Park, until the Silver Fox talked me into ghosting a memoir for a famous Hollywood comic of the 1950s, Sonny Day, a notoriously difficult nut who'd hired and fired every lunch-pail ghost in New York. But he hadn't encountered me. I'm plenty difficult myself. And my ego is so huge it recently applied for statehood. We fought like crazy, but ended up producing a major best-selling memoir. True, a couple of untimely deaths did occur along the way, but let's not dwell on that.

I bent over, kissed Alberta on the cheek, and gazed at her barely touched piña colada. "Since when do you drink anything other than straight bourbon?"

"I was feeling festive," she said dryly, lighting a Newport with a silver lighter. "Care to join me?"

"Have you ever known me to feel festive?" I slid into the booth across from her, ordered a Kirin beer for myself and a small platter of shrimp tempura for my short-legged partner, who has rather unusual habits—and the breath to prove it. She circled around three times under the table before curling up on my feet, where she waited patiently for her treat.

"And bring me a straight bourbon," Alberta said to our waiter.

"Not feeling festive anymore?" I asked.

"To be honest, I just realized I'm going to need something stronger because of what I'm about to tell you."

Right away, I felt my stomach muscles tighten. "You're not dropping me, are you? You sold my first two short stories to the *New Yorker*. You're the only agent I've ever had. I'll be lost without you. In fact, I doubt anyone else will take me on."

"I'm not dropping you, Hoagy. Stop being a neurotic writer."

"Is there any other kind?"

Alberta studied me through those glasses of hers. "Are you getting any writing done?"

"Feel free to ask me anything else."

"How are you holding up financially?"

"Try again."

"Okay, do you hear from Merilee?"

"She sent me a Christmas card."

"That was cordial."

"Wasn't it?"

Our waiter brought me my beer and Lulu her shrimp. I sampled my beer, found it a bit flat, and sprinkled some salt on it.

"I saw her in that lavish film adaptation of Zach's play," Alberta said. "I hate to say this, because I adore her so, but it's the first performance of hers that I haven't liked. She seemed to be going through the motions."

"I had the very same reaction. Mind you, I thought that his play was hugely overrated, not that I mean to sound bitter or petty."

"Of course not. You're a bigger person than that, dear boy."

"No, I'm really not. But it was nothing more than bad Pinter, and there's nothing that lies flatter and deader on the stage floor than bad Pinter. Putting it on film in the lush, green Dorset countryside didn't help it one bit. Just made it seem even flatter and deader. I could see it in Merilee's eyes. That she knew it was bad, I mean. Not that I've given it much thought."

"She did her best work when you two were together. You inspired her."

"It's true, I did. Right up until I broke her heart." I sipped my beer. "So what are we doing here? What's with all the secrecy?"

"There's someone whom I thought you should meet. Might be something extremely profitable in it for you."

"Another show-biz memoir?"

"Not exactly."

"Why didn't you just tell me about it over the phone?"

"Because if I had you would have said no."

"This sounds mighty promising."

"I've never lied to you, Hoagy. I've got mixed feelings about this one myself. But I figured it was at least worth a face-to-face conversation." She glanced up. "Ah, here he is . . ."

Our waiter was leading a tall, lean, extremely tanned man in his fifties who possessed an aura of confidence and power toward our table, and right away I understood why she'd been so secretive. The only people who are that deeply tanned in February are Left Coasters. We New Yorkers generally tend to develop a ghostly, slightly greenish pallor by mid-January. He was most certainly Hollywood from head to toe with his long, silver-streaked blond hair that he combed straight back and gathered in a pigtail. He wore a tweed jacket, a western-style flannel shirt with snaps instead of buttons, pressed blue jeans, and cowboy boots. He was handsome enough to be a movie actor but wasn't one, although he did appear quite often on television. He was Jack Dymtryk, one of the two or three top entertainment lawyers in the movie business. If one film studio or talent agency was negotiating to gobble up another one, they called in Jack Dymtryk. The man was a great white shark.

But that was only one of the reasons why I knew who he was.

The other was that he was the father of Nikki Dymtryk.

Jack greeted Alberta warmly and gave me an easy, relaxed grin. I stood and shook his hand. His grip was strong, his hand dry. He was an inch or two taller than me, which made him close to six feet five. On his left wrist he wore a Rolex Zenith Daytona chronograph, the watch of choice of professional racers.

"What do you drive?" I asked him.

"A Lamborghini Countach 5000 QV," he said as he sat, ordered a Perrier with a twist of lime, and gave Lulu a friendly pat on the head.

"That's the one with the longitudinally mounted V-12 engine and gull wing doors. Like it?"

"Love it. My wife, Pam, hates it. Or I should say hates the door. She's convinced it's going to fall on her and brain her, even though my mechanic has checked it three times. So I have to open and close it for her."

"That's because she wants to make a dramatic entrance and exit. She is an actress, after all." His second wife, Pam

Hamilton, star of the prime-time TV soap opera *Mill Valley*, was a gorgeous dark-eyed brunette in her midthirties, which made her at least fifteen years younger than Jack.

He gave me that relaxed grin again. "I guess you'd know all about that."

I sipped my beer in silence. At my feet, Lulu made a low, unhappy noise.

"Sorry," Jack said. "Didn't mean to summon sour memories."

"You didn't. They haven't gone anywhere."

"The surf was up Sunday morning," he said, deftly shifting topics. "I took the Countach out to my beach house up past Malibu in Trancas at seven A.M. and cruised PCH—Pacific Coast Highway—at a hundred miles per hour. My idea of a slice of heaven. So is my beach house. I have one of the last of the honest old shacks that's still left out there. I haven't gussied it up one bit since I bought it back in the sixties. I pull into my driveway, close my eyes and I'm the real me again, driving my VW bus with my board in back and the Beach Boys playing 'Surfin' Safari' on the radio."

"You like to surf?"

"Love it. My kid brother, Kenny, and I grew up in Santa Monica. The wrong side of the tracks but walking distance to the beach. Our dad was a plumber. Our mom waited tables at the Fox and Hounds on Wilshire. Surfing was my whole life when I was a teenager. And it's still how I maintain my sanity in this crazy business. Nikki and her sister, Lisa, who's two years older, practically grew up in Trancas when summer vacation arrived. I'd commute to the office as often as I could, and weekends we'd spend hours in the water together. Build a bonfire at night and eat s'mores. They loved it. So did Kenny, his wife Enid, and little Kenny Junior. They'd come out to stay all the time. And if Rita was on hiatus . . ." His first wife, Rita Copeland, had been a gorgeous TV actress, too. The man had a definite type. "We'd slip away to Europe for a genuine vacation while Kenny and Enid would stay out there with the kids."

Kenny was Jack's partner of sorts—the top business manager in town. He handled the financial affairs of everyone from moguls to major screen and rock 'n' roll stars. Worked out of the same suite of offices in Beverly Hills as Jack. Got his undergraduate degree at Dartmouth and his MBA from Wharton. Jack had never left home. Got both his BA and law degree from UCLA.

Our waiter brought him his Perrier and glanced down at Lulu's clean plate. "She wants seconds, maybe?"

Lulu let out a low whoop, her tail thumping.

"That's a yes," I said as he whisked her plate away, chuckling to himself.

"So this is the famous Lulu," Jack said, patting her some more.

"Indeed. I got her in the divorce. Lost the apartment, lost the '58 Jaguar XK150 . . ."

"And a genuine class act when you lost Merilee."

"Correct."

He took a small sip of his Perrier, letting out a rueful sigh. "I lost everything myself when my marriage to Rita imploded." Rita Copeland had been the star of a hit spy series back in the midsixties. Also one of my first adolescent crushes—right up there with Diana Rigg and Anne Francis. No one could flare her nostrils in the super sexy way Rita could. But she was over fifty now and didn't get offered many roles anymore. It's not a kind business for actresses who get paid to be adolescent crush objects. "Pam is wonderful. You'll have to come over for dinner when you come out."

I blinked at him. "I'm coming out?"

He frowned at Alberta. "You haven't filled him in yet?"

"I'm afraid Hoagy still has no idea why he's here. I've left the proposition entirely up to you." Alberta lit a Newport as the waiter arrived with another plate of shrimp tempura for Lulu. "But I should warn you that Lulu's a fast eater, so you have approximately sixty seconds to make your pitch."

"More like thirty," I said, not liking where this conversation was, or I should say wasn't, going. "What's this all about?"

His eyes met mine. "Nikki."

"Alberta was absolutely right. If I'd known that, I wouldn't have come."

The reason being that Nikki Dymtryk was the shallowest, sleaziest, most distasteful celebrity of the past several years, a potent downward drag on American popular culture who had, by the age of twenty-three, enjoyed a meteoric rise to superstardom despite a total absence of any acting or singing talent. Her one and only gift was knowing how to use her blond, beautiful good looks and killer bod to brazenly, calculatingly sleep her way up a ladder of so many male celebrities that she'd become famous for being famous. I considered getting up and leaving right then, but Jack Dymtryk was an important man and I owed him the professional courtesy of at least hearing him out.

But first let me tell you a bit more about Nikki. She never used her last name, by the way. She was simply Nikki, same as Madonna was simply Madonna. Except that Madonna could sing. Kind of.

Nikki's career—I guess I have to call it that—began in 1984 when she was a senior at Beverly Hills High. Nikki, her sister Lisa, Jack, and Rita lived in a hilltop mansion off Coldwater Canyon on a street that bordered Beverly Hills but was technically considered part of Bel Air. Still, Jack called in some favors and got her into Beverly Hills High, same as he had Lisa before her. Unlike Lisa, a serious and highly gifted student at the Otis Arts Institute whose field was fashion design, Nikki was a spoiled wild child who routinely ditched classes to get stoned with her friends. All she wanted to do was party. And she was so rich and beautiful that she was accustomed to taking and getting whatever—and whomever—she wanted. Seemingly, Jack and Rita made no effort to instill any personal discipline in her. They were much too preoccupied with their own lives. Jack was busy having a torrid affair with Pam. And Rita was trying, and failing, to keep her sexpot acting career alive by means of endless rounds of plastic surgery.

Nikki had the looks and the contacts to follow in her mother's footsteps, but no interest in acting, a career that requires training, discipline, and hard work. But she did have ambition, and launched her own career at age eighteen when she asked Jack to snag her and a friend backstage passes to a We Are You concert at the Forum. We Are You was *the* hottest boy band in America. Every teenage girl in the country was gaga over its four heart-throb members—especially lead singer Trey Sinclair.

Nikki promptly maneuvered her way into his bed and his life. When he left the band at her urging to launch a solo career, his first album, *Me, Alone*, became a mega platinum hit thanks in no small part to Nikki's appearance in the steamy video on MTV for his hit single, "Take Me," which consisted of her climbing in and out of bed with him wearing almost no clothing.

In fact, the video was so hot it inspired a hit song by the hip-hop artist H Rapper Brown (né Clarence Jackson) that was mostly a tribute to the awesomeness of Nikki's shapely ass, which led to Nikki modeling that shapely, oiled-up ass in *Playboy*. Practically overnight, Nikki had the distinction of owning the most famous ass in America. She and her famous ass promptly ditched Trey for H Rapper Brown, which did not go over well with Brown's rapper girlfriend, Lil' Bit'ch (née Diane Chichester), who shot up Nikki's yellow Porsche Carrera with a SIG when she spotted it parked next to Brown's Hummer at a club on Sunset that was popular with the young, hot and restless. Nikki was so thrilled by the bullet holes that she decided to leave them there as a mark of distinction. However, things soon turned seriously ugly when Brown got into a shoving match in a recording studio with Da Real (né Reggie Witherspoon), a rough-edged gangsta rapper from Compton who considered himself more authentically street than Brown. Angry words were exchanged by members of the two performers' posses, and later that night Brown was killed in a drive-by shooting at a fast-food restaurant. Da Real and his posse were questioned but not charged due to lack of evidence. A terrified Lil' Bit'ch decided to spend some quality time with her mom in Atlanta and disappeared from the LA scene.

An equally terrified Nikki made a quick career pivot to athletes. Even though she'd barely managed to graduate from Beverly Hills High, Jack had major pull at UCLA, where she was accepted—although she never attended classes. She was too busy seducing the Bruins' golden boy, all-American quarterback Rick Smith, who fell so madly in love with her that he wanted her to move to Buffalo with him when he was selected in the first round of the NFL draft by the Bills. Nikki took a pass, so to speak, and moved on to a Cy Young Award-winning pitcher for the LA Dodgers until his wife got wise to it. After that she changed food groups and jumped into bed with the young star of Steven Spielberg's newest film.

Practically every suburban teenage girl in America wanted to be Nikki. She was rich, blond, and beautiful. Wore incredible clothes. Slept with any hot, famous guy she wanted to. Had no cares or responsibilities. Didn't have to go to school or work or do anything except flit from one celebrity party to another. She was like a fantasy figure to them. She was also a major tabloid celebrity. It was impossible to sneak a peek at the front page of the *National Enquirer* or to flick on *Entertainment Tonight* without bumping into the dirty details of her latest sexcapade.

It was at this point that Jack Dymtryk was approached by a bright, inventive young producer-director who'd just left Merv Griffin Enterprises, the production gold mine responsible for *Jeopardy!* and *Wheel of Fortune,* to strike out on his own. It seemed he'd been having quiet conversations with a second-tier cable channel that was hungry for original programming, and had dreamed up *Being Nikki.* His insanely simple idea was, as the title suggested, to film Nikki being Nikki for an unscripted hour-long "reality TV" show that would run three times a week for twelve weeks and follow Nikki on camera living her fabulous life—shopping for clothes, lunching with friends, going out on the town with whomever she was out on the town with. Wherever Nikki went a camera crew would be right there with her. If she was at home with her family, then the camera crew would be there, too, which meant that Jack, Rita, and Lisa would serve as peripheral characters and go with the improvised flow. But, mostly, the camera would be on Nikki—from the moment she woke up in the morning until her head hit the pillow at night, wherever she was, whomever she was with. The young producer-director would be there at all times to steer things along and suggest ideas for improvised dialogue if the filming turned flat. And, naturally, whatever wasn't lively and frisky would be edited out. But he was positive that a) Nikki was a natural, and b) millions of teenage girls would tune in religiously to watch her living her fantasy life.

As I don't need to tell you, *Being Nikki* ended up becoming not only a major cultural phenomenon but a trailblazer that paved the way for other "reality TV" shows that would follow in the seasons to come, such as Fox's *COPS* and MTV's *Real World*.

Jack Dymtryk wasn't sold on the idea at first. But he was also no fool. If the show flopped, it would run for a month on an obscure cable channel and disappear. If it succeeded, then Nikki, who said she thought it sounded "kinda cool," would become famous beyond her wildest dreams. Rita was all for it. Anything to get back on camera. Lisa, who was painfully shy, wanted nothing to do with it—until, that is, Jack ran the idea past his brother. Kenny was immediately excited about the merchandising possibilities. Nikki was a style icon. Millions of girls wanted to wear whatever she wore. What if Lisa designed a line of sleepwear, sportswear, slinky party dresses, or whatever else she wanted for her? Possibly even branched out into skin- and hair-care products, too? All of which Nikki would wear or use in the show. The family would make millions. Kenny envisioned it as a family business enterprise—a Dymtryk co-production—with the lion's share of the licensing rights belonging to the family. And he was so gung ho that he convinced Lisa to go along with the idea. She designed a silky, slinky, curve-hugging sleep shirt for Nicki to wear to bed in the first episode. Within forty-eight hours of the show's premiere, girls were clamoring for it at every department store in America. They couldn't make them fast enough. And when Nikki dried off after a shower and rubbed her long, beautiful legs with an exotic lemon verbena-scented body lotion that Lisa had devised with an herbalist, it disappeared from the shelves overnight. And that was just for openers.

Being Nikki premiered in the spring of 1986 and garnered a huge amount of attention thanks to the obscenity-laced shouting match in the parking lot of Spago between Nikki and her current movie-star boyfriend—by now she'd moved on to sampling the Warren Beatty generation—and the champagne bottle she hurled at his Ferrari, missing it by ten feet and breaking the windshield of a limo that belonged to Max Diamond, the president of Panorama Studios. The police were called. Max, who'd been getting out of the limo at the time, pressed charges against Nikki. Jack had to fish her out of jail since her middle-aged movie-star boyfriend was long gone by then. There's no such thing as chivalry in Hollywood. Not since Errol Flynn died. Jack drove Nikki home, where she donned the sexy sleep shirt Lisa had designed for her, climbed into bed, and complained tearfully to a sympathetic Rita over the closing credits that all men were "shits." The word "shits" was bleeped out.

The next-day reviews of the premiere episode of *Being Nikki* called it everything from "utter garbage" to "a new low." *Daily Variety* labeled Nikki a "serial slut." The *Los Angeles Times* slammed the show, yet also grudgingly acknowledged that its star was a total natural on camera. "In fact," wrote the *Times*, "it's as if the camera isn't there at all." Meanwhile, her fans responded loud and clear. *Being Nikki* scored the highest ratings that its cable channel had ever received. And when the episode was repeated the following night, the ratings almost doubled. In the second episode, she met up with several friends at a Malibu beach house party, then ended up at another party at the house of a very famous British rock star, where she drank too much, had sex in an upstairs bedroom with a young actor whom she'd known for thirty minutes, and passed out. When she woke up in the morning, alone in bed, she didn't know where she was or how she'd gotten there. She did manage to get a lift home from a member of the catering crew, but she never did find her shoes. Or her panties.

Welcome to *Being Nikki*.

Not surprisingly, several prominent Evangelical Christian leaders called for an immediate nationwide boycott of any companies that sponsored the show, which not only failed but boosted its ratings even higher.

As the wildly successful Season One moved on to Season Two, the Dymtryk family became significantly more fractured and *Being Nikki* morphed into a real-life Hollywood soap opera. First, Jack gathered Nikki and Lisa around the dinner table to inform them in a halting, emotional voice that he intended to divorce their mother and marry Pam. Rita sat through her husband's announcement with remarkable calm because it so happened she had an announcement of her own to make—she'd fallen madly in love with George Moran, the burgundy-voiced six o'clock anchorman of one of LA's network news affiliates. George was a rising star who was targeted for a network anchor slot in New York. He was also fifteen years younger than Rita. No matter. Out moved Jack and in moved George, who married Rita after her divorce from Jack was finalized.

But George turned out to be not exactly who Rita thought he was. For one thing, the anchorman seemed to want a career in show business more than broadcast journalism. By eagerly joining the cast of *Being Nikki* his credibility was so seriously compromised that he was immediately fired as a news anchor—although he did latch on as an entertainment reporter for one of the local stations. His relationship with his older bride then took an unexpected twist when he informed Rita that he was having an affair with Rory Krieger, the house's thirtyish live-in pool boy and handyman. Rory, who had a scraggly Sundance Kid moustache and blond ponytail, hailed from Fresno and had made his way to LA in search of fame and fortune. He didn't get the fortune but he did get the fame when George announced he was moving out of Rita's luxurious master bedroom and into Rory's tiny room off the kitchen. Rita promptly took an overdose of sleeping pills and had to be rushed to the hospital to have her stomach pumped.

What with all these juicy domestic goings on, Nikki's bad-girl sex life began to get less and less screen time in a show that was supposed to be about her bad-girl sex life. As do all meteoric show-biz phenomena, *Being Nikki* hit a plateau. After three seasons, it was still popular but was no longer the sort of must-see TV that was chattered about at office watercoolers. The buzz was no longer buzzing.

And now the Silver Fox, Lulu, and I were having a clandestine drink in Trader Vic's with the Hollywood lawyer/power broker who was Nikki's father.

"I must confess to being a tiny bit lost. What am I doing here?"

"Excellent question," Jack responded. "Right to the point. *Being Nikki* has been a wild success but, just between us, the ratings for the twelve episodes of Season Three fell twenty percent below Season Two. The consensus from the focus group studies undertaken by the cable network was that the younger sisters of the girls who'd tuned in because they wanted to be just like Nikki don't want to be just like Nikki. They want to be just like someone new. Kenny has seen a slide in the sales of Nikki's clothing and beauty products, too. We haven't been canceled. They're perfectly willing to milk it for one more season. But I'm an adherent of the Branch Rickey school of talent management."

"As in it's better to trade a popular All-Star player one year too soon rather than one year too late."

"Exactly. We're pulling out while Nikki is still considered a hot commodity. Being candid, the decision didn't go down too well with the fifty-one people whose livelihoods depend on the show. I'm talking about cameramen, soundmen, electricians, production assistants, and so on. They were supremely pissed off, and I don't blame them one bit. It wasn't an easy decision to throw them out of work. But it was my decision to make and I made it. As a goodwill gesture, I gave each of them a five-thousand-dollar bonus, provided they signed a confidentiality agreement until we're ready to break the news. Which they did, grudgingly I'll admit, but so far each and every one of them has honored the agreement. The public doesn't know a thing about it yet. No one knows, because we want it to appear as if launching Nikki's newest venture is her own idea rather than something that was forced upon her by slumping ratings."

"And what is her newest venture?" I asked as I took a sip of my beer.

"She's going to become a best-selling author."

I did it. I actually performed a genuine, vintage-era Danny Thomas spit take. "Forgive me, but I truly didn't see that one coming," I said, glancing over at Alberta, who was carefully avoiding any and all eye contact with me.

"I've been working with Sylvia James, the editor in chief of Guilford House," Jack went on. "She approached us last fall with what, speaking candidly, sounded like a crazy idea. But after Kenny and I talked it over it started to make a lot of sense. Sylvia sees Nikki, who is currently twenty-three but would most likely be twenty-six by the time the book hits the stores, as someone who Guilford House can position as the next generation's Jackie Collins, which is to say an author of sexy, spicy Hollywood romance novels that would appeal to younger readers, who they happen to be losing in droves. Romance novels, as you no doubt know but I did not, constitute twenty percent of the adult fiction market. They're a vital part of the business. And Nikki has always been an avid fan of them. The bookshelves in Trancas are loaded with the paperbacks she used to devour on the beach. Sylvia has been desperately searching for a young author who can write books that are as racy and uninhibited as Nikki is, and it suddenly dawned on her, well, why not Nikki herself? Nikki's been involved with all sorts of famous men. She knows the movie scene, the rock music scene. And, naturally, readers will be keenly interested in trying to figure out how much of her book is a tell-all in disguise. Sometimes in fiction you can tell the whole truth in a way that you can't in nonfiction."

"Yes, I'm aware of that."

"I'm sitting here talking to a prestigious author and I just said something incredibly stupid, didn't I? What was it the *New York Times* called you? The 'first major new literary voice of the nineteen-eighties'?"

"Something vaguely like that. I don't recall the exact words," I said as Lulu coughed at my feet. She does that because she doesn't know how to laugh.

"Women of all ages will gobble up every word Nikki writes. She's a genuine celebrity. I can see her on *Oprah*. I can see her on *The Tonight Show*. I can see her on a national author tour signing books by the thousands at major bookstores. More importantly, so can Sylvia, who has given her a $250,000 advance with an option for two more books that would bring the total contract to a million dollars. We've already set the Dymtryk family wheels in motion. Lisa is planning to fly to Paris to study the latest designs in eyewear. She wants to put Nikki in a pair of glasses. And she's sketching out an entirely new wardrobe for her that's still sexy but less wild child and more creative freethinker."

"Sounds as if your operation is a well-oiled machine," I said. "You've got everything happening—except for the actual book. Only, Nikki won't be writing a single word of it, will she? You need someone to ghost it for her. Otherwise I wouldn't be here." On Jack's silence I said, "Am I getting warm?"

"Quite warm," he conceded quietly.

I turned to Alberta and said, "Sonny Day's memoir was one thing, but since when do I ghost spicy bodice rippers?"

She lit another Newport, dragging on it deeply. "I'll admit it sounds a bit daft at first, but you might have some fun knocking out a racy story chock-full of sex, drugs, and rock 'n' roll. And you'd be writing fiction again. Absolutely no one will ever know that you're involved. Sylvia is determined to promote Nikki as its author. She genuinely believes Nikki has franchise potential."

I considered this for a moment. "How many, Jack?"

"How many what?"

"How many female romance writers has Nikki already rejected?"

"Nothing slips by you, does it?" he said wryly. "Sylvia offered us our choice of three different women, all experienced middle-aged pros. Each one wrote Nikki the first sixty pages of the book as a kind of audition. Nikki hated their work so intensely that Sylvia tried giving a younger writer a shot. Still no luck. In fact, Nikki blasted Sylvia up, down, and sideways. Told her that every submission she was sending her came across like a crappy formula romance written by a no-talent hack."

"Because that's exactly what they were. Dumb your daughter is not."

"No, she's not. Nikki has a very keen bullshit detector. And, thus far, Sylvia has failed so miserably at finding her the right sort of writer that she suggested I phone Alberta, who's the most astute literary agent in New York, and pick her brain for some other names. Without so much as a moment's hesitation she mentioned you."

"Why me?"

"Because you're on Nikki's wavelength," he said. "You're a rebel. You did the punk-rock scene in the seventies. Had a coke problem. Know the ins and outs of show business. You're also a supremely gifted writer who's way out of the league of the others whom Sylvia has thrown at Nikki so far. I know you happen to be going through a tough time right now. We all go through them. Believe me, I have. When I split up with Rita, I lost nearly everything. All I managed to hold on to was my shack in Trancas. Hoagy, I'm betting that you can do what the other writers couldn't—find a voice for Nikki. I understand that you've lost your own. Maybe this will help you get it back. Meanwhile, you'll get paid $50,000 for your troubles."

"What percentage of the royalties are we talking about?"

"We're talking about no percentage of the royalties," he said, shifting gears from sympathetic confidante to slick Hollywood lawyer faster than you can say INXS. "That's nonnegotiable."

"In that case there's no point in talking any further," I said, climbing to my feet. "Sorry we wasted each other's time, although I genuinely enjoyed meeting you."

Jack glared at me before he let out an exasperated sigh. "You can tell how desperate I am, can't you?"

"It doesn't take a genius to figure that out—although I am one, according to the *Atlantic Monthly*."

"Okay, fine. If you can actually pull this off, I'll include royalty participation."

"I'll need that in writing," Alberta murmured at him.

"You'll get it."

I settled back down in my chair. "Anything else I need to know?"

"That you'd better not fail."

"I won't fail. But why do you say that?"

"Because I know Nikki, and she's going to lose interest in this whole idea very soon and go back to throwing her life away on drugs, parties, and lousy men." Jack ran his hand over his head thoughtfully. "None of the other writers spent any time with Nikki and got a chance to know her before they started writing. Sylvia assured me it wasn't necessary. Looking back, I think it was a mistake to not include her in the early stages of the creative process. What I'd like to do is fly you first class out to LA for, say, a week. You and Lulu both. Alberta has already informed me that you don't go anywhere without her." Under the table, Lulu's tail started thumping immediately. She loves LA in the winter. Balmy weather. Unlimited sushi. "I'll pay you ten thousand bucks out of my own pocket for your time. Rita has a half dozen guest rooms in the *Being Nikki* house. You can stay in one of them. Get a sense of who Nikki is. Listen to what she has to say. I think you'll find her quite intriguing. Just please . . ." He trailed off uncomfortably. "I would appreciate it if you didn't jump in bed with her."

"That would never happen. It would be unprofessional."

"Good," he said with obvious relief. "After a week, you can fly back home and write those sixty pages. You'll still come out ten grand ahead even if Nikki reads them and says no."

"She won't."

"Not exactly lacking in the self-esteem department, are you? Good. If Nikki thinks she can walk all over you, then we'll just be looking at another failed attempt." Jack Dymtryk gazed across the table at me. "Will you do it?"

I looked over at the Silver Fox. "What do you think?"

"Dear boy, if I didn't believe it was a good idea you wouldn't be here. Besides, look at it from another perspective. Exactly how were you planning to pay your rent next month?"

I showed Jack Dymtryk my most earnest smile. "When do we leave?"

CHAPTER TWO

We caught the 9:00 A.M. flight out of JFK the next day. I filled Lulu's antique black-leather doctor's bag with her water and food bowls, a one-week supply of 9Lives mackerel for cats and very unusual dogs, and her favorite snack—a jar of anchovies. She was very excited to be going on a trip. She's always sure that it means we're going to visit her mommy. I couldn't make her understand that her mommy was married to someone else now and that we weren't part of her life and she wasn't part of ours. But divorce is always hard on the little ones.

I didn't bother to bring my 1958 solid-steel Olympia portable, since I didn't figure on doing any typing. Just crammed my briefcase with notepads and reading material. Packed my toilet kit with, among other things, grandfather's straight razor, strop and my Floris No. 89 talc. Choosing what to wear was the hardest part. I was dressing for Nikki. The first impression I made on her would be critical. But I also had to be prepared for business meetings at Jack's Beverly Hills law office and dinners at chic restaurants. The *New York Times* weather forecast had said it would be in the seventies in LA for the next three days, which would make a nice change from the twenty-six degrees the weatherman on WNEW said was the current temperature in Central Park.

With Nikki uppermost in mind, I opted to go unshaven and dress in a navy blue turtleneck sweater that I'd had since college, torn jeans, a well-aged pair of black high-top Converse Chuck Taylor All Stars, and my 1933 Werber A-2 flight jacket. I didn't bother with a winter coat that I'd only need to get me to and from the airport. I'd hung my pinstriped charcoal suit, navy blue blazer, and a pair of pleated gray flannel slacks in my garment bag, which folded snugly in the medium-sized Il Bisonte suitcase that I'd bought in Milan back when I was in the chips. Underneath it I stowed my toilet kit, a pair of well-shined balmorals, shirts, non-torn jeans, T-shirts, socks, and so on.

We caught a cab on West End just after seven, made it out to JFK in plenty of time, and got settled into first class, which we had practically to ourselves that morning aside from a couple of Yushies—Young Urban Shitheads—of the Wall Street variety and the actor John Marley, who was famous for playing gruff studio boss Jack Woltz in *The Godfather*, the guy who woke up with his prized racehorse's bloody head in his bed. I sincerely hoped his presence on the flight wasn't an omen for Nikki's project. The stewardess paid almost no attention to me in my old turtleneck and torn jeans, but made a huge fuss over Lulu, whose tail thumped excitedly as we taxied from the terminal.

I decided to forego the subtle cultural nuances of *Caddyshack II* and make a serious effort to plow my way through *Hollywood Wives*, Jackie Collins's breakout 1983 best seller. It was, for about fifty pages, quite fascinating to read—a soap opera brimming with sexual and materialistic fantasies aimed at horny, bored suburban housewives. What it was not was something that would have much appeal to Nikki's hip young fans. She'd need a book that represented *her* Hollywood of wild parties, sex, drugs, and rock 'n' roll. My guess? The lunch-pail romance writers whose submissions she'd rejected didn't know a damned thing about that world.

I must confess that I maxed out on *Hollywood Wives* after fifty pages. Jackie Collins's overripe prose, shallow characters, and inane dialogue made my eyes start to glaze over. Happily, by then the stewardess was coming around with offerings. Lulu wheedled two shrimp cocktails out of her. I only got one, though I did get two Bloody Marys. My sirloin steak, whipped potatoes, and string beans all seemed to have been coated in a flavorless lubricant that made everything taste exactly alike. Lousy. I'm old enough to remember when the food in first class on a transcontinental flight was actually good. But it's not wise to dwell on such things. That's what boring, middle-aged men do. The ones who wear madras pants, belong to country clubs, and obsess about male-pattern baldness.

After lunch, I treated myself to my reading matter of choice. I was working my way through a collection of essays on film that James Agee had written in the 1940s, which is something I do every few years to remind myself what good writing is.

We made good time. Landed at LAX shortly before 11:00 A.M. PST. It can be quite lovely to fly into LA at night. The sprawling city's lights spread out below you like a blanket of sparkling jewels as far as the eye can see. Arriving during the day is a much different experience. You descend from the pristine desert blue sky into the toxic brown postwar hellscape of smog that we'd created in almost no time whatsoever. We'd even invented a name for it. We called it Progress.

As Lulu and I strolled across the terminal toward the baggage claim area, we passed a small gathering of limo drivers waiting to pick up passengers. Among them was a husky guy in his late forties brandishing a shirt cardboard that had HOAGY written on it with a black marking pen. I hadn't been expecting anyone to meet me, but he wasn't just anyone. As I came to a stop before him, I realized that this six-foot-four, 240-pound slab of man beef was Jack Dymtryk's brother, Kenny, the former Dartmouth offensive lineman who was the top celebrity business manager in town. I'd seen numerous articles about him in the *New York Times*. Kenny Dymtryk could not have looked less Hollywood if he'd tried. Partly it was his sandy hair that he wore in a circa-1957 buzz cut, and his earnest blue eyes, which had no trace of irony in them. Partly it was the roomy cut of his gray flannel suit, which shouted Brooks Brothers. He wore a white oxford cloth button-down with it, a striped tie, and genuine cordovan wing-tip shoes. Believe me when I tell you this—nobody in Hollywood wears cordovan wing-tip shoes.

He gazed down at Lulu, who studied him quizzically, before he grinned at me and stuck out a meaty hand. "I'm

Kenny. Jack told me to keep my eyes open for a basset hound. He said Lulu goes everywhere with you."

"That she does," I said, gripping his hand. "We're a team, like Moose and Squirrel."

Kenny frowned at me. "Moose and who?"

"I take it the names Boris and Natasha mean nothing to you. That you never watched *Rocky and Bullwinkle*."

"I'm afraid I didn't have time to watch cartoons when I was a kid. I had a paper route, mowed lawns . . ."

"You have my deepest sympathy. You were a culturally deprived child."

He let out a husky laugh. "If you say so."

"I wasn't expecting a high roller like you to chauffeur me around town," I said as we started our way toward the baggage claim area.

"Heck, I'm no high roller. I just help people handle their money. And I wanted to have a chance to meet you, because we probably won't run into each other while you're here. I'm at the office day and night, and Enid and I live in Pasadena, not the West Side. My brother loves the glitzy celebrity lifestyle. Enid and I don't. It was no accident that neither of us ever appeared on *Being Nikki*. Enid wanted nothing to do with endorsing Nikki's lifestyle. My wife comes from a very old, distinguished Philadelphia family. Her great-great-grandfather was the chief justice of the Pennsylvania Supreme Court. I met her when I was at Wharton and she was at Bryn Mawr. Her background is boarding schools and cotillions, and she's a deeply religious, conservative Republican, as am I. You don't run into many people like us in Bel Air or Beverly Hills, where pretty much everyone is left wing. Radicals, Enid calls them, although I'd hardly call Jack a radical."

"The two of you look nothing alike," I said as we waited at the baggage carousel for my luggage to arrive.

"So everyone says. I take after our dad, who was a Ukrainian plumber. Jack takes after our mom, who was Scandinavian. I know that you're primarily here to work with Nikki, but Enid sure would love to have you over for tea. You might find our house interesting. We own one of the gabled Greene and Greene bungalows on Hillcrest Avenue. It was built in 1907, which makes it a genuine historic landmark. Since you're a New Englander she thought you might appreciate it."

"That's very nice of her to invite me. I'll do my best to fit it in."

"Enid's also a big fan of your novel, and starved for intelligent conversation."

"She'll have to rely on Lulu for that part."

The suitcases started tumbling their way down the chute and around the carousel. When I spotted mine,

I grabbed it and we headed out the exit into the warm Southern California sunshine. My eyes started to sting immediately from the smog, which always takes me a day to get used to.

Kenny's car was parked curbside. The man could not have been more different from his brother in his choice of rides. He drove a boxy tan Volvo 240 station wagon. He opened the tailgate so we could deposit my bags in back alongside his gym bag and several pairs of size huge sneakers.

"Do you work out a lot?" I asked him.

"Try to. I turn into a fat blob if I don't. The gym that I go to has exercise bikes. I used to run every morning but my knees won't let me do that anymore. My orthopedist told me I have the knees of a seventy-year-old man. That's football for you. And I only played three seasons of Ivy League ball. Those NFL players must need crutches by the time they're forty."

Kenny slammed the tailgate shut and we got in. As he eased away from the curb, I lowered my window so that Lulu could plant her back paws in my groin and stick her nose out into the non-fresh air, her ears flapping in the breeze.

"No regrets though," he added. "I loved playing for Dartmouth. Not that we had a good team. We were just a bunch of big galoots clobbering the snot out of each other in the mud. But I loved the camaraderie. And I loved Hanover, New Hampshire. I felt more at home there than I do here, even though this is where I was born and raised. I was a top offensive line prospect coming out of Santa Monica High. USC offered me a full athletic scholarship, but I turned it down. I wanted to get into an Ivy League school, even though they don't offer athletic scholarships. And I did. Got into Dartmouth on brains, not brawn. Best four years of my life. I loved the place. I especially loved the people. They were genuine. Didn't have any kind of an agenda. Out here, almost everyone who I come in contact with does, and they're so greedy and cutthroat that I have to keep my guard up every minute of every day." He worked the Volvo out of the airport and onto the San Diego Freeway heading north toward Westchester and Palms.

"I understand that you and Enid have a son."

He nodded. "Kenny Junior. He's fifteen and goes to the top prep school in the area, the Buckley School in Sherman Oaks. They have the best record of placing students in the Ivy League, and his grades are excellent. Since I'm a Dartmouth alum, and have contributed quite generously for a number of years, we're hoping he'll be heading to Hanover in three years. Enid and I would very much like to join him. Buy a lake house or a small farm. Enid's been a good sport, but she isn't happy here. She'd love nothing better than to live like a real person again, if you know what I mean."

"I know exactly what you mean. Whenever I'm out here I feel like a stranger in a strange land. Jack told me that you folks do have a soft spot for his beach house in Trancas."

"We had a lot of fun out there when the girls were young and Junior was just a tyke," he acknowledged. "We even used to stay out there with the kids when Jack and Rita managed to squeeze in a trip somewhere. Lisa was a sweet, quiet girl. Just liked to sit on the deck and draw. But Nikki started to get headstrong and just plain nasty when she was, oh, thirteen or so. Would go off and do whatever she felt like. Refused to do a single thing that Enid told her to do. Even called her a 'nasty old bitch' right to her face. After that, Enid no longer enjoyed going there. Sometimes, she'd even stay in Pasadena with Junior so I'd have to watch the girls all by myself. And, believe me, I'm not much of a chef. The three of us roasted a whole lot of hot dogs over an open fire together."

"Did Nikki give you grief, too?"

"Not really. In fact, she'd get kind of sullen and pouty whenever Enid stayed in Pasadena. I think she missed having her around to torment," he recalled with a shake of his head. "We haven't been back to Trancas in years. But one thing hasn't changed—Enid and Nikki still can't stand each other." Kenny continued working his way north through the heavy freeway traffic toward Westwood, passing the off-ramps for Santa Monica Boulevard and Wilshire Boulevard before he got off at Sunset, skirted past the northern edge of the UCLA campus and the Bel Air Gate to Coldwater Canyon, where he made a left and started the steep climb into the high-rent district.

The houses on Coldwater were the usual mishmash of Spanish haciendas, Mediterranean villas, English Tudors, Greek Revivals, and center-chimney Colonials. All were immaculately well maintained, with spotless grounds. I saw no peeling paint. I saw no weeds. Such things are not allowed north of Sunset.

"No disrespect," Kenny said carefully, "but when I mentioned your name to Enid, she was surprised that an author as distinguished as you would consider hiring on to write Nikki's novel."

"I have two mouths to feed. And we both like to eat regularly."

"I don't mean to discourage you, but—"

"It's entirely likely, based on what's happened with the writers who've preceded me, that Nikki and I won't hit it off."

"Well, yeah. That about covers it."

"Not to worry. I'm not like the others."

He pondered this as he continued the long climb up Coldwater. "I've read about your drug problems, and about you and Merilee Nash splitting up. A real shame," he said. Lulu echoed his sentiment with a low moan of displeasure. "My work brings me in contact with so many gifted artists. It seems to me as if you, I don't know, pay a price for your gift. That you're more vulnerable to inner demons. Would you agree with any of that?"

"Only every word."

"This romance novel of Nikki's . . . what'll it be about?"

"I only know what your brother told me, which was barely more than a one-line idea. I haven't spoken to her yet."

"Not even on the phone?"

"Nope, but my sense is that it'll be exactly what her fans want—a racy behind-the-scenes look at the life of a character who bears a shocking resemblance to *her*. They'll want to know what really goes on in the VIP rooms at those clubs on the Strip and at celebrity parties in the Hollywood Hills. And they'll want heaping gobs of sex and drugs."

"Sounds about right," he said with more than a hint of distaste. "Speaking not only as her business manager but as her uncle, I'm concerned that she'll want to include experiences from her own life that the public aren't aware of. Things that might have a negative impact on her image."

"Meaning what, that she's gotten herself into some serious jams that Jack has managed to cover up?"

"No, not that I know of. But she does have a devilish streak, and there's just no telling what sort of secrets she might decide to spill."

I glanced over at him, wondering what he was concerned about. "It's going to be a romance novel, Kenny. Not a tell-all memoir."

"I realize that, but her fans will believe that every word is true."

"You're not wrong about that."

He continued the uphill climb in thoughtful silence. "It's going to make a fortune, isn't it?"

"If it's done right? I don't have a doubt in my mind."

Kenny slowed down for a signal at Cherokee Lane, made a right turn, and began an even steeper climb, then made a quick left at Bowmont Drive, where I recognized Julie Christie's house from the movie *Shampoo*. Then he made a quick right onto Hazen Drive, which was a very quiet dead-end road with the houses spaced far apart from each other.

"See that nice, cozy cottage up ahead there on the left? Rob Reiner and Penny Marshall used to live there when they were married. That's where Jack and Pam live now. Pam bought it two years ago with the money she's been raking in from playing the evil temptress on *Mill Valley.*"

"Is that where we're going?"

"Almost. Jack didn't have to move very far when he and Rita split up. The *Being Nikki* house, which now belongs solely to Rita, is right up at the top of the hill."

Hazen Drive ended at an ornate cast-iron gate mounted on stone posts. Kenny came to a stop, punched a code into the security keypad, and the gate swung open. As it closed behind us, he drove up a twisting driveway that ended at a three-car garage and driveway apron filled with vehicles. In the garage there was a powder blue Mercedes 560SL, a black BMW 325i convertible, and Nikki's infamous bullet-riddled yellow Porsche Carrera. Parked in the apron of the driveway were a white Toyota Corolla sedan, a beat-up blue Ford F-150 pickup truck, a much newer Jeep Wrangler, and two Kawasaki motorcycles.

Kenny came to a halt, shut off the engine, and we got out. It was so quiet up there that my ears started ringing. Lulu immediately nosed her way around the front yard, snuffling and snorting. Me, I gazed up at the house, which was quite familiar from the handful of episodes of *Being Nikki* I'd watched. It was an immense Spanish-style mansion that had been built in the 1930s, I'd guess, with an amazing hilltop view of the entire smog-shrouded San Fernando Valley.

Kenny fetched my bags from the back, slammed the tailgate, and stood there beside me, hugely. He wasn't any taller than me, but he was as wide as three of me. "I'm guessing it's a bit eerie to see it in real life."

"It is. I've strolled around studio back lots many times and it reminds me of one of those big, happy-family houses from fifties sitcoms like *The Donna Reed Show* and *Father Knows Best*."

Kenny let out a laugh. "Tell you what. If you can find *one* genuinely happy person in this house, I'll treat you to the biggest steak dinner money can buy."

We walked up a brick path to the front porch and rang the doorbell. No maid answered it. It was Nikki's mother, Rita, who greeted us, wearing a pink silk blouse and maroon slacks. I have to admit that standing there on the front porch, gazing at her in full sunlight, I barely recognized her as the Rita Copeland who'd been one of the fantasy crush objects of my early adolescence. It wasn't just that her plastic surgeon had pulled the skin across her face so tight that if she'd been a Dick Tracy character her name would have been Fridge Face. Or that when he'd removed the bags under her eyes, he'd also done something to her sagging eyelids so that she now looked vaguely Eurasian. It was also that her trademark 1960s mane of wavy, untamed ash-blond hair had been replaced by a chin-length shag that had been dyed a russet color tinged with henna that I suppose you'd call . . . actually, I'm not entirely sure there's a word in the English language for the color that her hair was. But it was distinctly matronly. *She* was distinctly matronly, as befitted a woman who was over fifty and weighed at least twenty pounds more than she had in her glamour-girl heyday.

"Rita, say hello to Stewart Hoag, the writer," Kenny said. "Likes to be called Hoagy."

"I'm so thrilled to meet you," I said to her. "I've been a huge fan since I was a teenager."

"Pleased to meet you, Hoagy," she said coolly, with what might or might not have been a smile. The poor woman could barely manage to move her mouth. She gazed down at Lulu. "And who is this?"

"My partner, Lulu. She does most of the heavy lifting."

"This is where I say good-bye," Kenny said. "Got to head back to the office."

"Thanks for the ride, Kenny. It was nice chatting with you."

"Likewise." He started to go but then stopped, squirming uncomfortably. "Rita, I'm afraid my prostate isn't what it used to be. May I duck into your powder room?"

"Of course."

"Thanks, old girl," he said, patting her on the shoulder as he darted inside.

"God, I wish he wouldn't call me that. Makes me feel like a nag who's been put out to pasture." Rita gazed at me as we continued to stand there on the front porch with my luggage. "I imagine you were expecting Consuelo to answer the door like she always did on *Being Nikki*. But Consuelo didn't really exist. We've never had a live-in maid."

"So, wait, Consuelo wasn't real life, she was 'reality' life? Boy, I sure am glad I'm not on a major psychedelic right now."

Rita looked at me disapprovingly before she said, "She was played by a very nice actress named Esperanza. In real life, we have two Guatemalan sisters who come three times a week to do the cleaning, laundry, and ironing. But it was suggested to us that Consuelo would fit our image better."

"So, in real life, who shops for groceries and does the cooking?"

"That would be Mona Shapiro, Nikki's personal assistant. She keeps track of Nikki's schedule, or tries to, and also helps out around the house. She's an excellent cook. And my husband, George, is quite a grill master."

"Mona didn't appear in *Being Nikki*, did she?"

"Correct. She didn't fit with Nikki's spontaneous image."

Kenny returned, looking a lot less squirmy. "Okay, I'm off." He handed me his card. "If it turns out that you have a spare couple of hours, Enid would love to have you over. I think you'd get a kick out of our house. The Greene and Greene bungalows are the highlight of any architectural tour of the southland."

"I'd like that. Thanks."

And with that he waved good-bye to Rita and went galumphing back down the path to his Volvo.

"Do come in, please," Rita said, turning slightly flustered. "I didn't mean to keep you standing out here on the porch like the Fuller Brush Man. We have a room upstairs all made up for you. It has a private bath and a lovely view."

She led us inside, trying to play the role of the warm, gracious hostess. And failing. Total despair radiated off her like the wiggly lines in an R. Crumb drawing in *Zap Comix*. On that subject of happy houses filled with happy people, Rita had to top the list of *not*, what with her first husband having left her for a beautiful, much younger actress, and her own much younger second husband, George, having announced to the world on *Being Nikki* that he intended to move in downstairs with Rory the pool boy.

I set my bags down in the entry hall with its antique grandfather clock and chandelier. To my right was the familiar dining room where many a *Being Nikki* scene had taken place. It was a formal dining room that seated at least twelve. To my left was the immense living room. The furniture in both rooms was nineteenth-century French provincial with elaborately carved legs. The living room sofa and chairs were upholstered in a deep purple satin that seemed poorly suited to the sun and fun LA lifestyle. Hanging over the fireplace was a formal oil portrait of Rita from her TV stardom days. Her back was to the artist and her head turned so that she was gazing over her shoulder. It was an old-fashioned star portrait. Think Loretta Young. The other paintings in there were middling French impressionists, most of them landscapes of the Provençal countryside. The living room was seldom used in *Being Nikki*. Much more of the activity took place in the huge step-down den, which ran the length of the back of the house and was a TV fantasy vision of LA, with its floor-to-ceiling glass view of the Valley, its mirrored, saloon-sized wet bar with a half dozen stools, Ping-Pong table, dart board, and a giant color TV that was situated in a seating area of casual furniture upholstered in bright blue cotton.

I heard the tromping of footsteps coming from what I assumed was the direction of the kitchen and in charged George and his lover, Rory, both of them devouring thick roast-beef sandwiches. George looked even more than fifteen years younger than Rita, practically young enough to be her son. With his big chest, broad shoulders, and unusually large, square-shaped head, it was if he'd been constructed to be a TV news anchorman. Although right now he sure wasn't dressed for the part. He wore a white T-shirt with the sleeves rolled up, blue jeans, and motorcycle boots. Rory, who was about George's age, was dressed the same way, though his T-shirt wasn't nearly as new and white. He sported a scraggly moustache and shoulder-length blond hair. Had a wiry build and roughneck swagger about him. His hands were big and work-gnarled.

"We're heading out, babe," George informed Rita in between bites of his sandwich.

"Where are you going?" Rita asked, her voice heavy with dread.

"Taking our motorcycles up around Franklin Canyon Reservoir."

She shot a glare at Rory. I'm certain she would have flared her nostrils angrily at him, too, if only she still could. "You have no work to do?"

"All caught up," he answered with a trace of country twang in his voice as he eyeballed me with cold hostility. "Who's this asshole?" he demanded, which I thought was a bit presumptuous for a pool boy to ask his employer. Not to mention crude. Then again, he was sharing a bed with the current man of the house so I suppose he felt entitled to say whatever he pleased. "And what's he doing here?"

"The name is Stewart Hoag," I said, sticking out my hand, which he refused to shake. Just stood and glowered at me. "Make it Hoagy. And, for future reference, I prefer it that people don't call me an asshole until they get to know me better."

Rory raised his chin at me. "So you're a wise guy. I don't like wise guys."

"Remind me again why I'm supposed to care about what you like or don't like."

"Real glad to know you, Hoagy," George interjected in his rich burgundy voice as he shook my hand. His was soft and a bit moist. "And we're all friends here," he said in a placating voice. "Am I right?"

"By all means," I said.

Rory didn't go near that. Just continued to glower, which seemed to be his go-to facial expression. Something told me that the two of us weren't going to be exchanging Harry and David fruit baskets at Christmas. "You still haven't told me what you're doing here," he said.

"Nothing slips by you, does it?"

Rita let out a miserable sigh. "Hoagy is out here from New York for a few days to talk to Nikki about her book."

"Oh." Rory relaxed his manner slightly. "So you're a writer."

"That's the general idea, though the *New York Review of Books* would disagree with you vehemently."

"And you have a beagle." Rory bent down to pet Lulu, who immediately backed away, growling at him. "Not real friendly, is she?"

"She usually is, but she's very sensitive to insults. Lulu's not a beagle. She's a basset hound." A basset hound that possessed keen instincts about people.

Rory frowned. "You make it sound like she understands what people say."

"Only if they speak English. Her French is terrible."

Again, he raised his chin at me. "You chumping me?"

"Wouldn't dream of it."

"Good, because that would be a really, really bad idea."

"I'll be sure to put that at the top of my list of things to remember."

"Come on, let's go," George said to him.

And off they went, but not before Rory gave me another menacing look.

Rita shook her head disgustedly. "I'm terribly sorry about that."

"About what?"

"That an author of your caliber had to get stuck talking to such human trash. Imagine how it makes me feel to marry a handsome, successful younger man only to lose him to that greasy hooligan. Some nights I feel like barging in on them in bed together and pumping them full of bullets."

"You own a gun?"

"Of course. Everyone who lives in these hills has a gun. It's not as if any of us has forgotten the Manson killings. You don't? Own a gun, I mean."

"Don't need one. I have Lulu. How did Rory come to be employed here?"

"A neighbor had hired him to do some odd jobs around the house, and one day our pool boy wandered off and didn't come back. They're a notoriously unreliable lot. So Jack hired Rory to do some repairs and he ended up moving in."

I heard the Kawasakis roar to life outside and off they went.

"Shall I show you to your room now?"

"Is Nikki here?"

"Yes, she's outside in the pool."

"I'd like to pay my respects first. Alone, if you don't mind."

"You want to establish a rapport. I understand perfectly. Just go out the French doors by the Ping-Pong table and follow the flagstone path."

The flagstone path made a sharp left turn before it led me to the swimming pool, which was big enough to get in a rigorous workout swimming laps, and deep enough to sport a diving board. But Nikki wasn't swimming laps or honing her diving skills. She was floating around on a blue lounge raft wearing a pair of Ray-Bans and nothing else. Her display of nudity wasn't intended to shock me. Had nothing to do with me at all. It was obvious that she always sunbathed nude. Her body was golden brown from head to toe with not a single tan line anywhere. She had a beautiful body, long-legged and broad-shouldered with small, perfectly shaped breasts and not a trace of flab at her waist, thighs, anywhere. She wore her long blond hair tied up in a topknot, the better to expose her neck and shoulders to the sun's rays. She wore black nail polish on her toes, none on her fingers.

"That's okay, don't dress up on my account," I said as Lulu immediately began running back and forth from one end of the pool to the other barking her head off. She has a mighty big bark for someone with no legs.

Nikki peered at me coolly over her Ray-Bans. "You must be Stewart Hoag," she said in that familiar husky voice of hers.

"I must. Make it Hoagy. And that's Lulu who's playing lifeguard."

"Why on earth is she doing that?"

"She's afraid that you're going to drown."

"Is she ever going to stop barking?"

"Not until you get out of the water."

"She's not going to jump in and try to rescue me, is she?"

"Can't. She doesn't know how to swim. Just sinks to the bottom like a stone, glug-glug."

"I thought all dogs could swim."

"She's not like other dogs."

"Yeah, I'm getting that." Nikki squinted at a large wall clock on the side of the house. "Well, I have to get out anyway." She paddled the lounger with her hands over toward the pool's ladder. "Tommy is coming to pick me up soon."

Tommy, her latest conquest, was the young actor who'd landed the starring role in Scorsese's next film.

"I was under the impression that we were going to talk about your novel."

"Sorry, no time. A bunch of us are heading out to a bowling alley in Riverside that hasn't changed a bit since the fifties. Supposed to be totally bitchin'."

"I see. And when will you be back?"

"Today? I won't. Tommy's throwing a bash tonight at his new house in Laurel Canyon and I'm sort of like the hostess. But we can talk about it tomorrow." As soon as she reached the ladder, Lulu stopped barking and joined her there to say hello, her tail thumping. "Oh, you're a sweet girl, aren't you?" Nikki cooed as Lulu licked her face. "Jeez, her breath is kind of . . ."

"She has unusual eating habits."

"What does she eat, dead seals that have washed up on the beach?"

"You're remarkably close. What time?"

"What time what?"

"What time can we talk tomorrow?"

"We'd better get something straight. I don't like to be pinned down."

"And I don't like to be jerked around. I just flew three thousand miles to talk to you about a project your father swore to me is very important to you. If it's not, I'm going to be on the first flight back to New York."

"Like I said, we'll talk tomorrow. Just chill, will you, cuz?"

"I'm very chill. And don't call me cuz."

Her big, sky-blue eyes narrowed. She seemed to regard me as an adversary. Perhaps she regarded most people that way. I didn't know yet. I also had to remind myself that even though she'd been famous for a whole lot of years she was still just a twenty-three-year-old kid. She looked me over, softening slightly. "Nice pair of Chuckie T's. Look like they have some miles on them. How long have you had them?"

"Since my senior year of high school."

"Oh, yeah? Where was that?"

"A small brass mill town in Connecticut that you've never heard of."

"Did Daddy work in the mill or own it?"

"Take a wild guess."

"Owned it. You reek of being a major-league Wasp."

"Big expert on major-league Wasps, are you?"

"Oh, yeah. My Aunt Enid is the queen bee. It oozes from her pores. You'll have to meet her."

"I intend to. I've been invited to Pasadena for tea."

"Twenty seconds."

"Excuse me?"

"That's how long it'll take before she tells you that her great-great-grandfather was chief justice of the Supreme Court of the state of Pennsylvania. She's a stuck-up bitch."

Nikki looked me over me some more. "My dad gave me a couple of your short stories. He said they were published in the *New Yorker* before you became a famous novelist and then crash-landed on coke. Now you're a major burn-out case or you wouldn't be here."

"All true."

"And you used to be married to Merilee Nash."

"Also true."

"What's she really like?"

"I'm not here to talk about her. Did you read my short stories?"

"Haven't had the time."

"Make the time."

"Are you deaf much? I told you, I *don't* like to be pinned down."

"Well, guess what? That's too damned bad. I'm merely laying out a simple scenario. If you haven't read them by the time we talk tomorrow, I'm out of here—as in see you, so long, sayonara. Got it?"

She didn't bother to respond. Too busy squinting at the wall clock again. "Shit, Tommy's going to be here any second." She slid off the lounger, planted a foot on the ladder, and climbed out of the water, treating me to a full-on naked view of the most famous ass in America—which was, I'll admit, pretty spectacular. But I was married to Merilee when she was still in her twenties, don't forget, and hers took a back seat to no one's, as it were.

Nikki dried off hurriedly with a towel. "Pool's not real clean, is it?" she observed. Leaves and dead insects were floating on its surface. "Rory's the worst pool boy on Hazen Drive. Also total scum. When he came to work here, he pulled me aside and whispered in my ear that he intended to stick his tongue up my ass. I slapped his face so hard I gave him a nosebleed. He left me alone after that and moved on to George. He swings both ways, same as George."

"What do you make of him?"

"Who, George? Total idiot. He had a big, big future and killed it when he married Mom and became a character on my show."

"Why do you think he married her?"

"Because he's more interested in social climbing than working for a living."

"Did she know he was bisexual?"

"Hadn't a clue. Mom . . . how shall I put this? Mom isn't real swift. She was a hot young actress with a great bod who never had to use her brain to do things like make decisions. Now the poor thing is totally dazed and confused." Nikki set the towel aside and threw on an oversized Magic Johnson Lakers jersey. "I hated the pages that those other writers sent me."

"So I understand. That's why I've been called me in. I specialize in difficult cases."

Nikki let out a laugh. "I'm a difficult case?"

"That all depends."

"On what?"

"Whether you genuinely care about this book or if it's strictly your family's idea for how to keep you in the limelight."

"No, no. I'm totally into the idea. I think it would be fun to be an author."

"That's the most hilarious line I've heard in years."

"Then why aren't you laughing?" She didn't bother to wait for my reply. Was already hurrying back inside the house to get dressed.

I watched her go, enjoying the feel of the warm sunshine on my face. A horn honked at the foot of the driveway. And honked again, impatiently.

A moment later Nikki, barefoot, came dashing out the same French doors wearing her Magic Johnson jersey and tight jeans, her long blond hair hastily combed out. She was carrying a slinky-looking black dress in a plastic dry-cleaner's bag, a pair of black stiletto heels, and a shoulder bag that doubtless contained her makeup, hairbrushes, and other essentials for Tommy's party.

He honked again.

"Coming, baby!" she called out as she went running down the driveway.

I watched her go, trying to decide if she was going to be worth my time and effort. I wouldn't know for certain until we had an actual conversation, but my initial impression was a resounding no.

"Don't get too comfortable, girl," I said to Lulu. "I don't think we're going to be here for long."

Lulu responded with an unhappy whimper.

My bags had vanished.

Someone had toted them away. I wandered up a grand curving staircase, where more middling French impressionist paintings lined the wall, to the second floor. The first room I arrived at was a bedroom that had been converted into an office. A young woman in a polo shirt, jeans, and Nikes was perched on the edge of a desk talking on the phone to someone about a dinner reservation for eight on Friday night.

"Yes, I *totally* promise that Nikki will be a member of the party. Okay, great. Thank you." She hung up the phone, flashing a smile at me. "Spago. *The* toughest reservation in town. Wolf would have squeezed her in at the last minute but I don't like to leave things to chance. I'm Nikki's personal assistant, Mona Shapiro. I make sure the trains run on time and fend off the tabloids." Mona was alert, take-charge, and talked very fast. "You're Hoagy. And that's Lulu, who is adorable. Come here, you." Lulu moseyed over and got her ears scrunched. "You'll find your bags in your room. It's at the end of the hall."

"Thank you, Mona."

Mona was a nice-looking blond who wore her hair parted down the middle with a couple of purple streaks in it. Her brown eyes were lovely, her lips full, her body toned and fit. Back home in the mill town where I grew up she would have been the prettiest girl in my high school. Out here in sunny Southern California, where the most beautiful women in the world congregated, she was just another blond. Her cheekbones were ordinary. Her chin receded slightly. Out here, she was a personal assistant.

"How did you end up working for Nikki?"

"I was her best friend in high school. She stole my first boyfriend when I was fifteen. In fact, she stole any boy I took an interest in. That's Nikki. The only rules she's ever lived by are her own. That's why she became so famous. Millions of girls wish they had the nerve to do what she does."

"Which is what, exactly?"

"Give the whole world the finger. She does whatever she pleases. Sleeps with any guy she wants. Dumps him whenever she wants. They admire her. I must confess that I'm partly responsible for her behavior. I turned sixteen a year before she did. Had a driver's license and my own car. Late at night I'd drive over here, she'd sneak out of the house and we'd go to frat parties at UCLA. Get bombed, get laid. We were such bad girls. Never went to school. Just ditched class, swam in her pool, and got stoned. No one was ever around. Lisa was a full-time student at Otis. Rita was still getting guest shots and going on auditions. And Jack worked twenty hours a day, plus he had girlfriends up the wazoo. He was a total hound. He drank a lot in those days, too. He doesn't anymore. Pam cleaned up his act. And I cleaned up mine. Nikki didn't. She just kept right on partying. Made an entire freaking career out of it."

"Did you resent it when she became so famous?"

"At first," Mona admitted, continuing to perch on the edge of the desk. "I'm only human. Nikki isn't. There's something otherworldly about her. Besides, she's been a loyal friend to me. Gave me this job, which pays me enough so that I have my own apartment in Westwood. If it weren't for her I'd be waiting tables at Hamburger Hamlet. I work hard but it's like Mr. Toad's Wild Ride around here. Never a dull moment. And I have a great boyfriend, Bobby, who was the assistant director on *Being Nikki*. Although he is *totally* bitter that Jack pulled the plug on the show. Bobby was hoping to get another year of experience under his belt so he could hook on with a network series. He's been banging on doors. No luck, so now he's back to making money the way he used to," she said unhappily.

"Which is doing what?"

"Working as a driver for Daylite Courier. They deliver hundreds of pouches filled with manuscripts, contracts and casting reels every day back and forth between studios, stars, agents, producers . . . They're the biggest outfit in town. The business wouldn't run without them. Neither would half of the talent," Mona added, arching an eyebrow.

"Meaning?"

"Meaning Daylite is the biggest drug dealer in the entertainment industry. Pot, acid, coke, smack, quaaludes, painkillers, you name it. Bobby walks in and out of the offices of major studio executives all day long carrying pouches filled with dope. He was lucky he never got busted before. And I hate that he's back to doing it again, because you just know that if something goes south it's Bobby who the cops will land on, not Daylite. They'll say they had no idea that a rogue driver was using their perfectly legitimate service as a way to peddle dope. If he gets busted, it will be *so* unfair. He's a really, really good guy. Hell, I may end up marrying him. He'd have to ask me, of course," Mona said with a laugh. She glanced down at Lulu, then back up at me. "But Nikki and me, we're good. I consider myself very lucky. I really do."

I nodded, unconvinced. She was only human, like she'd said. It had to piss her off that life had made Nikki into a famous reality TV star and her into Nikki's paid slave whose boyfriend, an assistant director, was back to dealing drugs because *Being Nikki* had gotten yanked off the air due to Jack Dymtryk being a disciple of the Branch Rickey school of talent management. "So the two of you have stayed friends?"

"We still like each other, sure. But we move in totally different circles, as in she hangs with celebs and I don't. Which reminds me, you're expected for drinks and dinner at Jack and Pam's house at six o'clock. And when Pam says six, she actually means six, not the socially correct six fifteen, because she has to be in the makeup chair tomorrow morning at five thirty. They live right down the street."

I nodded. "Kenny pointed the house out to me."

"And now I imagine you'll want to unpack. Also meet Lisa. She and Nikki could not be more different. Lisa's a total loner. Sometimes she doesn't come out of her room for days. You have the rest of your afternoon free unless you have other plans."

"That all depends. Do I have enough time to make it to Pasadena and back by six o'clock? Kenny's wife, Enid, invited me over for tea while I'm here, and based on my initial conversation with Nikki there's a decent chance I'll be leaving tomorrow."

Mona blinked at me. "It was *that* bad? They sure are having a hard time getting this book off the ground."

"Maybe she doesn't really want to do it."

"No, she does. She desperately wants people to think she's smart. In answer to your question you've got plenty of time. I'll call Enid and see if she's free at, say, three o'clock? If you stay an hour, you should be able to beat the traffic back in plenty of time."

"Sounds perfect. Is there a car I can use?"

"You can take Nikki's. Nothing like cruising around Pasadena in a yellow Porsche Carrera that's full of bullet holes," Mona said, grinning at me.

I heard sobbing now coming from behind the closed door of the bedroom directly across the hall. "Rita?"

Mona nodded.

"She do that a lot?"

"I dunno, does every day count as a lot?"

Lisa's room was the one right next door to Mona's office. Mona told me Lisa always kept her door closed so she could focus on her work, so if I wanted to introduce myself I'd have to knock. I knocked. A voice hollered something unintelligible in response

I chose to interpret it as an invitation to come on in. I went on in.

Lisa's room was large and sunny, though aside from the narrow daybed tucked in a corner it was really more of a designer's work space than a bedroom. There was no chest of drawers. No desk. No armchair to curl up in to watch TV. No TV. Just creative clutter. A large, square worktable was heaped with sketchpads and clear plastic boxes filled with spools of thread, buttons, snaps, zippers, and a gazillion other things. There was also a giant glass jar full of Milky Way, Snickers, and Baby Ruth candy bars. One entire wall was shelves stuffed with bolts of material. Another wall, this one covered in cork, had dozens of sketches pinned to it. There was a glass display case filed with *Nikki* skin- and hair-care products. There were two dressmaker's forms on steel rollers, both of them Nikki's size, I imagined, since Nikki was Lisa's only client. One of them had some sort of thigh-high kimono thingy draped over it, loosely basted together, the other a double-breasted navy blue blazer that was currently armless. There was a coatrack filled with Lisa's signature *Nikki* creations—her slinky silver sleep shirt, dark-wash, skin-tight stove-pipe jeans, tie-dyed thong bikini, sleeveless black minidress, splatter-art skirt, and urban chic gangsta hoodie that dated back to Nikki's H Rapper Brown phase. Lisa had been crafting her sister's look since long before *Being Nikki* became a reality TV sensation. Nikki's wardrobe was a big part of her mystique. No one else dressed like she did—thanks to her big sister, Lisa.

Or I should say her older sister, Lisa, because standing there before one of the dress forms, studying the armless blazer, her brow furrowed in concentration, Lisa Dymtryk was no more than five feet four. She was a pale, round-faced young woman with dark brown hair that she wore parted down the middle and cropped at her chin. She bore no resemblance whatsoever to her tall, famous blond sister or to her tall, blond surfer-dude father. She must have inherited her genes from Rita's side of the family. She was chunky through the hips and haunches. Not so much fat as built like a tank. She was dressed in worn, chalk-marked *bleu de travail*, the blue cotton-twill workman's jacket and pants that are ubiquitous in France, and a pair of clogs.

Lulu studied Lisa curiously from the doorway. We both did, since she was gazing in our general direction yet was so lost in thought that she seemed completely unaware that we were standing there.

I cleared my throat, startling her. "Yes, what is it you want?" she demanded.

"Just to say hello. I'm Hoagy. The short-legged one is Lulu. We'll be bunking down the hall. Your father flew me out here from New York to talk to Nikki about ghosting her book."

"Oh, I see." Lisa nodded to herself. "Well, good luck. You're the first candidate that Dad has flown in, so he must have high hopes for you. And I am *loving* your leather jacket. Talk to me about it."

"It's a 1933 Werber A-2 flight jacket. I bought it in a used-clothing store in Provincetown back in the seventies."

She approached me and ran a hand over it, somewhat reverently, before fingering the lining. "I'm going to need a Polaroid of that before you leave. Have you met Nikki yet?"

"Just now. We had a brief, highly unproductive conversation before she left to go bowling in Riverside. She told me she won't be back until tomorrow."

Lisa bent down and gave Lulu's ears a gentle tug. "Nikki has the attention span of a flea. She's also inconsiderate beyond belief. But, hey, she's my kid sister."

"Kind of hard to believe."

"Why, because I'm so short, fat, and ugly?"

"Don't put words in my mouth. Especially those. No, because you're so serious and talented. Mona also told me you're not the least bit socially inclined. You've had so much to do with making Nikki famous. Do you envy her?"

"Envy her? God, no. She's desperately searching for joy and never finding it. All she ends up doing is hurting other people."

"Have you ever had any desire to break away and launch your own clothing line?"

Lisa frowned. "Why would I want to do that?"

"To make a name for yourself. Plus the family has made millions of dollars off you. If you went out on your own, those millions would all be yours."

"When it comes to money, I've already made enough that I'm set for life. Besides, I like this arrangement. I'm left alone to do my thing. And I have *carte blanche* to go anywhere in the world and try out anything I want."

"Your dad told me you're flying to Paris to look at eyeglass frames."

"That's right. I want her wearing glasses when she goes on tour to promote her book. They won't have prescription lenses. Her vision's perfect. But I'd like to create a hip, scholarly image for her. I'm thinking about new-wave tortoiseshell horn-rims, which could work as sunglass frames, too." Lisa moved back over toward the dress forms, her voice rising with enthusiasm. "This is a blazer I'm working on for her. I see her wearing a blazer and slacks. I may even put her in a man's dress shirt and necktie."

"I often wear silk polka-dot bow ties. I have a couple with me if you want to look at them. The colors will really make those blue eyes of hers pop on TV. And if you put her in a man's dress shirt I'd recommend French cuffs so you can design cuff links for her. You might also think about going all out and putting her in a man's suit. Pinstriped, maybe, with pleated slacks. She's definitely got the legs for pleats. Strickland & Sons, Savile Row, make mine. If you stop off in London, tell them you'd like to see samples of what they've made for me. Ask for Mr. Tricker."

Her eyes widened. "Wait a sec, I remember you now. You're *Stewart Hoag*. You used to be big."

"I *am* big. It's the books that got small."

"Sure, you wrote a huge best seller, married Merilee Nash, and *GQ* said you dressed like a Hollywood leading man from the 1930s."

"That's me. I chose what I'm wearing right now because I wanted Nikki to connect with me, and she did. Noticed these old Chuck Taylors of mine right away. But I've packed a few dress things if you want to look at them later."

"Can I look at them now?" she asked me eagerly. "I'll help you unpack."

"Uh, sure, okay. Let me find my room."

"I know where it is." She darted out the door and started down the carpeted hall. Lulu stayed with her. I brought up the rear. "This is Nikki's room," she called to me over her shoulder, indicating a closed door that was three doors down the hall from hers. "And this one is yours," she said, arriving at an open door at the end of the hall.

My room was spacious, with a king-sized four-poster bed, desk, its own bath, and a terrace with a view overlooking the Valley. My suitcase was parked at the foot of the bed along with Lulu's black-leather doctor's bag and my briefcase.

"I love that doctor's bag," Lisa exclaimed.

"I keep Lulu's supplies in it." I carried it into the bathroom and gave Lulu an anchovy to let her know she was home. Filled her water bowl and set it on the floor along with her dinner bowl, which would remain empty for now since it wasn't dinnertime. Then I set my suitcase down on the bed.

"Il Bisonte," Lisa said admiringly.

I unlocked it, opened it, and lifted out my folded garment bag so that I could show her my bow ties and the French cuffs on my dress shirts, along with Grandfather's cuff links, which I'd tucked into an inside pocket of the suitcase. "You can really go to town with cuff links. They're a lot of fun."

"God, I love these," she said, cradling them in her pale, chubby hand. They were twenty-four-karat gold martini shakers.

"My grandfather had style."

I unzipped the garment bag and hung my charcoal pinstriped suit, navy blue blazer, and gray flannel slacks in the closet, spreading them apart so that they could drape freely.

Lisa turned on the closet light and checked out each article of clothing, fingering my blazer's material. "I would swear this has cashmere in it."

"Of course it does," I said, removing my balmorals from their shoe bags and setting them on the closet floor.

Lisa studied them closely. "Nikki has really long feet. I don't see her in heels, and low pumps are a yawn. But a knockoff of a man's balmoral might be interesting."

"I have a two-toned pair for the warmer months. She'd slay in those. And you can go crazy designing socks for her."

"*Socks!*" Her eyes gleamed with delight. "Wow, I had no clue you were going to be such a fount of ideas."

"That's me. A fount."

"While I have you captive can I ask you something else? I'm trying to figure out what type of pen she should use for autographing books. What do you use?"

"A Waterman."

She looked at me blankly. "A what?"

I reached into my briefcase for my gold Waterman fountain pen. "Lisa, if you can return the fountain pen to mass popularity I'll kiss you on both cheeks."

She immediately blushed bright red. "May I try it?"

I dug out a notepad, uncapped it for her, and said, "Give it a go."

She drew some squiggles on the page, then tried out her signature with a dramatic flourish. "I've never used one of these before. It's so different from a ballpoint pen. So much more . . ."

"Elegant?" I suggested.

Mona appeared in the doorway, looking slightly surprised to find the reclusive Lisa with me. She handed me a neatly typed sheet of paper. "Enid will be delighted to welcome you for tea at three o'clock. I've typed out the directions for how to get to there. Also her phone number in case you get lost."

"I won't. Lulu has an unerring sense of direction."

"And here are the keys to Nikki's Porsche."

"She won't mind me driving it?"

"Won't care a bit. The car means nothing to her. The remote control to open the front gate will be in the glove compartment."

"Thanks very much. You're incredibly efficient."

"Just doing my job," Mona said with a smile as she left us.

"Wow, this is so beautiful." Lisa was back in my closet, where she was examining the lining of my suit. "I am definitely going to need Polaroids."

"Knock yourself out. But right now I have to change clothes. Something tells me that Enid would not appreciate me showing up in torn jeans and ratty old sneakers."

"And you'd be right. I should warn you that she thoroughly disapproves of us. Thinks we're nothing but a bunch of immoral, sex-crazed druggies."

"Even you?"

"Me she just considers weird."

"I don't think you're weird at all. In fact, I rather like you."

Lisa scurried out, blushing bright red once again.

CHAPTER THREE

O kay, Mona was wrong.

The remote control to open the front gate wasn't in the Porsche's glove compartment, although I did find two healthy-sized doobies in there, which prompted Lulu to let out a warning growl from the passenger seat when she got a whiff of them. She's very protective of me. Guards against any and all enemies who wish to do me harm, especially when that enemy is myself.

I had to fish around for a good five minutes before I finally found the remote underneath the driver's seat, along with a fistful of parking tickets, an empty half-pint bottle of Jose Cuervo Gold, and a pair of beat-up, ripe-smelling red rubber flip-flops that doubtless could have sold for six figures on the underground celebrity-perv-memorabilia market if I had no moral code whatsoever.

It can be an expensive nuisance sometimes, this moral code of mine.

The Porsche was a thing of beauty, provided you didn't mind the four bullet holes in the driver's side door. I rather liked them. Not just anyone could drive around in a yellow Porsche Carrera coupe that wore the 9mm battle scars of a fanatically jealous Lil' Bit'ch. It was one of a kind.

Lulu settled in comfortably in her seat. She's always appreciated a choice ride, and even though she'd never groused I knew she missed the XK150. She'd loved that Jag almost as much as I had. The Porsche started up with a rear-engine roar that immediately made me aware that it had considerably more power than the Jag. As I backed out of the garage, I rolled down Lulu's window so she could stick her nose out if she wanted to, which she did, then turned around in the apron and eased the car down the driveway, its engine burbling. I used the remote to open the gate and drove slowly down the hill past the house where Jack Dymtryk now lived with his beautiful young wife, Pam. I could feel the car straining to go as I hung a left on Bowmont, drove by Julie Christie's house from *Shampoo*, made a right on Cherokee, and went down the steep hill to Coldwater, where I made a right turn per Mona's typewritten instructions and floored it, working my way out of first gear into second and third as Cold-water climbed its way up, up past Upper Franklin Canyon Reservoir. The Carrera handled snugly and responsively on the curves as I maneuvered my way through the busy midday traffic.

When Coldwater crested at Mulholland, I downshifted and wove my way down, down, down into Studio City. I hit a red light at the intersection of Coldwater and Ventura Boulevard, home to the landmark Sportsmen's Lodge, a wonderfully kitschy survivor from the Rat Pack days. Back in its heyday the Lodge had boasted exotic gardens and man-made streams stocked with rainbow trout that kids fished for while their parents were knocking back martoonis and giant slabs of prime rib inside the sump-tuous dining room. More recently, it had gotten a bit seedy, and you no longer saw anyone fishing for anything. But the hotel was still popular with New York actors who were in town to shoot sitcom pilots or guest shots on the soundstages of the Radford lot, which was walking dis-tance away.

After the light turned green, I got onto the Ventura Freeway, heading south toward the Oak Knoll section of Pasadena, which held the distinction of being not only the oldest and most beautifully preserved section of the greater Los Angeles area but also the exclusive domain of its old-money Wasp elite. According to Mona's directions, Pasadena wasn't much more than a twenty-mile drive on the freeway, but one of the whimsical pleasures of LA life was that its dense freeway traffic made it impossible to estimate how long a twenty-mile drive might take. It wasn't my lucky day. I hit a dead stop bumper-to-bumper bottleneck at the intersection of the Ventura and Hollywood freeways that made forty minutes disappear with a poof. But once I cleared that I sped my way through Glendale, got off at exit 13B, and followed Mona's directions to St. John Avenue, near the lavish Huntington Museum.

It was a staid, prosperous neighborhood. The tree-lined streets were wide, the houses substantial and traditional. I'd felt certain I would get stares from people on the street as I drove along in the bullet-riddled yellow Porsche, but there didn't seem to be anyone out on the streets. They were so devoid of people I felt as if I'd wandered into one of those nostalgic time-travel episodes of *The Twilight Zone*. As I drew closer to Hillcrest Avenue, my destination, the houses started getting much older and much, much grander, and soon I found myself in a historic enclave of gabled Greene and Greene pre-1910 Arts and Crafts "bungalows," which is to say enormous mansions, all of them lovingly preserved and surrounded by acres of manicured gardens. The Greene and Greene bungalows were so rare and prized that architecture students from all over the world made pilgrimages to study them, photograph them, sketch them, bask in them.

And Kenny Dymtryk, a plumber's son from Santa Monica, and his wife, Enid, actually lived in one.

I pulled into their driveway next to a red Saab. Kenny drove a Volvo, Enid a Saab. They were clinging to their East Coast identities by their fingernails. When Lulu and I got out, I discovered that not only was it ten degrees hotter in Pasadena than it had been on Hazen Drive but that the smog was suffocating. Yet that didn't seem to deter anyone from living there. It was incredibly quiet aside from the sound of a gardener hosing down the sidewalk in front of the historic bungalow across the street. No specks of dirt allowed.

I strolled to the covered front porch and rang the bell, properly decked out in my navy blazer, crisp white shirt, polka-dot bow tie, gray flannel slacks, and balmorals. Based on how Nikki had described Enid I was expecting a demure, girlie-girlie finishing-school princess wearing white gloves and pearls. Enid was anything but that. She was tall and rangy, with short dark hair streaked with gray. Not exactly pretty. She had an overbite and too much jaw. But she was attractive in a healthy, tomboyish way.

She was wearing a pale blue spread-collar blouse, a pair of gabardine slacks, and pumps. No pearls. No jewelry at all besides her wedding ring. On her throat, I noticed, she had a significant, jagged scar.

"You must be Mr. Hoag," she said, shaking my hand firmly.

"Make it Hoagy. The short stack is Lulu."

Enid's face lit up. "Oh, I *love* bassets. I had one when I was a girl. Mr. Bumble was my best friend. Are you going to be my friend, Lulu?"

Lulu, who is an Olympic caliber suck up, rolled over on her back and offered Enid her belly, tongue lolling out of the side of her mouth.

"What a cutie." Enid knelt to pet her and got a happy whoop in response. "Say, her breath . . ."

"She has rather unusual eating habits. Lovely home you have here. In fact, this entire neighborhood is amazing."

"That's kind of you to say. I feel at home here. You see, my great-great-grandfather was chief justice of the state of Pennsylvania . . ." Chalk up one to Nikki. ". . . And I grew up on the Main Line in a community of old, established homes where there was a sense of history, continuity, and decorum. A much more structured and formal environment than you find out here. I even went to cotillions. Mind you, I was no porcelain doll. More like a moose," she said with a laugh. "It wasn't until I met Kenny that I found a man who I could actually look up to. Plus he was so strong and handsome he made my heart flutter. When he decided to make his mark out here working with his brother, Jack, I resisted the move, but there's no denying that he's done very, very well for himself. When we got here, we went house hunting on the West Side, since that's where Jack, Rita, and the girls lived and the office was in Beverly Hills. But I didn't like any of the neighborhoods we looked at. I felt very uncomfortable surrounded by so many show-business types, if you know what I mean . . ."

I tugged at my ear. "Yes, I believe I do." *Show-business types* was an age-old expression employed by upper-crust anti-Semites so that they could avoid having to say the word *Jews* aloud.

"Our realtor finally steered us here to Pasadena. Our first house wasn't nearly this grand. But Kenny became very active with the local Republican Party, made excellent contacts with the right sort of people, and we were able to buy this place eight years ago. We feel very fortunate. They so seldom come on the market."

I nodded. Couldn't imagine how much money and pull it took to land a Greene and Greene house.

"We've kept the furniture and lamps that came with it. They belong here. Do come in, please."

The living room was dark and cool in contrast to the bright sunlight outside, and exquisitely furnished in the spare, functional Arts and Crafts oak furniture of the period, which was more delicately proportioned than the sturdier Craftsman style that came along a couple of decades later. There was a loveseat with matching side tables, a pair of armchairs, coffee table, sideboard cabinet. For lighting there were several priceless Dirk van Erp copper table lamps with mica shades. There were no rugs on the polished oak floor. No works of art hanging from the oak-paneled walls. The room itself was the work of art.

Enid steered us down a hallway past Kenny's study, which had floor-to-ceiling bookcases and a vast oak desk, then led us through a sunny day room and out onto a flag-stone patio where a glass table was set for two, complete with ironed linen napkins. The patio was surrounded by a rose garden. Beyond the rose garden there was a huge expanse of lawn and, past that, an orange grove.

An actual uniformed maid rolled an actual tea cart out to us as we sat at the table. The cart was laden with platters of cucumber sandwiches and smoked-salmon sandwiches on thin slices of white bread with the crusts cut off. There was also a plate of cookies, two tall glasses, and a pitcher of iced tea with wedges of lemon floating in it.

"Iced tea is my chief concession to Southern California living," Enid confessed. "If you'd prefer hot . . ."

"No, iced will be fine."

The maid poured me a glass, set it on the table next to me and offered me the sandwich platters. I helped myself to one of each before she rolled the cart over toward Enid.

"Now, Lulu, you come over here and sit with me because we're going to be good friends." Lulu obeyed at once, hoping there was a reward in it for her. "I adored Mr. Bumble so. Cried and cried when he passed on. I'd love to have a dog now, but this house is so precious we're deathly afraid of marring the floors with barf stains, scratches, and the like. Living here is like living in a museum. It's a privilege. But I do miss having a dog." She helped herself to a couple of sandwiches before she said, "I don't suppose there's anything here that would be of interest to Lulu, is there?"

Lulu let out a low whoop.

"She'd be very interested in one of those salmon sandwiches."

Enid looked at me in surprise. "She eats smoked salmon?"

"Loves it. Just be careful or you might lose a finger."

She offered Lulu one of the little salmon sandwiches—which immediately disappeared. "My goodness. Okay, you get one more but that's it or you'll get spoiled. I don't believe in spoiling pets." The second one disappeared even faster than the first before Lulu returned to me and curled up at my feet.

"It's a genuine honor to meet you, Hoagy. I enjoyed your novel so much that I read it twice. And yet, as much as I enjoyed it, I felt that you treated your father unfairly."

It never fails to amaze me how freely total strangers volunteer blunt criticism of my work right to my face. Do they slam their doctor, dentist, or car mechanic that way? Never. Yet I'm someone who has dared to go public with my innermost feelings, so as far as they're concerned that makes me fair game.

"All angry young novelists are hard on their fathers," I said. "That's why we become angry young novelists."

"Have the two of you mended fences?"

"No, he still hasn't forgiven me for refusing to join the family brass mill. Blames me for it going under, and always will, even though nearly all the other brass mills in Connecticut had already vanished. His world had changed. He couldn't accept that, so he chose to take it out on me." I swallowed the last of my cucumber sandwich. "Tell me about yourself, Enid. Did you have a career before you married Ken?"

She let out a polite laugh. "The only job I've ever held was as a summer camp counselor. Believe it or not, I'm an honest to God housewife. I never wanted anything more than to marry a good man and raise his children. I had some difficulties delivering Junior so God didn't bless us with another child, but Junior's a wonderful boy. He's fifteen, already a strapping six feet three, and his grades at the Buckley School are excellent. He has basketball practice this afternoon so you may not see him. What with Kenny being a Dartmouth alum, and generous benefactor, we're hoping Junior will be admitted there. And it's my heart's desire that if he . . ." She hesitated, gazing across the lawn at her orange grove. "That if he's admitted, we'll move to Hanover ourselves. Kenny was very happy there."

"Yes, he mentioned that when he picked me up at the airport."

"He did?" Enid's somewhat horsey face lit up. "It delights me to hear you say that. I'd hate to think it's nothing more than a pipe dream of mine."

"You're really that unhappy out here? Look at where you're living. It's paradise."

"Oh, I keep plenty busy," she allowed. "We belong to the country club so I can play golf or tennis nearly every day, and I do a lot of volunteer work at our church. But I've never felt comfortable out here." Her mouth tightened. "Being candid, I also can't stand my in-laws. Jack has always been a slippery operator and philanderer. Rita is a self-absorbed, clueless dimwit who gobbles so many tranquilizers and sleeping pills that she barely knows what day of the week it is. As soon as she started to lose her looks, Jack traded her in for Pam. And what did Rita do in response? Married a young homosexual."

"George is a young bisexual, actually."

"If he sleeps with their greasy pool boy, then that makes him a homosexual," Enid insisted.

"If you say so."

"I do say so. And, my God, what has that fool woman done to her face? I barely even recognize her as the Rita who I once knew."

"It's a cruel business. Actors are allowed to age. Actresses aren't. Not unless they're incredibly gifted, in which case they can continue to pursue their careers on stage. But Rita was never a powerhouse in the talent department. Just a sexy young thing who is no longer a sexy young thing."

"Not to mention she's an awful mother. Totally failed to instill Christian values in Nikki. That girl is a foul-mouthed tramp who'll do *anything*. Why, she even had sex with one of those rap musicians from the ghetto. My God, that's like jumping into the water with an alligator."

I blinked at her, startled.

"Not that I'm a racist or anything," Enid added hastily.

"No, of course not. You just don't care for alligators."

Now it was her turn to blink at me. "Lisa's the only one for whom I have any use. She's smart, serious, and works hard. I just wish she'd devote her talents to someone besides her awful sister. They repeatedly asked me to appear on *Being Nikki*, you know. Kenny, as well. I flatly refused. I would not endorse that filth. Nor would Kenny." She finished her iced tea, dabbing at her mouth with her linen napkin. "Would you care to stroll the grounds?"

"I'd love to."

"Lulu won't tinkle on anything, will she?"

"She wouldn't dream of it. Mind you, I might."

Enid raised an eyebrow at me. "Bit of a teaser, aren't you? I must tell you that I don't care for teasers."

"I'll try to remember that."

"See that you do," she said abruptly, as I wondered how Kenny could stand to be married to this woman. I was itching to make a mad dash for the Porsche and burn rubber out of there.

Instead, I followed her through a wrought-iron garden gate between two rosebushes and joined her as we crossed several acres of lawn in the direction of the orange grove, Lulu ambling happily along beside us. Enid's stride was long and athletic. This was no casual, relaxed stroll. But nothing about Enid was casual or relaxed.

"Kenny did mention you enjoyed spending time at Jack's beach house in Trancas," I said.

"That was quite a long time ago. It must be ten years since I've been back there. Junior couldn't have been more than five then. The girls were teenagers. I did enjoy Trancas. It reminded me a bit of Cape Cod. Remote and quiet, and that house of Jack's was an honest beach house. Nothing fancy. I loved to jump in the water and swim. The Pacific is so warm and blue, with those wonderful crashing waves. I could stay in that water for hours. If Rita's shooting schedule permitted it, she and Jack loved to travel together. They went to Europe for a month one summer, I remember. Kenny and I stayed in Trancas for the entire time with the girls, who loved to spend their summers there. Kenny would be on the phone working all day, but he loved it. So did Junior."

"Sounds idyllic."

"It was. And Nikki was still a perfectly nice young girl in those days. But she . . . changed when she was thirteen. Became wild, disrespectful, and impossible to control. Jack and Rita should have taken a much firmer hand with her, in my opinion. But they couldn't be bothered. Jack was too busy running around with other women, and Rita's acting career was slipping away and she was in a terrible state. So they let Nikki get away with murder. Lisa was an angel. She'd sit on the deck reading fashion magazines and drawing pictures. But Nikki was a horror. She'd just take off up the beach whenever she felt like it to smoke pot and do God knows what else with some boy or another. Wouldn't tell me where she was going or when she was coming back. Just did whatever she felt like. When I tried to put my foot down, she told me to f-u-c-k off. I must confess that there were times when she made me so angry I'd invent a dentist's appointment for Junior and tell Kenny I had to head home to Pasadena for a day or two. Anything to get away from her. It meant that Kenny had to take care of the girls by himself, but he didn't mind. Lisa was no trouble at all, like I said, and with Nikki he adopted the same attitude that Jack and Rita did. Shrugged and let her go her own way, which I found totally unacceptable. I went back to Trancas less and less after that summer, and would have nothing more to do with Nikki if I could help it."

The orange grove smelled remarkably fragrant, especially considering I'd been in midwinter New York City that very morning, where absolutely nothing was fragrant, unless you're partial to bus fumes and raw sewage. Lulu moseyed her way along, nose to the ground, snuffling and snorting happily.

I stood there gazing at the historic Greene and Greene bungalow that Enid and Kenny called home. It was just as majestic from the back as from the front. "How many bedrooms does it have?"

"Anywhere between eight and ten depending on whether you count the second-floor sitting room and sewing room as bedrooms. The realtors do, the architectural historians don't."

"Still, that's a lot of bedrooms for a family of three."

"Too many. I'm reaching a stage of my life where I'd prefer something much more modest. I keep remembering this dear old farmhouse up in Brooklin, Maine, where my Bryn Mawr roommate lived. She invited me home over Christmas break freshman year. The house had a huge, homey kitchen that was the center of family activity. She had a sister and two brothers, and there was so much laughter and gaiety and love in that kitchen. Her mother still cooked on an immense, old wood-burning stove, and there was a trapdoor in the ceiling directly over it that she opened to warm the upstairs bedrooms, which were unheated. I would love to be baking cookies in that little farmhouse right now," she said as we began striding back toward her landmark mansion.

"What do you think of this idea of turning Nikki into a romance author?"

"Do you want an honest answer?"

"Generally."

"I think it won't pass the smell test. No one will be fooled into thinking she's actually capable of writing a book. God blessed that girl with a beautiful face and a gorgeous body. Given Jack's connections she could easily have followed in Rita's footsteps and landed acting roles on TV. And if she'd possessed genuine talent and a sense of purpose she could have attended a prestigious drama school like your ex-wife did and be on her way to a stage and screen career of great consequence. I admire Merilee Nash tremendously. She has not only beauty but class and breeding."

"She's a Miss Porter's girl."

"As am I, so I've always felt she's a kindred spirit. I'm sorry you two didn't make a go of it."

"That was my fault."

She looked at me sternly. "I hope you learned something from the experience."

"I did."

"And what was that?"

"Cocaine's a really bad thing to get addicted to," I said as Lulu let out a low moan of agreement.

Enid shook her head at me disapprovingly. "How does a man who's as bright as you are let that happen? You should have known better."

"It's complicated."

"That's what people always say to me when they want me to mind my own business. 'It's complicated.' I suppose you think I'm an annoying prude just like the West Side Dymtryks do, but I can't help how I was raised. And I'm proud to be who I am."

"As well you should be," I said, wondering how many more minutes I could stand to be with this woman. I glanced at Grandfather's Benrus as we worked our way back toward the patio. "Sorry I won't get a chance to meet Junior, but I have to be getting along. I have a six o'clock dinner engagement. But I want to thank you. This has been a real pleasure."

"It's been a pleasure for me, too, Hoagy," she said as she led me back inside her cool, silent museum of a house. "I've never had a chance to chat with a celebrated author before. I'll n-never forget this afternoon." Enid's eyes suddenly began to puddle with tears. She struck me as a deeply unhappy person whose inner torment led to dark, scary places where I really didn't want to go. And then there was that jagged scar on her throat.

We made our way back through the living room to the front door and out into the bright sunlight of the front porch, where she shook my hand with a firm grip and patted Lulu on the head. "I pray every day that Junior will be admitted to Dartmouth. I'm so desperate to get back to where I belong, with people who share my values. You must think I'm a terrible snob."

"Not at all. You know what makes you happy and what doesn't. That puts you ahead of eighty percent of the American population. May I ask a personal question?"

"Of course."

"How did you get that scar on your throat?"

Enid's hand went to it instinctively. "When I was twelve, I developed a tumor there. It wasn't a malignancy but I would have become unable to speak if it had been allowed to grow, so it had to be removed. Rita's always telling me that a cosmetic surgeon could make the scar disappear, but I don't believe in hiding life's scars. They're part of the sum total of who we are."

"That would be terrible"

She frowned at me. "What would?"

"To be unable to speak. You were lucky that the operation was a success."

"Yes, I was. I still am. I've always been lucky," she said, though absolutely nothing in her voice indicated that she believed that to be the case.

CHAPTER FOUR

T hanks to the rush-hour traffic it took me nearly twice
as long to make it back to Hazen Drive from Pasadena
as it had taken me to get there. But I was still back in time
to open a tin of 9Lives mackerel for Lulu and to change
into a chambray shirt, non-torn jeans, my Chuck Taylor's,
and my Werber's flight jacket in case it got chilly, which
it often did at night in LA. Mona had emphasized that
when Pam extended a 6:00 P.M. invite, she meant 6:00 P.M.,
so Lulu and I left at 5:55, armed with the keypad code to
open the front gate. I saw no sign of Rita, the lady of the
house, or her husband, George, the square-headed former
anchorman, or Rory, the scruffy, hostile pool boy. Mona

was on the phone and didn't notice me. Lisa's door was closed. The *Being Nikki* house, I was discovering, didn't feel like a house at all. More like the partially abandoned set of a cancelled TV series.

It took three minutes to stroll down the block to the former Rob Reiner-Penny Marshall house. It wasn't a large house. Almost a cottage, really. The garage door was open. Parked inside were Jack's red Lamborghini Countach, a truly remarkable-looking machine, and a tasty silver BMW 3.0 CS Coupe from the early 1970s that I assumed was Pam's. BMW hadn't made many of them and they were quite precious. I was about to ring the front doorbell when I heard voices out in back. I took a brick path around to the floodlit backyard, where Jack was chatting amiably with Rory, who was using a net to clear out the leaves that had fallen into the small, kidney-shaped pool. It was not a large backyard. No lawn whatsoever. Just a retaining wall that surrounded the pool and a raised flower bed brimming with hibiscus, bougainvillea, bottlebrush, and camellias.

"Permission to enter," I called out.

Jack smiled at me. "Come on in, Hoagy. You've already met Rory, I imagine."

"I have, but I didn't realize you worked here, too, Rory. Were you part of the divorce settlement?"

Rory treated me to his trademark glower, convinced that I was mocking him. At my feet, Lulu let out a low growl. She smelled trouble on him. Hell, I smelled trouble on him, too, and I'm not even a scent hound. "I do a half dozen pools on Hazen," he said in a low, quiet voice before he stashed the net in a tool shed. "Sorry again to show up so late, Mr. D. Things just got super squirrely today." Apparently, taking a midday motorcycle ride to Upper Franklin Canyon Reservoir with George was Rory's idea of super squirrely.

"Not a problem," Jack assured him. "Have a good evening."

I smiled at Rory as he left, and got that same glower in return. I still couldn't figure out why he'd taken such an instant dislike to me. I wasn't the least bit interested in George. Or in Nikki, for whom he no doubt still harbored those same unwholesome carnal desires. Yet he clearly seemed to think that I represented a threat to him. Either that or he was just a prick. You have to consider all the possibilities.

There was a trestle table under a pergola off the French doors to the kitchen. A wood-fired grill was heating up, and some good smells were coming out of the kitchen. I could see the lovely Pam in there. Also a man wearing an apron and a chef's toque.

"Come on around so I can give you a proper greeting at the front door or Pam will scalp me," Jack said as he led us up the brick path to the driveway, closing a gate behind us. With his relaxed manner, pigtail, and LA-casual denim shirt, khakis, and beat up Top-Siders, I was struck again by how totally different he and his plodding right-wing brother were. "So how did you and Nikki get along today?"

"We didn't."

"Sorry?"

"I talked to her out by the pool for a grand total of five minutes before she took off to go bowling in Riverside, which she considered a matter of much greater importance than this book project. Tonight she's helping her boyfriend throw a party at his house and won't be home until the wee hours, if at all. I informed her quite plainly that if she can't make some serious time for me tomorrow that I'll be on the first flight home to New York."

Jack ran a long, tanned hand over his silver-streaked blond hair, frowning. "Genuinely sorry about that. I did impress upon her how important it was to make time for you today, but that's Nikki being Nikki. She always has to be the rebel. Back when she was a teenager virtually everyone thought Rita and I went too easy on her, but they had no idea just how headstrong she was. If we'd been more strict with her, I can guarantee you she would have run away with a heavy-metal band when she was fifteen, ended up on heroin, and probably be dead by now." He started to open the front door, then stopped. "I hope you have a patient streak."

"I don't."

"In that case, I hope she gives you the time and attention you deserve tomorrow. If she doesn't, so be it. I won't blame you one bit if you walk away."

"Jack, are you familiar with an outfit called Daylite Courier?"

"Sure thing. Daylite's been around since the fifties. They started with three drivers and one phone. Now they have two hundred drivers and a twenty-four-hour switchboard staffed by something like three dozen operators."

"Sounds like you know a lot about it."

"I know a lot about a lot of things." His eyes narrowed slightly. "Why are you asking me about Daylite?"

"What sort of a reputation do they have?"

"Reputation?"

"Have you ever heard any ugly whispers about them?"

"Such as that they're the largest drug dealer in Hollywood? Everyone knows that."

"Including the LAPD?"

"Including the LAPD, but Chief Gates is well aware that the entertainment business is one of the engines that drives the economy in this city, not to mention shapes its image, so the LAPD looks the other way. Daylite's clientele is studio bosses and world-famous celebrities. It's not as if we're talking about black teenagers selling dime bags on street corners in South Central."

"So who are we talking about?"

He frowned at me. "Sorry?"

"Who owns Daylite Courier?"

"That piece of information is confidential, I'm afraid."

"Meaning it's a client of yours."

"Meaning it's confidential. May I ask why you're so curious?"

"Nikki's assistant, Mona, mentioned it to me. Her boyfriend, Bobby, was the assistant director on *Being Nikki*."

"Sure, I remember Bobby."

"It seems he's had to go back to work for Daylite as a delivery driver ever since you canceled the show. Couldn't find a position anywhere else. She's terrified he's going to get busted."

"He won't, but we can't have Nikki's personal assistant running around with a drug dealer, can we? The tabloids would eat that up. I always liked Bobby. Good kid. Worked hard. I'll call Steve Cannell in the morning and see if he can use him. Steve's got so many shows on the air he can always use an extra hand. Besides, he owes me a favor." Jack patted me on the shoulder as he opened the front door. "I'm glad you brought this to my attention, Hoagy. Now *I* owe *you* a favor," he said, so smoothly that he left me with more questions than answers.

Inside, the living room and dining area were furnished in a modern Scandinavian style, very spare, very chic. There were a few interesting pieces of modern sculpture. Not a whole lot else. They were not into clutter.

"This is quite nice," I said.

"I wish I could take credit for it, but I can't," he said as I heard more noises and conversation from the kitchen. "Pam furnished it long before I moved in on her. She's very big into what they call elegant minimalism. I offered to buy us a bigger place but she didn't want one. We're really quite happy here. We have a master suite. Her gym is in one of the spare bedrooms. I have my office in the other. We don't need anything more. And if we get a hankering for more elbow room we head to Trancas for the weekend."

"Sounds ideal."

"Beats that mausoleum at the top of the hill. Seeing as how Nikki made herself unavailable how did you spend your afternoon?"

"I had tea in Pasadena with Enid."

His blue eyes widened in surprise. "What on earth for?"

"I was invited."

"What was your impression of Enid?"

"That she doesn't seem particularly happy here."

"She isn't. Neither is Kenny, even though he grew up here. It won't surprise me one bit if they pack up and head back east one of these days."

"Will you be okay with that?"

"I'll miss Kenny. He's my kid brother, and he's done more than I could have imagined to generate a family fortune out of *Being Nikki*. But there's no reason why he has to be here if he doesn't want to be. His other clients' business affairs can be taken over by someone else in the office, or he can continue to handle them by phone. That's not so unusual. My own stockbroker lives in New York. We talk on the phone once or twice every day." Jack ran his hand over his hair again, which he seemed to do when he was mulling something over. I sincerely hoped he didn't play high-stakes poker, because it was a definite tell. "Kenny and I grew up in the same house. Hell, the same bedroom. But we were always different. I was the surfer dude who liked to party. He was the football player who went to church every Sunday with Dad. School was easy for me. Kenny had to work his tail off. Never had fun. Never dated girls. Just studied. And when he did finally start dating, he chose Enid, who's the most uptight, self-righteous snob I've ever met. Nikki goes out of her way to be horrible to her. She does have a mean streak. Got that from me. I'm not the nicest guy in the world. You don't become an A-list entertainment lawyer by being Mr. Rogers."

"How does Nikki get along with Kenny?"

"Well enough. She doesn't have very much to do with him. It's Lisa who does, what with all the fashion and beauty products she's created." He glanced over in the direction of the kitchen, lowering his voice slightly. "Did you get a chance to talk to Rita?"

"I did. She doesn't seem to be a particularly happy either."

"What gave you that impression?"

"She told me that some nights she feels like barging in on George and Rory in bed together and pumping them full of bullets. She owns a gun, you know."

"Never forget that Rita's an actress. Believe me, that will never happen. She'll just take tranquilizers and weep. I genuinely feel badly about what happened between us. But I had to follow my heart. I love Pam. And, for what it's worth, I advised Rita *not* to marry that blockheaded anchorman. I thought he was an opportunist. Little did I know that he'd take up with Rory."

"What's *his* deal?"

"Who, Rory? He's just your average no-class handyman—aside from the fact that he's sleeping with my ex-wife's husband." Jack smiled warmly as Pam Hamilton came breezing in from the kitchen. "Ah, there you are."

"Here I am. I'm supposed to call you Hoagy as opposed to Stewart, right?" she said to me cheerfully, showing me her dimples and perfect white teeth. "I'm so glad you could join us. Dinner will be ready soon, and I did *not* make it myself. We have a chef on call if I'm short on time. I must warn you it's not a very elaborate meal. I have to watch my diet or I turn into a blimp."

"I find that hard to imagine."

"You and I are *definitely* going to be friends," she said with a laugh.

I liked Pam right away. She was relaxed and unpretentious—a second-generation Hollywood performer who'd made her first on-screen appearance when she was six. Pam was in her early thirties now and had a curvy but trim figure, flawless milk-white skin, pillowy lips, and dark bedroom eyes under carefully sculpted brows. She'd combed out her shiny black hair so that it was parted down the middle and fell to her shoulders. As the resident bad girl on *Mill Valley*, she wore it piled in an elaborate coif that doubtless took the stylists an hour to construct. She was casually dressed in jeans, a burgundy cotton pullover sweater, and Arche slip-ons.

"And this must be the famous Lulu," Pam said as she sat down on the sofa. Lulu immediately joined her there and was treated to a belly rub, which set off all sorts of argle-bargle noises. Lulu loves to be doted on, especially by gorgeous, cuddly ladies. "You're a sweetie, aren't you? I'll bet you're just dying to lick my nose, aren't you?"

"Be careful what you wish for," I warned Pam, joining them on the sofa as Jack settled in an armchair.

"Hoagy, it's such a treat to have you here," she said. "I love to be around writers. My dad was a screenwriter, as you may know. It was so much fun when he'd have his buddies over for Sunday brunch. They had such quick wits."

"I hope you're not expecting anything like that out of me."

She let out another laugh. "Somehow, I knew you were going to say that."

Pam's father, Arthur Hamilton, had written several popular screen comedies in the fifties before he moved on to writing and producing TV sitcoms. Her mother, Kim Dale, had been a contract player at Metro who specialized in playing the leading lady's wisecracking best friend before she moved on to a solid career in sitcoms herself.

"Are your folks still with us?"

"In a manner of speaking. They moved to Palm Springs about ten years ago. I can't stand the place. It's practically a Hollywood retirement village. But they love it. Their friends live there. They play golf. Go out to dinner together. And I do understand how they feel. This is not a good town to grow old in. You get reminded ten times a day that you're a has-been. Better to cash in your chips and leave." She sat there, stroking Lulu. "So I have to ask you something, if you don't mind."

"You want to know what Merilee's really like," I said.

Her eyes widened in surprise. "How did you . . . ?"

"Everyone asks me that."

"And what do you tell them?" Jack said.

"That she's a terrific person. Down to earth, smart, funny. She doesn't take herself too seriously. The work, yes. But herself, no."

"I'm just so in awe of the depth that she brings to a role," Pam said.

"As am I."

Pam tilted her head at me slightly. "You still love her, don't you?"

"I'll love her until the day I die. But when I didn't have a second book in me, I ended up making a total mess of things."

"Do you think you ever will have a second book in you?"

"I believe I will. I have to believe I will. But sometimes it takes years for another idea to percolate, and unfortunately that's not how the publishing business works. I wrote a red-hot first novel and they heaped a lot of money and pressure on me to deliver a second one right away. I wasn't up to the task, so I self-destructed and drove her away. Not a day goes by that I haven't regretted it." On Lulu's grumble I added, "*We* haven't regretted it."

Pam took my hand and squeezed it. "I didn't think I'd survive after my own first marriage fell to pieces." She'd been married to a TV Western star who was a champion hell-raiser. "But then I met Jack and I've never been happier."

"That goes double for me," he said. "Hey, I'm being a terrible host. I haven't offered you anything to drink. A client of mine just sent me a case of wine from his vineyard up in the Napa Valley." This was the new Hollywood thing—buying vineyards and competing over who could make the best wine. "I uncorked a bottle before you got here so it could breathe. We haven't tried it yet. It's a Burgundy. Are you feeling adventuresome?"

"Absolutely. Let's give it a try."

He went over to the bar in the den, poured three glasses from the bottle, handed Pam and me ours, then sat back down with his.

I sampled mine. I'm not a big Burgundy fan. It tends to be too heavy for my taste. This one was so heavy I immediately had visions of Lucy and Ethel standing in a barrel stomping on the grapes in their bare feet.

Pam took the tiniest of sips before she put her glass down on the coffee table and didn't look at it again. She clearly didn't care for it either.

Jack sampled it carefully before he said, "I love this guy, but I'm switching to an ice-cold Corona long neck. Care to join me, Hoagy?"

"I wouldn't say no. And you needn't bother with a glass."

"My kind of beer drinker. A sherry for you, sweetheart?"

"Just a bit, please."

He poured a small glass of sherry and brought it to her, then went into the kitchen, got two beers out of the refrigerator, popped them open, and returned with them. After he'd handed me one and we'd each taken a gulp, sighing contentedly, he said, "I am informed that dinner is ready whenever we are."

We brought our beers with us. Pam left her sherry glass in the kitchen and poured herself a glass of Perrier. We sat at the table outside under the pergola. There was a light, cool breeze but it was very comfortable out. The on-call chef, who was young and Asian, had prepared grilled teriyaki chicken thighs, brown rice, and a salad of grated jicama, cucumber, and mango. It was very simple but also very tasty. And it worked wonders for getting the taste of Lucy and Ethel's feet out of my mouth.

"This is delicious, Brad," Pam said to the chef as she took careful bites of the small portions she'd taken.

He thanked her, closed the French doors, and got busy cleaning up.

"My acting career hasn't exactly had the same trajectory as Merilee's," Pam said wryly. "When I was six years old, the studio was positive I was going to be the next Natalie Wood. Then I moved on to playing wholesome, clean-cut teenagers. After *Easy Rider* came out, I wasn't exactly the type that they were looking for anymore so I quit the business. Enrolled at USC, majored in history, and tried living a totally normal life. But I soon found that a totally normal life is incredibly boring so I stuck my toe back in the water and started doing guest shots on episodic TV. I'd always been prepared and professional, and my folks were well-liked, so the networks found a niche for me. I played sympathetic young schoolteachers, sympathetic young mothers, sympathetic young police officers. And now, at long last, I've finally graduated to playing a full-fledged slut. It's really fun playing a bad girl for a change. *Mill Valley* is pure fluff but it's popular and we have so many characters and subplots that I don't have to work super hard. It's not like playing the lead role in a detective show where you're stuck in a trailer out in Pacoima for fifteen hours every day. And I do love it when the tall guy and I can get away to Trancas for the weekend."

Jack sipped his beer, smiling at her fondly.

"Sounds as if life is good," I said.

"Never better," she responded. "I just wish I could get him to stop working so hard. The phone is always ringing." As if on cue, it rang inside the house. "See what I mean?"

He got up to answer it.

"Let the machine take it, Jack," she pleaded. "We're eating."

"Sorry, I can't. I've got some major irons in the fire right now and timing is everything." He took it in the kitchen, where Brad was wiping down the stove. He was only on for a second before he returned and said, "Actually, it's for you, Hoagy. Nikki's assistant, Mona. She apologized but said it's important."

I got up, went inside, and picked up the phone. "What's up, Mona?"

"I'm so sorry to bother you but I just got the strangest phone call here from *Merilee Nash*. She said she needs to speak with you."

I considered this for a moment. Why on earth would Merilee need to speak with me? And what could possibly be so urgent that she'd figured out how to track me down in LA? "Did she leave a number where I can reach her?"

"She's waiting to hear back from me, and when she does, she'll call you there. I know it's none of my business but she sounded . . . upset."

"Okay, I'll wait right here for her call. Thank you." I hung up, stepped outside and said, "Please excuse me, but I have to wait for a call. Shouldn't be long."

"Go right ahead," Jack said.

Pam nodded in agreement as the phone rang.

I went back inside, Lulu following me this time, answered it, and said, "This is Hoagy."

"It's me, darling," Merilee said with a distinct quaver in her voice.

A wave of panic washed over me instantly. I knew that quaver. It was her bad-news voice. My imagination raced, wondering if the next words out of her mouth were going to be *grapefruit-sized tumor.* "What's going on, Merilee? And how on earth did you find me?"

Lulu whimpered at my mention of her name, gazing up at me imploringly.

"I-I left a half dozen messages on your machine, but when you didn't return any of my calls, I tried Alberta. She told me you were out in LA on a potential project and gave me the number of the house where you're staying. The woman who answered the phone was nice enough to find you for me. Hoagy, we . . . need to talk." Now she sounded as if she were on the verge of tears. "Can you come over this evening? I hate to bother you but it's *terribly* important."

"Merilee, I'm in LA, remember?"

"So am I. I'm at the Four Seasons. Rob Reiner wants me to do a project for Castle Rock. I got in a few days ago."

"Amazing. This is a small town the same way New York is."

"How so?"

"At this very minute I'm having dinner in the house that Rob used to live in when he was married to Penny Marshall."

"Who lives there now?"

"Pam Hamilton and Jack Dymtryk."

"Don't trust that man. He's the sort that gives lawyers a bad name."

"I didn't realize they had a good name. So we're both here at the same time. What a pleasant surprise." On her silence I said, "Or not. I'll be finished here at eight thirty, nine at the latest. Pam has an early makeup call. Shall I meet you in the bar there?"

"No, what I have to tell you is very private. I . . . don't want anyone eavesdropping. Besides, Lulu is bound to make a scene."

"That's because she misses you terribly."

"Come up to my suite. I'm in 1031."

"Merilee, what on earth is—?"

"I'll fill you in when I see you. And please tell Pam that I saw her in an episode of *Cagney & Lacey* a while ago and thought she was wonderful."

I hung up, my head spinning. Then I shook myself and went back outside, Lulu sticking close to me.

"Is everything okay?" Pam asked me, her brow furrowing with concern.

I sat down. "I truly don't know. That was Merilee. She needs to see me, and she sounded very upset."

Jack studied me with concern. "So are you flying back tonight?"

"No, she's here in town talking to Rob Reiner about a project. I'm meeting her at the Four Seasons later. Oh, and Pam? I'm supposed to tell you that she saw you in an episode of *Cagney & Lacey* and thought you were wonderful."

Pam's eyes widened. "She *said* that?"

"She did."

"I may faint."

Jack reached over and stroked her arm affectionately. "Listen, guy, if you want to cut out right now we won't be offended."

"Thanks, but she's not expecting me until nine o'clock. Besides, I'm hungry and this meal is delicious."

We went back to eating.

"So, tell me, do you get along well with Nikki?" I asked Pam.

Pam let out a laugh. "Does anyone? She doesn't think I'm an evil home-wrecker who broke up her happy home if that's what you're wondering, because she knows she didn't have a happy home."

"Exactly," Jack said.

"I guess you'd call our relationship civil. We're different ages and we move in different social circles, but she comes over and uses the pool here whenever the gardeners are up at their house ogling her and making lewd comments. She's always welcome here. So is Lisa, but Lisa mostly stays in her studio and works. I don't think that poor girl has any fun at all."

"I'm guessing Lisa doesn't have a boyfriend."

Pam finished her small portions of dinner and patted her mouth with her napkin. "Not that I'm aware of. She's Nikki's polar opposite."

"I think Lisa's very talented," I said. "But I'm afraid I told her something this afternoon that she didn't care to hear."

Jack gazed across the table at me. "Which was . . . ?"

"That she ought to strike out on her own."

He sipped his beer, nodding. "I agree with you."

"You do?"

"I keep telling her that very same thing myself. But she lacks the confidence to launch her own clothing line. It's just not in her nature. She's content to stay in Nikki's shadow, or seems to be."

I cleaned my plate and drank down the last of my beer.

At my feet, Lulu immediately started whimpering impatiently.

Pam looked at her in amazement. "My gosh, it's almost as if she knows you're about to go see Merilee."

"Believe me, she knows," I said. "Would you mind terribly if I skipped out on dessert? Merilee did sound awfully upset."

"Of course not," Pam said. "It was such a pleasure to meet you. Come back any time."

"Thanks, it was nice meeting you, too. Dinner was superb. And I love your house."

Jack walked me out front by way of the brick path. "Do you have wheels?"

"I've been using Nikki's Porsche."

"I hope everything is okay with Merilee. If I can help in any way, just holler, okay? And *please* let me know if Nikki makes time for you tomorrow, because if she doesn't I intend to intervene. This is an important project for us."

"May I ask you a strictly personal question?"

A brief look of dread crossed his face. Just a flash, but it was there. "By all means."

"Do you believe that she genuinely wants to do this book?"

He looked at me in relief. So much relief that I wondered what he'd been afraid I was going to ask him. "I do believe it," he said with total conviction. "Nikki's one hundred percent committed to it. She just . . ."

"She just what?"

He ran his long, tanned hand over his silver-streaked blond hair. "She just doesn't know it yet."

⚭

The Four Seasons, which was on Doheny in Beverly Hills, catered to the show-business crowd—so the valet parking guy was not the least bit fazed by the bullet holes in Nikki's Porsche. Just handed me my stub and wished me a good evening. The concierge and desk clerk paid me and my short-legged friend no mind at all as we strolled across the lobby toward the elevators and took one to the tenth floor.

Merilee hadn't been wrong about Lulu making a scene. She could smell Merilee's Crabtree and Evelyn avocado-oil soap from halfway down the corridor, made a mad dash to 1031, and pounced on the door, letting out a wail that was worthy of the large, demonic hound in *The Hound of the Baskervilles.*

When Merilee opened it, Lulu charged into the room, yelping until Merilee joined her on the floor of her suite's sitting room and hugged her and let her lick her face all over. "Yes, I've missed you, too, sweetness. Yes, I have. Is Daddy feeding you enough treats? I'm sorry there are no anchovies in the minibar."

"No anchovies in the minibar?" I said in astonishment, closing the door behind me. "I'm shocked, shocked. And to think that this used to be a first-class hotel."

When Lulu finally calmed down, Merilee stood up, tossed her waist-length golden hair, and gazed at me with those mesmerizing green eyes of hers, which right now happened to be red and swollen from crying. I hadn't seen her in over two years but the effect she had on me was the same as ever. My heart started pounding. My knees went weak. I could barely breathe. It was no different from that very first time I'd seen her seated at a table with a mutual friend at the Blue Mill on Commerce Street down in the Village. A fragile little creature Merilee Nash was not. She stood six feet tall in her white gym socks. Was wearing her complimentary Four Seasons terry-cloth robe over a sweatshirt and sweatpants. No makeup. She never wore any unless she was working. Didn't need any. Not with

*

those eyes and sculpted cheekbones and her trademark high forehead.

She leaned over and kissed my cheek. "Thank you so much for coming, darling. Can I offer you anything besides an anchovy? A beer?"

"I'm all set, thanks."

The suite's sitting room had a sofa and an armchair. She settled on the sofa with her legs curled under her. Lulu immediately joined her and got fussed over some more. I sat in the armchair, studying my ex-wife. Clearly, she was emotionally distraught, but I hadn't the slightest inkling why. She'd tell me when she was ready, and no sooner.

"Alberta was a bit unclear on the phone about what it is you're doing out here," she said, gazing at me.

"That's because it's a deep, dark secret."

"In that case, do tell."

"I may be working for Nikki."

"Ghosting her memoir?"

"Nothing quite that dignified. Guilford House has decided that she has a major future as an author of hip, steamy Hollywood romance novels."

"You're kidding me, right?"

"I wish I were. Obviously, they need someone to write it for her . . ."

"Obviously."

"And, apparently, she's not easy to please. So far she's dropkicked four lunch-pail romance writers, all women. She wants something that'll break the mold. Something explosive. Something *Nikki*. Out of sheer exasperation Jack sought out Alberta's advice and she suggested that perhaps a male novelist with Hollywood ties and a punk-rock era background who happened to be flat broke might have better luck. I'm picturing it as a giddy fantasy of what it's like to be a wild and sexy aspiring actress. Lots of glitz, sex, parties, drugs, and . . . did I mention sex?"

"You can write that in your sleep."

"Which would be great. It would leave my days completely free. Jack's paid me ten thou to fly out here and meet her. I got in this morning and she gave me five minutes of her time before she took off to go bowling in Riverside. Right now she's in Laurel Canyon at her latest boyfriend's party. If I don't get her complete attention for a solid hour tomorrow morning, I'm flying straight home. But if I do end up ghosting it, I'll get paid fifty thou. Alberta thinks it could actually be good for me. Start me writing fiction again, even if it is trash."

"It won't be trash if you write it. What's more, I agree with Alberta. It might be a good thing for you to write someone else's fiction. Unless, that is, you have an idea of your own."

"Nothing yet. Not a thing."

"I read the Sonny Day memoir, you know."

I looked at her in surprise. "Why, no, I didn't know."

"I thought you did a wonderful job of capturing his voice."

"Thank you, Merilee. That's kind of you to say."

"But what a strange, disturbing story it turned out to be."

"It certainly wasn't what I was expecting."

She hesitated, tilting her head at me slightly. "How are you, um, feeling these days? You certainly look healthy and fit."

"I'm fine. Haven't touched any coke in three years. Keeping busy, as you can see. I'm just . . . wistful. I miss our sunshine days."

"I know," she said softly, her eyes shining at me.

I gazed out the terrace doors at the lights of downtown LA in the distance. "So what does Rob Reiner want?"

"It seems he's had a dream for years to film a remake of his all-time favorite Hollywood romance."

"*Wuthering Heights*?

"Guess again."

"*Now, Voyager*?"

"Guess again."

"*An Affair to Remember*?"

"Guess again."

"Abbott and Costello Meet Frankenstein?"

"Okay, now you're just being you. *Random Harvest* with Ronald Coleman and Greer Garson."

"That's a hell of a good movie."

"It is. I've always adored it. And he's got a verbal commitment from Jeremy Irons to play Smithy *if* the right actress agrees to play Paula."

"And I'm guessing that you're the right actress."

"Jeremy seems to think so. So does Rob."

"And what do you think?"

"I'm hesitant, honestly. Greer Garson was *so* fabulous in it. I'm not convinced that I can bring anything fresh to the role. So I stroll over to Castle Rock every day and Rob and I talk it out. He's a genuinely nice guy, full of ideas and enthusiasm. And he likes working with actors. Started out as one himself, you'll recall."

"That's right. He was Meathead in *All in the Family*. How's the script?"

"Getting better and better. Three different writers have worked on it so far. And Rob and I have been tweaking Paula's dialogue."

"Is Jeremy here, too?"

"No, he's in London." She fell into an uneasy silence. Took a deep, ragged breath and let it out slowly before she said, "And he's not the only one who is . . ."

I frowned. "Meaning?"

"I-I'm divorcing Zach," she informed me with that same quaver in her voice. "He's moved out of the apartment and gone back to London. I wanted you to hear the news from me rather than read about it in Liz Smith's column."

I nodded calmly even though I was doing cartwheels inside. For the first time in years I had an actual chance to get back to where I once belonged. I still believed that we were meant to be together. Had never stopped believing it. "What happened?"

"Marrying Zach was a mistake, that's what happened. You knew it, too, didn't you? But you were too much of a gentleman to say anything."

"You and I weren't speaking at the time, actually."

"Yes, but you always see things more clearly than I do. When I was in his play on Broadway after you and I split up, he swept me off my feet. His West End hit was now a Broadway hit. He'd sold it to the movies for a fortune. He was hard at work on a new play, and just so confident and full of energy and ideas."

I nodded knowingly. "Everything I wasn't."

"Let's not go there, please. That's not my point. All I meant was that he was wonderful to be with . . . until he wasn't. Making the movie was a miserable experience. He fought constantly with the director, who banned him from the set. So then he started fighting with me. When the movie flopped, he blamed everyone but himself. And when his new West End play closed after eight performances, he pouted like a little boy. I . . . I was fooled by him. He's not a man. He's also not a major talent. Just someone glib who has no genuine depth." She looked at me steadily with those green eyes. "Not like you."

"Why, Merilee, that's the second nicest thing you've ever said to me."

"What's the nicest?"

"'Are you going to tear my blouse off or do I have to do it myself?'"

She let out a laugh that quickly turned into tears.

I got up, shoved Lulu over to make room on the sofa—amidst a great deal of protest—and gave my sobbing ex-wife a hug.

She held on to me tightly. She's strong. I'm talking boa constrictor strong. "I feel so, so emotionally wrung out. It's truly been a welcome distraction to work with Rob. He's incredibly upbeat and creative."

"Does he want to film *Random Harvest* on location?"

"Absolutely. Liverpool, the country village, all of it—which will be marvelous, although I must admit that there was a magical charm to that sweet little cottage of theirs on the MGM soundstage."

"And will you still call out, 'Oh, Smithy?' when he finally finds his way back there?"

"I have to. It's one of the most famous lines in movie history. I just don't know if I can measure up to Greer Garson. She was so strong, so *alive*."

"It was a different era, and you're a different kind of actress. Less theatrical, more reality-based," I said as her eyes studied mine. "You'll bring new dimensions to Paula that she didn't. And you'll be great. I have total faith in you."

"Bless you for that, darling."

"Kind of odd, isn't it? The two us both being out here at the same time."

"It is," she agreed. "Especially because you abhor coincidences."

"I do?"

"You once told me that you considered coincidences the hallmark of shlock storytelling."

"Yeah, that sounds like me. I may only be here until tomorrow, like I said, but if I end up sticking around maybe we can get together."

"I'd like that. Call me when you know what's going to happen with Nikki." She reached for a Four Seasons notepad on the end table, scribbled a phone number on it, tore off the sheet, and handed it to me. "Here's how you can reach me at Castle Rock. And thank you so much for coming over. I feel much better now. I'm sorry I was so emotional."

"Never apologize for being your genuine self."

"Wise words. Who was it that said that?"

"I did, just now. And I'm truly sorry about Zach."

"No, you're not. You're as happy as a clam at high tide."

"I never could fool you, could I?"

"Don't even bother to try, handsome."

"Well, I'd better head on back to Chez Dymtryk. Come on, Lulu."

Lulu didn't get up from the sofa. Didn't so much as budge.

"Come on, girl," I said as I started for the door.

She still didn't budge.

"Sweetness, you have to leave," Merilee said, her eyes getting shiny again. "I'll see you again before you go back. I promise."

Lulu stirred grudgingly, making low, unhappy noises, and made a slow Bataan death march across the sitting-room carpet for the door.

Merilee joined us there, patted Lulu, and gave me a hug. Not a quick hug. A lingering one, before she pulled away and said, "I'm glad you're healthy again. May I ask you a personal question?"

"You can ask me anything, Merilee."

"Are you seeing anyone?"

"A therapist, you mean?"

"No, I mean do you have a woman in your life?"

"Oh." I tugged at my ear. "Yes, as a matter of fact I do."

Her green eyes searched mine intently. "Tell me about her. Who is she?"

"You."

It was past eleven o'clock by the time I worked Nikki's Porsche back up Coldwater to Hazen, Lulu continuing to grumble unhappily in the seat next to me. I finally had to tell her that if she didn't shut up I'd cut off her anchovy treats for a month. All the lights in the *Being Nikki* house were out except for a porch light and one upstairs light, which I guessed was a nightstand light in my room that Mona had left on for me before she took off. She was a pro, that one. I hoped she found something more productive to do with her life than making dinner reservations for Nikki.

I parked the Porsche in the garage. As I got out, I smelled cigar smoke coming from the direction of the backyard and heard a man clearing his throat. I opened the gate, strolled back there, and in the blue lights of the pool, spotted George stretched out on a lounge chair in jeans and a hooded sweatshirt, puffing on a cigar and sipping from a brandy snifter as he gazed out at the lights of the San Fernando Valley.

Lulu moseyed over and nudged his arm with her head to say hi.

George slowly turned his large, blocky head and gave me a half wave. "Care for a nightcap?"

"I'm good, thanks."

"Rory conked out an hour ago. He puts in a hard day of work. I don't do much of anything, so I have trouble sleeping sometimes. And when I do my, wheels start spinning."

I rolled a lounge chair over next to his and stretched out. Lulu managed to make herself comfortable on my legs with her head on my tummy. "Anything in particular worrying you?" I asked him as I stroked her.

"My future, or total lack thereof. I've fucked up my life big time."

"Big time as in you were in line for a network anchor slot in New York and instead you got married to Rita, became a regular on *Being Nikki*, and now you're a lowly entertainment reporter for a local station?"

"That pretty much covers it. I'm genuinely fond of Rita, and our relationship was intensely sexual at first. But she's in her fifties and not as active as I'd like to be. When I met Rory, a jolt of electricity went through me. I've never understood why, but when it comes to men, I've always been attracted to poor white trash, which Rory most definitely is. I knew instantly that the two of us would end up in bed together. I just hadn't anticipated that it would be on national TV. Rita intends to divorce me, so it'll be no more sipping brandy by the pool for this reporter. I'll be living in a one-bedroom condo in Encino cranking out two or three stories a week and spending the rest of my time being a public laughingstock. I doubt I'll see much of Rory anymore because, well, why would he bother?" George glanced over at me. "Can I let you in on a little secret? I was never really on New York's radar screen. That was just a rumor that my agent started. I hit my ceiling as a local news anchor. I'm not network material. Not nearly smart enough. I'm just a dumb cluck who has a good voice and can read a prompter."

"If I'd known you were holding a pity party, I'd have gone straight to bed."

"Sorry, I'm just not feeling really proud of myself right now."

"You're a young guy. You've still got plenty of time to change careers. Was there anything else you wanted to do before you got into TV journalism?"

"Actually, that's what I was just thinking about. What I really wanted to be was an actor. And I still figure that if a total stiff like Lee Majors can be a TV star, why can't I? The guy can't act a lick and he hasn't missed a day of work since *The Big Valley*. I took drama classes in high school and college. Maybe I ought to hook on with a top acting coach like Jimmy Best and see what I can do. I'm plenty comfortable in front of a camera. And I enjoy a fair share of notoriety, which casting agents love."

"Sounds like a plan. Where did you grow up, George?"

"You're looking right at it. A tract home in Van Nuys. My dad's a pharmacist at a Rexall in Encino. My mom's a kindergarten teacher. I studied broadcast journalism at Arizona State. Wanted to be a drama major, but one of my acting teachers steered me to broadcast journalism because he said I had a strong on-camera presence and a *sonorous* voice. That was the word he actually used. I had to look it up in the dictionary. I must admit he gave me good advice. As soon as I got my degree, I instantly landed a weekend anchor slot at a station in Tucson, then became their five o'clock anchor before I ended up right back here in my hometown. LA is considered a stepping-stone for the networks. Tom Brokaw and Connie Chung both came out of here. And there was every reason for people to think I had a shot, too." He reached for the decanter and poured himself another slug of brandy. "I was the only one who knew I didn't stand a chance." He paused, puffing on his cigar. "One Sunday afternoon I emceed a charity event in Newport Beach that Rita was hosting. We got to talking and hit it off right away. I have to confess, I was madly in love with her when I was thirteen."

"Ditto. There was Diana Rigg. There was Anne Francis. And there was Rita Copeland. She was one hot babe."

George chuckled softly. "Ain't that the truth? And when I looked at her that day in Newport, I still saw the same Rita Copeland of twenty years earlier. When we got married, the tabloids made a great big joke out of our age difference. It's perfectly okay if the man is older, the way Jack is older than Pam, but when the roles are reversed, it's a whole different deal. We didn't care. We were happy and had a very healthy sex life for a while, like I said. But I couldn't keep away from Rory. The attraction was too strong."

"How well do you and Nikki get along?"

"She thinks I'm a phony opportunist who snatched up her mom on the rebound because I smelled money. As for me, I can't stand the spoiled bitch," he said with sudden savagery. "She's a taker who leaves a trail of ruined lives in her wake and doesn't give a shit. I'm just sorry she wasn't *in* that Porsche when Lil' Bit'ch shot it full of holes." He glanced over at me. "I guess I shouldn't say things like that, but this is not my first brandy."

"And what about Lisa?"

"She's so quiet I hardly know she's here. Just works on her clothing designs in her room. There's something strange about her. She reminds me of a little girl sitting on her bedroom floor dressing her Barbie dolls. Except she has her very own life-sized Nikki dolls to play with. There's Hollywood Nikki. There's Malibu Nikki. Lisa hardly ever leaves the house. Has no man in her life. She just plays with her Nikki dolls. I find it weird. Don't you find it weird?"

IF YOU WRITE THIS BOOK YOU WILL DIE

Those were the words that were typed on the piece of paper that I found waiting for me in my bed when I crawled under the covers. Just what I needed after a long, exhausting day. A death threat. Unless, that is, there was some other way to interpret it.

IF YOU WRITE THIS BOOK YOU WILL DIE

Nope. It was a death threat, no question, typed on a plain sheet of typing paper. I stared at it a moment before I fetched the directions to Pasadena that Mona had typed for me on her IBM Selectric. I examined the two sheets of paper carefully by the bedside light as Lulu watched me curiously from the foot of the bed where she'd sprawled, ready to call it a night.

They hadn't been typed on the same typewriter. Entirely different font. Which ruled out Mona, unless she had a second typewriter in her office. But why on earth would Mona leave me a death threat? Had her bitter boyfriend, Bobby, put her up to it? What could he hope to gain by doing that?

So who else had access to my room, owned a typewriter, and, for some reason, didn't want me to write Nikki's steamy romance novel? Lisa? Hell, she was already designing the wardrobe for her sister's book tour. Rita? She seemed way too overwhelmed by her own woes to care one way or the other about her younger daughter's foray into new-wave bodice rippers. George? What further harm could the novel do him? Rory? He'd made it plain that he had no use for me and wanted me gone. But direct physical confrontation struck me as more his style. Besides, I doubt that he even knew how to use a typewriter. Nikki herself? Was it possible Jack was totally wrong about her and that she wanted nothing to do with this book? Was that why she kept rejecting writers? Was that why she'd avoided me today? It was certainly a possibility, but *why* wouldn't she want to do it? She'd merely be called upon to promote the damned thing. Self-promotion was what she was good at and, seemingly, lived for.

IF YOU WRITE THIS BOOK YOU WILL DIE

I'd been threatened before, when I ghosted the Sonny Day memoir, but that book had involved deep, dark show-biz secrets that would have a serious bearing on someone else's future career. This *wasn't* a tell-all memoir. It was fantasy escapism. No animals would be harmed in the making of this motion picture. So why on earth did someone want to scare me off?

I tucked the note in the nightstand drawer. It would be something else to talk to Nikki about tomorrow, if indeed we did talk. I also decided I'd head home tomorrow whether we did or we didn't. I'd had enough of this nuthouse.

And in case you're wondering, the answer is yes, I did get up and lock my bedroom door before I turned off the nightstand light and fell into an exhausted sleep.

CHAPTER FIVE

I was still sound asleep when someone knocked loudly on my door at 7:00 A.M. and called out, "Room service!"

I staggered out of bed in my Sea Island cotton boxers, and opened it.

It was Nikki, looking impossibly perky and fresh-faced. Also outrageously sexy in her trademark slinky, curve-hugging sleep shirt. Her nipples poked right through the clingy silver material. She was carrying a tray that was laden with a French press coffeemaker, two mugs, and the *Los Angeles Times*. "It's currently fifty-seven degrees in the southland," she announced in a loud, clear voice. "But it's supposed to get up to seventy-four by this afternoon, so it's me for the pool later."

"I think you've missed your true calling," I said, yawning hugely as I propped up my pillows and climbed back into my nice warm bed. "You should have been a weathergirl."

Nikki put the tray down on the desk, worked the French press expertly, and poured out two mugs of steaming, fragrant espresso as Lulu watched her guardedly from the bed. "Did you know it's *freezing* in here?"

"I like to sleep with the windows open."

"Can I climb in there with you?"

"That's up to Her Earness."

Lulu considered it a moment before she moved over to give Nikki space. True, Nikki was young, sexy, and mostly naked. But business is business.

Nikki handed me my mug, set hers down on the other nightstand, turned back the blanket, and stretched her long, smooth, gorgeous bare legs under the covers, pulling the blanket back up.

I sipped my espresso, which tasted even better than it smelled. "Did you make this?"

"Of course," she said, sipping hers. "Why do you look so surprised?"

"I had no idea you were so multifaceted."

"There's a lot about me you don't know, and will never find out. By the way, you're not in bad shape for a guy your age."

"'A guy my age?' I'm thirty-five. There are professional athletes my age who are still performing at the top of their game. Besides, I'll have you know I was once the third-best javelin-hurler in the entire Ivy League."

Her sky blue eyes gleamed at me over the rim of her mug. "Little bit touchy, aren't you, cuz?"

"And don't call me cuz." I took another grateful sip. "So what's brought on this heartwarming display of domesticity?"

"Couldn't help it. I'm so incredibly excited I'm about to burst."

"And why is that?"

"Well, if you'll shut up I'll tell you. I was still incredibly wired when I got home from Tommy's party so I—"

"Which was when?"

"This morning."

"So you haven't gone to sleep yet?"

"I was still wired, like I said. Are you even listening to me?"

"I'm listening. I'm just not totally awake yet."

"So I got into bed and read those two *New Yorker* short stories you wrote when you were still in your early twenties. My dad had them Xeroxed for me. They're all about being young and crazy back in the New York punk era. Getting high, bopping around on a motorcycle at four in the morning . . ."

"Yes, I remember. Some of it, anyhow."

"Let me tell you, I was knocked out. The characters are so *real* that they jump right off the page at you. I mean, you're incredibly talented."

"Tell me something I don't already know."

"And modest, too." She grinned as she lay propped up against her pillows next to me. It was hard to believe that she looked so bright-eyed and beautiful after going a night without sleep. The wild life still hadn't left its mark on her. But she was only twenty-three. It would catch up with her soon if she kept on partying the way she did. "I've got to read your novel now, too, which is supposed to be amazing. Anyway, I want you to write my book. You and nobody else."

"I see . . ."

"Try and sound a little more thrilled, will you?"

I pulled the death threat from my nightstand drawer and handed it to her. "It seems that not everyone agrees with you."

She stared at it. "What's this shit?"

"Found it when I got into this very bed last night."

She handed it back to me. "My mom," she said airily. "She probably mixed her pills with too much booze and was reenacting an episode of her old spy show. She does that sometimes. Slips back into character and can't tell TV from reality. And, believe me, three seasons of *Being Nikki* wasn't exactly healthy for her between the ears."

"Does she have a typewriter?"

"There's a typewriter around here somewhere. Mona has one for sure."

"This wasn't typed on Mona's."

"I really wouldn't sweat it. This house is full of wackos, but we're harmless. The important thing is that I want *you* to write my book, not one of those lady authors. You *get* me, which is weird because you don't have a vagina."

"Not that I'm aware of." I drank some more espresso, which I needed a whole lot more than she did. "Before I say yes I'd like to know some things about you."

"Fire away. I'm all yours until nine, when I have to go visit one of my ex-boyfriends at Cedars-Sinai."

"Which one?"

"Teddy Bear." The Teddy Bear to whom she was referring was the drummer for one of rock 'n' roll's longest-running British supergroups. "He OD'ed on smack at a party two nights ago. Almost didn't pull through."

"I could have sworn I read in the *New York Times* that he was admitted for an emergency appendectomy."

She looked at me with pity in her eyes. *Pity.* "You don't actually believe those stories, do you?"

Nikki had an uncanny ability to make me feel naïve, even though I had a decade on her and had been around the block more than a few times myself.

She held her mug in her long, slender fingers, gazing down at it. "So what do you want to know about me?"

"Why you crave so much attention."

"I don't."

"Oiling up your bare butt in *Playboy* isn't exactly avoiding it."

"That was a hoot. Do you honestly think any other eighteen-year-old girl in America would have said no if she'd been asked?"

"Fair point."

"What else do you want to know?"

"I'd like to understand who you really are."

She stuck out her succulent lower lip. "Is that so important?"

"Yes, if you want to be a character who jumps right off the page."

"Okay . . ." She set her empty mug aside. "Very few people know this but I'll tell you. I don't have the slightest idea who I really am. Not so much as a clue. I have no idea what I want to do with my life, so I'm having fun while I can and maybe someday I'll figure it out."

I studied her curiously. "That's it? That's all you've got?"

"I'm afraid so."

"Don't buy it."

"Why not?"

"Because I don't think you're that shallow. I think you have a brain, a million things you want to do with it, and that you're running away from them."

"What, you think I want to cure cancer or something?"

"Do you?"

"Just out of curiosity, what are you basing this on?"

"Instincts. You're not a bimbonic airhead slut. There's a lot more to you than the public realizes."

She gazed at me mischievously. "Are you hitting on me? I mean, we're in bed together. We're wearing very little clothing, and you keep staring at my nipples."

"It's rather difficult not to."

"So are you getting ready to jump my bones?"

"Nope."

She raised an eyebrow at me. "Sure about that?"

"Positive. We're going to be working together. It wouldn't be professional."

"What if we weren't? Going to be working together, I mean."

"Still nope."

"Why not?"

"I'm involved with someone else."

"Who? Wait, don't tell me—it's your ex, Merilee Nash. Am I right?"

"What makes you say that?"

"Because if there's one thing I know, it's guys. Not that I understand any of you, because I don't. Earth to Hoagy—she's married to someone else now."

"Doesn't change how I feel about her. Which brings me to my next question. Have you ever been in love?"

She stiffened slightly. "God, why would you ask me *that*?"

"The character I'd be creating has to bear a resemblance to you. That's what your readers will want. I'm thinking about a young, aspiring actress who'll do anything to make it. It'll be a behind-the-scenes look at what that really means. Being lied to. Being used. Producers who promise you an audition if you'll have sex with them. The real deal."

"Ooh, I like that. And you for sure know a lot about actresses."

"So have you?"

"Have I what?

"Ever been in love?"

"Why does that matter?"

"It's a romance novel, remember? That means you need a great love. It may not be the guy your readers approve of, but you have to carry a torch for somebody. Maybe you end up with him in the end. Maybe you don't. We won't know until I write it."

She nodded. "Okay, sure. I see what you mean. Yes, there was someone once."

"Who was he?"

She looked down at Lulu, stroking her. "My secret."

"As in you're not going to tell me?"

"Correct."

"Why not?"

"My secret."

"Was he your first?"

She colored slightly, clearly uncomfortable. I'd struck a nerve. "How did you know that?"

"Wild guess. How old were you?"

"Fourteen. And I know what you're going to say—I was too young, as in statutory rape too young. But I didn't care. When I was fifteen, I moved on to banging guys at UCLA frat parties. I'd get so bombed I used to wake up at three A.M. in some guy's bed and couldn't even remember who he was."

"You're lucky you didn't get pregnant."

"I did. Twice. Mona took me to the abortion clinic both times. You don't need parental consent in California. My parents never knew. Still don't."

"Was your first love a classmate or someone older?"

Her mouth tightened. "I told you already. My secret."

"One of your teachers?"

She flared at me angrily. "Stop asking me about him, because I won't tell you. I've never told *anyone*, and I never, ever will. So just forget about it, okay?"

"Okay. Do you think you'll ever fall in love again?"

"God, I hope not."

"Why not?"

"I don't want to get hurt again."

"So he hurt you?"

"I told you, we're *not* talking about him."

"You're the one who brought up getting hurt."

"After that, I made a lot of stupid mistakes with a lot of stupid guys. When I was eighteen, nineteen, I made a complete ass out of myself. We all do that when we're that age. You did, didn't you?"

"Oh, most definitely."

"Thought so. I could tell from your short stories. The only difference between us is that I was a rich, good-looking Hollywood brat—so every single stupid thing I did was splashed all over the tabloids. It wasn't fair, really."

"I totally agree. We should all be given the chance to be young and stupid without the whole world knowing about it. But are you honestly telling me you weren't provoking the media just a tiny bit by dumping Trey Sinclair for H Rapper Brown? And by pissing Lil' Bit'ch off so much that she shot your Porsche full of holes? That isn't exactly flying under the radar."

She let out a snort. "Okay, so maybe I poked the media a bit. That was part of the fun. And it *was* fun, damn it. I loved every minute of it—until Rapper got killed by Da Real's posse. That was a genuine wake-up call."

"Clearly. You moved on to married baseball players instead."

"That was harsh."

"You're right. I apologize."

"Besides, I've settled down a lot since then. I'm not interested in one-night stands anymore. I'd much rather be in a steady relationship."

"Are you in one now?"

"I don't know," she said glumly. "Tommy's an actor, which means he's more wrapped up in himself than he is in me. I also think he's dogging me with a model who was at his party last night. They were super friendly. Do I get to ask you a question now?"

"Absolutely. Fire away."

"I want this book to be super sexy. Do you write good sex scenes?"

"I wouldn't worry about that part."

"I'm talking kinky, like threesomes."

"I wouldn't worry about that part."

"So you've been in threesomes?"

"I think we've pretty much exhausted this topic."

"I'm sorry, it's just that I can't figure you out. You have this serious, distinguished reputation, except now that I've read your stories and we've talked some I can tell that deep down inside you're still a wild man."

"And this is a problem for you?"

"No, I'm glad. The samples that the other writers submitted were straight out of 1957."

"Don't kid yourself. Nineteen fifty-seven was plenty kinky. It was just kept under wraps in those days."

"Really? I didn't know that."

"So today you learned something."

"Anything else you want to know about me?"

"Why do you still live at home? When I was your age, I wanted nothing more than to get far, far away from my parents."

"Well, for starters, my dad doesn't live here anymore and my mom's so loopy she's not really *here*. I come and go as I please. Everything I want is here. Mona helps me keep my shit together. Besides, I love Lisa and she hardly ever leaves. I'd miss her."

"Do you think you'll ever get married and have kids?"

Her eyes widened in alarm. "Where did *that* come from?"

"Do you?"

"Who knows? I'd have to fall in love with someone again, which I'm not that anxious to do. He'd have to be a guy who's serious but also has a silly side, like you and Lulu do. Someone who's not a bullshit artist. And he'd have to genuinely like me for who I am."

"You're not proposing to me, are you?"

"In your dreams," she said, punching me on the shoulder.

"Are you sorry that *Being Nikki* has ended its run?"

"Actually, I'm thrilled. It was all getting to be too much. I felt like I had to keep living up to this image that the tabloids had created. I was never as out of control as they made me seem. I'm just someone who takes what I want. If a guy does that, people admire him. If a girl does it, they stick all kinds of slut-bomb labels on her. Actually, I thought that would make a good title for my book."

"What, *The Slut Bomb*?"

"No, *The Girl Who Took What She Wanted*. What do you think?"

"I like *The Slut Bomb* better." Again, she slugged me on the shoulder. "Okay, that's starting to hurt. *The Girl Who Took What She Wanted.* That isn't bad, actually. It makes your character sound bold, gutsy."

"Mostly, I want her to be someone who lives in the moment. Does what she wants, when she wants, with whoever she wants. Which pisses certain people off."

"Are we speaking of anyone in particular?"

"My Aunt Enid, just for starters."

"We had tea together yesterday in Pasadena."

Nikki rolled her eyes, "Isn't she awful?"

"I'd vote for joyless and miserable. I felt sorry for her."

"Don't. She's a total bitch."

"She didn't have much nice to say about you either. Told me you used to delight in tormenting her in Trancas back when you and Lisa were teenagers."

"It's true, I did. It was fun. And *so* easy. She's convinced I'm going to burn in hell for eternity. But that's her problem, not mine."

I finished my coffee, thinking that I hadn't been so different from Nikki when I was twenty-three. Just angrier and more driven to prove my worth. I was only a year older than her when I'd published those short stories and then buckled down and started my novel. It had meant giving up a lot—not only partying, but severing ties with the first great love of my life and breaking her heart. But I was committed to proving myself to my father. Hell, to the whole world. And so I did what I had to do. Nikki didn't strike me as someone who burned with intensity the way that I had. Possibly she never would. Not unless she found something that she truly cared about the way her sister had, but that takes a special kind of single-mindedness, bordering on lunacy. "Tell me about Lisa."

"What about her?"

"The two of you are so different."

"Totally. I was the bad girl who ditched class. She was the straight-A student who did all her homework and didn't drink or do drugs. She was also terrified of boys. Still is. If she'd just get some sun and exercise and stop mainlining candy bars, she'd be real cute. But, I swear, it's almost like she *wants* to be unattractive."

"Why would that be?"

"She's super shy. She's never had a serious boyfriend that I know of. Just stays in her studio and does amazing work. She's so talented."

"Does she socialize at all?"

"She's still friends with a group of her old class-mates from Otis. They go out together for Chinese food sometimes, that kind of thing. And please don't ask me if she's still a virgin because I'm afraid I think the answer is yes." Nicki took my empty mug from me and climbed out of bed. I'd like to tell you that I didn't stare at her barely covered ass as she stood there returning our mugs to the tray. But it was impossible not to stare. What's more, she knew I was staring. Expected me to. She turned to me with a curious look on her face. "So does she make it?"

"Does who make it?"

"My character. The actress who gets boned by scuzzy producers. Does she become a movie star?"

"Good question."

"I'm waiting for a good answer."

"She has to, yeah, otherwise your readers will be disappointed."

"Gotcha. So do you have everything you need for now? Are we good?"

"I think so, yes. In fact, I'm raring to get started. I'll head back to New York tonight. If I have any more questions, I'll call you. What's the best number to reach you at?"

"My private line." She took a pen from the desk, grabbed my hand, and wrote her number on the back of it. Then she turned my hand over and gazed at my palm for a moment with grave scrutiny before she gave my hand back to me and said, "I have a good feeling about us."

"I'm glad. So do I. I'll send you some pages in a few weeks to find out if you like where I'm going or if I'm way off target."

"I can't imagine you will be, unless you totally fuck it up. But that'll never happen. You need to make a good impression."

"On you?"

"Not me, silly man. On Merilee."

I tugged at my ear. "You're not as dumb as you look."

"Keep it to yourself, okay? I like to catch people by surprise."

"Not to worry. Your secret is safe with me."

Nikki picked up the tray and started for the door. "And now I am out of here because I really do need to get to the hospital to see Teddy Bear."

"Who has *not* been hospitalized for an emergency appendectomy."

"Correct."

"I am now clued in. Thank you."

"Sure thing. It can definitely get weird out here. You want my advice, cuz? Just remember that you're in Hollywood, where everything's possible and nothing is real."

"Hello . . . ?"

"Morning, cuz. What's up?"

Merilee fell silent at the other end of the phone line before she said, "Hoagy, is that *you*?"

"Nobody but."

"Since when have you taken to calling people 'cuz'?"

"Since I just had coffee in bed with Nikki. French press espresso that she made herself. Damned good, too. She delivered it to my room at seven o'clock sharp, pronounced that she was freezing cold—since, as you may recall, I like to sleep with the windows open—and jumped into the feathers with me. She had on one of her trademark slinky sleep shirts, and there is not much to those, let me tell you."

"Oh . . . ?" There was a slight edge in Merilee's voice now.

"Why, Merilee Gilbert Nash. If I didn't know you better, I'd swear you were jealous."

"Who, me? Never. Well, okay, maybe a tiny bit. You are a man, after all, and therefore a complete idiot around a gorgeous, frisky young babe."

"I'm also a free agent. I don't belong to you anymore."

"You'll always belong to me, darling. Don't you know that?"

"No, I don't. You married someone else, remember?"

"You do *not* need to remind me."

"Besides, it was strictly business. And Lulu was right there to chaperone. It seems that Nikki actually sat down and read a couple of my early short stories and, unlike the other writers they tried teaming her with, she seems to think we're on the same wavelength."

"The same wavelength? You and Nikki? Imagine that."

"Now you're mocking me. I wish you wouldn't. I need this job."

"Sorry, darling. I didn't mean it to sound as if I were taking it lightly."

"We talked over my ideas for the book. She liked them. She's actually not nearly as shallow and stupid as I thought she'd be. I think we can work together. And, more importantly, so does she. So the job's mine. I'm officially ghosting a steamy Hollywood romance novel for Nikki Dymtryk. Okay, this is the part where you get to congratulate me."

"Congratulations, darling."

"Thank you. I just have to phone Jack to let him know it's a done deal and then Lulu and I will be on the redeye back to New York tonight so I can get started at the typewriter. I was wondering if I could buy you lunch before I go. Or will you be in conference with Rob?"

"Actually, Rob's tied up until midafternoon today screening a rough cut of his new romantic comedy, *When Harry Met Sally.*"

"Terrible title. Who's in it?"

"Billy Crystal and Meg Ryan."

"Whew, talk about a combustible duo. They'll generate so much raw animal heat the screen will burst into flames."

"Actually, I'm hearing good word of mouth about it."

"I'll borrow a car and pick you up at your hotel at noon. Deal?"

"Deal. Do I need to dress up?"

"Nope."

"Where are you taking me?"

"To the one place I absolutely must go whenever I visit LA."

Pink's, which is on the corner of Melrose and La Brea, has been serving the best chili dogs in LA since 1939. It is not Lulu's favorite lunch spot, because there is absolutely nothing on the landmark hot-dog stand's menu to interest her. But she'd be plenty happy riding there in her mommy's lap in Lisa's black BMW convertible, which Lisa assured me she wouldn't be using. In fact, judging by its odometer, she rarely did. The car was two years old and had less than five thousand miles on it, which is more like two *months'* worth of driving in LA. It was plenty peppy and handled well, and by noon it was warm enough that I could put its top down.

Merilee was waiting for us outside the Four Seasons next to that stupid real-as-life statue of a human being that never moves. Because, dig, it's a statue. Heavy, huh? She was wearing a denim cowboy shirt, narrow-wale corduroy pants, and cowboy boots. I was wearing my torn jeans, ancient Chuck Taylors, and a long-sleeved faded yellow Izod shirt.

When we got to Pink's, Merilee and Lulu grabbed a vacant picnic bench while I ordered us four chili dogs topped with grated cheddar cheese and raw onion, and a pair of large root beers. When I brought them to the table, we dove right in, savoring their deliciousness, while Lulu made do with the rare pleasure of curling up on her mommy's feet.

"It meant the world to me that you stopped by last night," Merileee said when she paused to sip her root beer. "I was feeling *so* low. To be honest, I wasn't sure you'd be willing to come."

"Are you kidding? I'll always be here for you, even if you go off and get married again. Just promise me it won't be to Harrison Ford."

"Why, what's wrong with Harrison Ford?"

"He's better looking than I am. Seriously, Rob Reiner cast *Billy Crystal* as the leading man in a romantic comedy?"

She arched an eyebrow at me. "Why are you obsessing about him?"

"Because his face looks like someone sat on it when he was a baby and didn't quite squish it back into shape properly. Plus his voice is irritating, his hair is irritating . . ."

"I suppose you're going to start in on Meg Ryan now."

"No, I don't have a problem with her," I said, going to work on my second chili dog. "Aside from her pert-and-perky thing. She's always pert and perky. Her character could be just about to stick her head in an oven and she'd still play it pert and perky. And is it just me or is there something strange about her gums?"

"Hoagy, we are not going to talk about Meg Ryan's gum tissue. New subject, please."

"Fair enough. But you're not nearly as much fun to dish with as you used to be. Zach has earned himself a punch in the nose."

She went nowhere near that. Just devoured her chili dog in silence. One of the most amazing things about Merilee is that she eats like a longshoreman and never puts on a pound. Two teenage girls approached our table shyly and asked her for her autograph. She cheerfully complied. They thanked her before scurrying back to their table.

"How long are you planning to stay out here?" I asked her.

"Another few days. Then it's home to New York to wait for the latest draft of the script to arrive. Jeremy intends to fly in soon. We'll try reading some scenes together to see how they play. Rob will join us."

She signed another autograph, this one for a polite, elderly female tourist from Ohio, before we finished our root beers and deposited our trash in the container. Then we piled into Lisa's BMW and I drove us back to the Four Seasons. It was a nice, warm, sunny afternoon to be driving in a convertible with a beautiful movie star and a mouth-breathing basset hound. I suppose there are worse cities to live in than LA, but there are so many that are nicer. San Francisco, if you want to stay on the West Coast. Me, I'll never lose my love for New York, Paris, London, or Secaucus, New Jersey.

When I pulled into the hotel's driveway and stopped next to that stupid statue, Merilee and I gazed at each other for a long moment. I was smiling at her gallantly, or at least I told myself I was. She looked as if she was about to start sobbing again.

"I'm so glad we were able to do this, darling," she said, with that quaver in her voice. "See each other again, even for just a little while."

"That makes two of us." Lulu let out a low, unhappy moan from her lap. "Correction, three of us."

"So you're really flying back tonight?"

"If I can book us two seats in first class. I haven't called yet."

"You can phone the concierge from my room, if you'd like. He'll take care of it for you."

"That's okay, I can call as soon as I get back to . . ." I trailed off, noticing that she was gazing at me in that way of hers that makes the lower half of my body do strange, warm things. "Sure, that sounds like a good idea."

We got out of the car. I gave the valet parker the keys. He gave me a ticket. Then we strolled inside with Lulu and got in an unoccupied elevator. I punched the button for the tenth floor.

As the doors closed, I said, "I wonder if it's snowing in—"

And never finished the sentence. Couldn't. Merilee had grabbed me by the shirt and clamped her mouth over mine. She does that. Kisses me unexpectedly. Usually it's after she's had a few drinks. She was quite sober now, although Pink's chili dogs do back a wallop.

We stood there kissing passionately as the elevator made its way up to the tenth floor, Merilee running her hands under my Izod shirt and up my bare chest.

We barely managed to make it to her room fully clothed.

❧

"Wow . . ."

"Wow. . . ."

"Was that . . . incredible or what?" she gasped.

"Incredible. Let me tell you, we really, really need to eat at Pink's more often."

Merilee let out a giggle as we lay there under the sheets, flushed and drenched in perspiration. Lulu watched us from the armchair near the bed, her tail thumping happily.

"I must confess I don't know what came over me, darling. Except that when we pulled into the parking lot, I suddenly realized I had to have you. Okay, that was a lie. I wanted to jump you last night when you came over and were so sweet to me, but I was afraid you'd think I'd become a loose woman."

"On the contrary, I would have swelled with pride, as it were."

"I guess the old magic is still there," she said, snuggling against me.

"I guess it is."

She glanced at the bedside clock radio. "My God, it's nearly three. I have to get ready to meet with Rob. Do you want the first shower? You were always faster than me."

I climbed out of bed and took that fast shower, toweled off with one of the Four Seasons' plush, thirsty towels, and put my clothes back on. While Merilee was taking her shower I phoned down to the concierge and had him book me two first-class seats on a redeye flight to JFK that night.

Merilee came out a few minutes later in her complimentary terry-cloth robe with her waist-length golden hair in a bun. She gazed at me, glowing.

I looked back at her, long and steadily. "So what happens now?"

"Darling, I have absolutely no idea, other than to say it was a mad, wonderful impulse and I have no regrets. But I also can't handle any complications in my life right now. Let's talk it out when we we're both back in New York, okay?"

"Fair enough, but I picked up today's lunch tab so dinner's on you."

"The Blue Mill? Liver and onions with bacon and extra mashed potatoes?"

"You've always known the way to my heart." I kissed her tenderly. "Okay, I'm out of here. Have a good meeting. We'll talk when you get home."

She knelt and said good-bye to Lulu, who looked up at her curiously, wondering what was going on between us. Merilee had no way of telling her since we had no idea ourselves. "I'll see you soon, sweetness," was the best she could come up with.

Then it was her turn to kiss me tenderly and out the door Lulu and I went. I can't speak for Lulu but I was feeling more buoyant than I had in years.

The valet parker fetched Lisa's BMW. I tipped him ten bucks and drove up Coldwater to Cherokee, made that right turn and steep climb, then took the left at Bowmont and drove past Julie Christie's house from *Shampoo* before I made a right onto Hazen—where I ran smack dab into a crime scene. Four black-and-whites, an unmarked Ford Crown Vic sedan, an ambulance and a county coroner's van were clustered around a house about halfway up the street.

It was Pam Hamilton and Jack Dymtryk's house.

I came to a stop, feeling my stomach muscles tighten. Right away, I knew we weren't going to be catching the redeye back to New York that night.

CHAPTER SIX

I pulled up alongside of a uniformed patrolman who was so clean-cut, square-jawed, and athletically built that he looked like an extra from *Adam-12*, as did a freakishly high percentage of the sworn personnel on the LAPD. Jack Webb, aka Joe Friday, the image-conscious actor-producer who gave us *Dragnet* and *Adam-12*, was responsible for that. Reality and fantasy held hands on the day Webb died in 1982. Every police station in the city flew its flag at half-mast. I know you think I'm kidding but I'm not.

"What's going on?" I asked the patrolman.

"Please move along, sir," he said.

"The people who live here are friends of mine. I ate dinner here last night. What's happened?"

"Again, sir, please move along." He was robotically polite. Another Webb fetish.

It was at that moment I spotted someone striding up the brick path from the backyard whom I'd gotten to know when I ghosted the Sonny Day memoir, which, as I believe I mentioned, had turned kind of messy.

Detective Lieutenant Emil Lamp's eyes widened in surprise when he noticed me idling there. "Cheese and crackers, is that *you*, Hoagy?" he called out in that chirpy voice of his. "What in the holy heck are you doing here?"

"I was just about to ask you that myself, Lieutenant," I said, my stomach knotting up with dread.

Emil Lamp was the LAPD's go-to celebrity homicide ace—and as unlikely looking an ace as you'd ever come across. He was a fresh-scrubbed, pink-cheeked, eager young guy who bore a striking resemblance to Howdy Doody. Wore a tan suit, yellow oxford button-down shirt, striped tie, and a pair of nubucks with rubber soles. Lamp specialized in high-profile cases because he and his nubucks were uncommonly skilled at not stepping on famous, sensitive toes. He was extremely solicitous and tactful. Also razor sharp. "I sure didn't expect to see you again," he said to me as he approached the BMW.

"I didn't expect to see you again, either, Lieutenant. And something tells me I'm not going to be happy that I have."

Someone in a Bentley who wanted to get by me and go further up Hazen honked his horn and hollered at me to get the hell out of his way. Rich people who live on exclusive canyon roads tend to be impatient. Also assholes.

Lamp glanced around and said, "Hoagy, why don't you pull into that driveway across the street?" Which I did. He waved the outraged grouch in the Bentley on through and joined me. Lulu stuck her paws on her rolled-down window and let out a whoop. She had developed a fondness for Lamp. "Hey, Lulu!" He scratched her head affectionately. "Hoagy, is it my imagination or have her ears gotten longer?"

"No, they're the exact same size. I measure them every week."

"How's the writing coming? Get an idea for your second novel yet?"

"Afraid not."

"Sorry to hear that. I sure did enjoy your first one."

"Lieutenant, I don't mean to be rudely abrupt, but would you kindly tell me what the hell's going on here?"

"You first. What are you doing here?"

"Staying up at the top of the hill at the *Being Nikki* house. Now that Nikki's show has been cancelled, which I believe is still a trade secret, a prominent New York publisher has approached Nikki's dad, Jack, about turning her into an author of spicy romance novels targeted at a hip young audience."

"Which I'm guessing she would not actually write herself. You would."

"Correct. Her job is to get a ton of airtime on TV talk shows promoting the book and no doubt make it into a huge best seller. Lulu and I flew in yesterday morning to meet with her. I had dinner right here at this very house last evening with Jack and his lovely wife, Pam Hamilton. And now I'm officially out of patience, Lieutenant. Are you going to tell me what's happened here or do I have to call your mother?"

"Sorry, but there's a way that we have to go about these things."

"*What* things?"

Lamp stroked his chin thoughtfully. It looked so peach fuzzy it wouldn't have surprised me if he still didn't need to shave more than three times a week. "It's half past three. Where have you been this afternoon?"

"Having lunch with my ex-wife."

His face brightened. "Miss Nash?"

"Correct. She's in town to talk to Rob Reiner about filming a remake of *Random Harvest*. That's it. I'm all done answering questions. Your turn."

"Fair enough." Lamp's face tightened. "Hoagy, I'm sorry to say you're not going to be ghosting that romance novel for Nikki. She's no longer available to do any book promotion—or anything else. Pam Hamilton finished filming her scenes for *Mill Valley* this afternoon at two o'clock, stopped off at the supermarket on her way home, arrived at about two forty-five and began unpacking her groceries in the kitchen when she looked out the French doors and discovered Nikki floating facedown in her pool in a yellow thong bikini with the back of her head bashed in. There's a five-pound sledgehammer lying by the side of the pool with blood on it."

I sat there in stunned silence. This day was turning into a rollercoaster ride of emotions. First the sheer bliss in Room 1031 of the Four Seasons. Now a horrific gut punch.

"We don't know yet if Nikki was already dead when she hit the water or if she drowned," Lamp went on. "The county coroner just arrived and has to get her body back to the lab. They've removed her from the water and covered her body with a beach towel that was on a lounge chair near the pool. Pam said it wasn't one of her towels, so Nikki probably wore it draped around her when she strolled down here. No sign of any shoes or sandals."

"She was probably barefoot. Ran barefoot down the driveway yesterday to meet her movie-star boyfriend,

Tommy, when he picked her up. Any idea what time it happened?"

"All I can tell you so far is that the blood on the sledge was dry when the first responders got here. On a fairly warm, sunny day like today it takes blood about an hour to dry. As a rule, the coroner goes by body temperature with floaters and the water temperature is a major factor. Since she was found in a heated pool with the temperature set at seventy-eight degrees he should be able to determine a pretty accurate time of death. There doesn't appear to be any evidence of sexual assault. No obvious scratching or bruising. Her bikini wasn't torn. But he won't know anything for sure until he gets her on the table and conducts a thorough autopsy. He might find traces of someone else's skin or blood under her fingernails, that sort of thing. I've spoken to Nikki's assistant, Mona Shapiro. She told me the gardeners were working up at the big house when Nikki wanted to take a swim and they enjoy making lewd catcalls at her so she left the house at around one o'clock to stroll down here. My guess? It happened not long after she got here, but that's just a guess. We've canvassed the neighbors. None of them saw a thing. In fact, there's hardly anyone around. Just a few housekeepers. We'll keep after it, but these houses up here are set far apart and well back from the road. People value their privacy."

"Pam mentioned to me last evening that she'd given Nikki permission to use the pool whenever the gardeners up at her place were annoying her."

"So she told me. She was, *is*, utterly devastated. Said that when she saw Nikki floating out there, she let out a shriek, called 911, and then called Jack at his office. He got up here almost as fast as the emergency responders. I'm guessing he floored it from Beverly Hills in his Countach and ran every red light."

"Where are he and Pam now?"

"Up at the big house, along with the whole rest of the family and Mona, who told me that she and Nikki were best friends in high school. She's real shaken up. They're all shaken up."

I heard the faint sound of a helicopter overhead heading toward us. Then another. Then another. The TV news choppers were arriving.

"I don't have to tell you that this is going to be a media shitstorm, do I?"

"No, you do not. Somehow, that movie-star boyfriend of hers got wind of it and showed up here ten minutes before you did in a Range Rover with a couple of buddies, totally crazed. I guess he was seriously in love with her."

"She told me he was dogging her with a fashion model."

"Well, he sure *seemed* upset."

"There's a reason why they call them actors."

"He demanded I let him go in the backyard so he could see her body."

"Did you?"

"Oh, heck no. It's an active crime scene. No one's allowed back there until our forensics people have a chance to process it. He stomped around and cussed at me but finally left. Now we're setting up barricades on Bowmont and at the foot of Cherokee on Coldwater to keep the media and the lookie-looks away." He paused, exhaling slowly. "I've already received a personal call from Chief Gates, who is not anyone's idea of a patient man. He made it clear to me it's imperative that I have her killer in custody within twenty-four hours or I'll be spending the remainder of my career issuing parking tickets in Boyle Heights."

"That'll never happen. I have complete confidence in you, Lieutenant. I assume you know that the same pool boy, Rory Krieger, worked both houses. In fact, he was cleaning the pool here when I showed up for dinner last evening. If you're a *Being Nikki* fan or follow the tabloids, you'll know Rory as the hot and heavy bed partner of Nikki's stepfather, George."

"Yes, I'm aware of that."

"You may not be aware that Rory put a move on Nikki before he settled for George. Whispered comments in her ear about certain unwholesome things that he'd like to do to her with his tongue. She responded by slapping him hard enough to bloody his nose. So there was no love lost there."

"That I didn't know. We definitely want to have a conversation with Rory. He doesn't seem to be up at the big house, though his truck and motorcycle are there. Must be working around the neighborhood somewhere. He'll turn up. And if he doesn't we'll turn him up." He scratched Lulu's ears, squinting at me in the sunlight. "What's your plan?"

"I expect I'll go up to the house and pay my respects. Then move out of the room that I've been using and give them their privacy. Lulu and I are booked on a redeye flight back to New York tonight."

"Any chance I can talk you into sticking around town for a day or two?"

"Is this one of those 'Don't Leave Town' ultimatums?"

"Oh, heck no, Hoagy. It's nothing like that. You were a lot of help to me on the Sonny Day case, and I'd like to tap into your insights. You know these people. You understand them."

"I would hardly go that far."

"Have you got a place where you can stay tonight?"

"Possibly. I'll make a call from the house."

"Super. I'd appreciate it. I should be able to get away from here in a couple of hours. How about we meet at

Chuy's at, say, six o'clock? I'll have some forensics details by then. Maybe learn more from the coroner."

"Sounds good. And I'll be able to give you a play-by-play of what I pick up from the family. We can compare notes." I fell silent for a moment. "Nikki told me this morning she was on her way to Cedars-Sinai to visit an ex-boyfriend who OD'ed a couple of days ago. Famous British rock 'n' roller. The press thinks he's recovering there from an emergency appendectomy."

Emil Lamp frowned at me. "You're telling me this why?"

"Because the image of Nikki wasn't the real Nikki."

He put his hand on my shoulder. "I'm sorry about this, Hoagy."

"Me, too."

"But it's awfully good to see you and Lulu again. There's nobody else around quite like the pair of you."

"God, I certainly hope not."

Jack's Countach was crowded in the apron of the driveway with Kenny's Volvo, Enid's Saab, Mona's Toyota Corolla, George's Jeep, Rory's Ford-150 pickup, and the boys' Kawasakis. Nikki's bullet-riddled Porsche was parked in the garage next to Rita's Mercedes. The sight of it there hit me harder than I'd expected. I pulled Lisa's BMW into its garage space, then Lulu and I got out and went up the front path. The front door to the house was unlocked.

The first thing I saw was Rita standing in the middle of the living room clutching on to her ex-husband and wailing, "My *baby's* gone, Jack! I held her in my arms when she was born and now she's *gone* and I'll never, ever see her again!"

"I know, Rita. I know." Jack held his sobbing ex-wife in his arms, looking both grief-stricken and incredibly uncomfortable. "They'll find out who did this awful thing to her and he will be one sorry son of a bitch."

"But it won't bring her back!"

"You're right, it won't," he said, his voice heavy with sadness.

She released him and reached for her glass on the coffee table. Whatever she was drinking was brown and had two ice cubes in it. My guess was Scotch, and she'd had plenty. Her arm wavered more than slightly as she grabbed it, and the rim of the glass conked unappealingly against her top teeth when she gulped some down.

Jack, who Lamp told me had sped to the murder scene straight from his office, wore a handsomely tailored black Armani suit. I'd only seen him in casual clothes before. Dressed for work, he looked much more like the powerful Hollywood shark that he was. He gazed at me, tight-faced, before he said, "This has to be the worst day of my life. And poor Pam, finding Nikki floating there in our pool. I won't ever forget her voice on the phone when she called me. She was hysterical, Hoagy. Utterly hysterical."

"How is she doing now?" I asked as Lulu stood beside me, gazing up at him.

"Better. Nursing a glass of wine at the bar the last time I checked on her."

"And how are *you* doing?"

"Nikki was the best and the worst of me. She *was* me. I don't know how I'll get through this. I really don't." He ran his hand over his hair. "I guess you and I won't be in business together after all, will we? There's no book without her."

"No, there's not. A shame, actually. Nikki and I had a terrific talk this morning. Really hit it off. I think we would have worked well together."

"I'll talk to Alberta when I get a chance. See if we can arrange some form of compensation for your time."

"You've already done that, Jack. You don't owe me anything."

"So you'll be heading back to New York?"

"Actually, Lieutenant Lamp has asked me to stick around for a couple of days."

Jack's eyes widened slightly. "He doesn't consider *you* a suspect, does he?"

"No, not at all. Or at least I hope not. But our paths have crossed before."

"You must be referring to that Sonny Day mess."

"I am. He told me he'd value my input on this. I came here to pack my bags, actually. Doesn't seem appropriate for me to stay here any longer."

"Have somewhere else you can stay?"

"I believe so."

"Good. I've booked us a suite at the Beverly Wilshire since our house is now a fucking *crime scene*. Plus Pam won't go back there. What I'd really like to do is jump in the Countach and floor it to Trancas fast enough to break the time barrier. Hurtle back to when I had my VW bus, my board, ten dollars in my pocket, and was the happiest dude in the world. Back in those days the people I loved didn't get their heads bashed in by some . . . some . . ." He trailed off into pained silence. "I've been hearing helicopters circling overhead for the past half hour. Pretty soon the tabloid scum will be trying to climb over the walls here. We'll all be better off staying somewhere else."

"Yes, we will."

"I like the way you handle yourself, Hoagy. If I stumble upon a project that I think might be a good fit for you, I'll be sure to contact Alberta. I hope we actually do work

173

together sometime." Then he murmured something about wanting to check up on Pam and went striding off.

Next I encountered Mona, who was making her way toward the stairs from the kitchen with a sandwich on a plate and tears streaming down her face.

"I'm so sorry, Mona."

Her lower lip quivered. "Nikki was my best friend *ever.*"

"I understand that she left here at about one o'clock to swim in Pam and Jack's pool."

Mona nodded, sniffling. "The gardeners. They were making those juvenile hissing noises and catcalls at her. They're such jerks."

Lulu began sniffing at Mona's Nikes with keen, busy-nosed interest.

"Why's she doing that?" Mona asked, looking down at her.

"Couldn't say. She doesn't tell me everything."

"Oh, wait, I bet I know. I just made a tuna sandwich. Spilled some of the oil from the can on my sneakers."

"Then that's your answer. I'll be clearing out of the guest bedroom."

"You don't have to do that."

"Yes, I do. But I was wondering if you could do me a small favor."

"Sure. Anything."

I handed her the sheet of Four Seasons notepaper on which Merilee had scribbled the number where I could reach her at Castle Rock. "That's the phone number of Rob Reiner's assistant. Could you please tell her that I need to speak to Merilee as soon as she has a free moment?"

"Not a problem. I'm on it. And, hey, guess what? Bobby got a call first thing this morning from Steve Cannell's right-hand man. They're in need of an assistant director and he wants Bobby to come in for a talk."

"Well, that's one piece of good news," I said, wondering if there were any strings Jack Dymtryk hadn't been able and willing to pull if it had to do with protecting his precious Nikki's reputation.

"Yes, it is. I'll feel *so* much better if he's no longer working for Daylite Courier. And so will Bobby."

I glanced up the grand, curving staircase. "How's Lisa doing?"

"I wouldn't know. She hasn't left her room."

"I have her car keys."

"Hold on to them. You'll probably need them before she will."

"Thanks, I'll do that."

Kenny and Enid were seated together on the living-room sofa staring straight ahead in such grief-stricken silence that it was as if they were in a trance. They didn't even notice me standing there before them until I cleared my throat.

Enid stirred slightly before she nodded at me and said, "Hello, Hoagy."

Kenny continued to gaze at me blankly before he blinked and his eyes came back into focus. "Oh, hey, Hoagy. Forgive me. This isn't how things are supposed to . . . I guess I'm still in a state of shock."

Enid cast a frosty look at him. "Yet surely you can't be surprised."

He frowned at her. "What's that supposed to mean?"

"The way she lived, the people with whom she consorted . . . this sort of thing was inevitable."

"Don't say that!" Kenny erupted at her angrily. "Don't even think it!"

"Well, forgive me for speaking my mind," Enid huffed.

"I can't," Kenny said. "I don't."

As the two of them sat there bickering, Lulu was busy sniffing the trouser cuffs of Kenny's navy blue suit, snuffling and snorting.

"Why is she doing that?" he asked me.

"Offhand, I'd say she smells something that interests her."

"I'll bet I know what it is," Enid said. "Kenny, you had a mayonnaise stain on them, remember? From a sandwich you wolfed down at your desk. I took them to the dry cleaner last week. He got it out, but he must have used a solvent that left a residual odor."

"Sure, that would explain it," I said, even though Lulu had never shown the slightest interest in residual cleaning-solvent odors before.

My short-legged partner then proceeded to begin sniffing delicately at the cuffs of Enid's light tan gabardine slacks. Enid stiffened, crossed her legs, and gave Lulu a bonk on the nose that jolted her hard enough to back her off, whimpering in protest.

"Oh, I'm sorry, Lulu. I didn't see you there." Enid reached down to pet her but Lulu hid behind me, deeply offended.

Me, I wondered why Enid had refused to submit to a scent inspection.

Kenny ran a meaty hand over his face. "I rushed over here as soon as I heard the news. I was out of the office, meeting with a prospective client and his manager at the Record Plant recording studio on the Strip. A British rocker named Nigel Hamer whose second album just went platinum. I'd invited them to come up to the office but Nigel doesn't 'do' offices. While I was there I overheard a couple of people talking about Nikki out in the hallway. They'd just heard the news on their car radio. I couldn't believe what I was hearing so I called Jack. His secretary, who was weeping, said he'd already taken off. I called home and left Enid a message on our machine. Then I mumbled an apology to Nigel and his manager and drove straight here. As soon as Enid got home and heard my message, she joined me."

"Where had you been?" I asked her.

"At our church," she responded. "Sorting donations for the annual clothing drive."

Rita chose that moment to stagger her way toward me. "So awful, Hoagy," she sobbed, hugging me tightly. "So awful."

"I'm truly sorry, Rita. Were you here when Nikki left to go swimming?"

"No, I was at the beauty parlor." Which explained the strong scent of gel in her hair. She also reeked of a heavy, fruity perfume. "Sal had a perfume sample for me to try out. Please tell me you like it."

"I do like it," I assured her.

Lulu, who is allergic to most alcohol-based perfumes, did not. She began to sneeze so violently that I swore her ears would start pinwheeling around fast enough to lift her right off the ground.

Rita watched her curiously for a moment before she plopped down in the armchair next to the sofa, shook a couple of pills from a bottle that was in the pocket of her sweater, and downed them with the glass of Scotch that was never far from reach.

"Go easy, old girl, Rita," Kenny cautioned her.

"Go to hell, Kenny," she responded.

Kenny grimaced at her before he turned to me. "Hoagy, I sure am sorry you flew all the way out here from New York for a project that's never going to happen."

"Don't give it a moment's thought. You've got plenty else on your mind."

Enid just sat and eyed me coldly. I had no idea why. I thought we'd gotten along pretty well when I visited her for tea. But for some reason she'd decided she didn't approve of me.

George was standing by himself over by the floor-to-ceiling windows in the den, gazing out at the smog over the San Fernando Valley. He wore a corduroy sports jacket, jeans, and a pair of hiking shoes.

I made my way over toward him. Lulu, who was anxious to get away from Rita's perfume, joined me. George didn't turn his big, blocky anchorman's head at the sound of my footsteps on the terra-cotta tile floor. Just gazed out at the Valley.

I gave him a pat on the back and told him how sorry I was about what had happened.

He nodded grimly. "Life's full of surprises. Amazing just how many of them are totally shitty."

Lulu sniffed his jeans, found nothing of interest, and stretched out on the floor, yawning hugely.

"Is Rory here?"

George shook his head. "He told me this morning he was totally slammed today. I've been plenty busy myself. Just got here. But he's no doubt seen all the police cars in the neighborhood and heard about what's happened."

"Surprised he didn't come right home."

"Don't be. Rory goes his own way."

"You said you were plenty busy yourself. Doing what?"

"The station likes my 'Yesteryear Profiles' of old-time movie stars. I spent a couple of hours this morning doing a sit-down on-camera interview with June Allyson. She was terrific. Reminisced about the old days at MGM. Told me some great stories. Then my crew and I went back to the station to put the footage together. I was preparing my voice-over when I got the call from Rita."

"She's pretty shook up."

"Pretty blitzed, you mean. I'm going to have to put her to bed soon."

"I wouldn't wait too long," I said, noticing that Pam was sitting by herself on a stool at the mirrored saloon-style bar sipping a glass of white wine. I excused myself and joined her.

"How are you holding up?" I asked, sliding onto the stool next to hers.

"Jack keeps asking me that very same question. I still don't have an answer. I'll have to get back to you." Pam made an effort to smile at me but couldn't quite manage it. Just let out a ragged breath, her gorgeous dark eyes puddling with tears that spilled down her cheeks. I offered her the linen handkerchief from the back pocket of my jeans and she took it, dabbing at her eyes. "Thank you. I can't seem to stop doing that. Seeing Nikki floating there in the pool was . . . it was the most awful thing I've ever seen in my life. I can't stop seeing her there. I'll never be able to stop seeing her there."

"Yes, you will. We're self-protective creatures. It'll recede into your memory. Won't go away completely, but the visceral pain will."

"That sounds suspiciously like the voice of experience."

"Only because it is. Feel like talking about it?"

She shrugged her slim shoulders in the powder blue knit top she was wearing. "They didn't have any more scenes for me to shoot today, so I clocked out early. Did some grocery shopping on my way home. I was putting them away and fretting about the last scene I'd filmed, wondering if I should have delivered one of my lines differently. I was totally preoccupied with myself, in other words."

"Just like all the rest of us are."

"I suppose." Pam took a small sip of her wine. "I must have been in that damned kitchen ten whole minutes before I looked out the French doors and saw her floating there with her head bashed in and . . . her blood in the water."

"What did you do?"

"You mean besides scream? I called Jack. He told me to call the police and that he'd be right home. They got there before he did, along with an ambulance. Asked me some questions."

"Such as?"

"Did I remember seeing anyone driving away from the house as I was coming home?"

"Did you?"

"No, I didn't. Who notices such things? I don't. By then Jack had made it home. He got me out of there and walked me up here with his arm around me. I don't even remember what we talked about. I was still in such a state of shock. All I kept thinking, *keep* thinking, is what if she was still alive when I got home? Could I have saved her if I hadn't been so obsessed with that stupid line of dialogue?"

"I can assure you that the answer is no. The homicide detective who's in charge of the case just told me that her blood on the sledgehammer was dry, which means she'd probably been floating there at least an hour."

Pam gazed at me hopefully. "For real?"

"For real."

"Well, that does make me feel a tiny bit better. Thank you for telling me."

Lulu whimpered at Pam from the floor at the foot of her stool.

"Why is she doing that?"

"She knows you're upset and wants to cheer you up."

"What a sweetie." Pam got down off her stool and sat on the floor. Lulu licked her face and then climbed into her lap, resting her head on her shoulder. Pam hugged her and scrunched her ears. "Thank you, Lulu."

Jack appeared, smiling at Pam fondly as she snuggled there with Lulu. "I don't know about you, hon, but I vote we make a beeline for the Beverly Wilshire, tell them to hold all calls, and make the world go away—at least for a little while."

Her eyes gleamed at him. "That suits me."

I was ready to pack my things and get gone myself. I crossed the living room and headed upstairs. Mona was just getting off the phone in her office. "That was Rob Reiner's secretary," she informed me as I stood in her doorway.

"Merilee is in conference with Rob and his brain trust, as she called them, but they should take a break soon. She'll tell Merilee that you need to speak to her. She knows how to reach you here."

"Thanks, Mona."

"I'll be sorry to see you and Lulu go," she confessed. "It was nice to have some friendly company around here. It was bad enough listening to Rita sob all day over George and Rory. Now it's going to be a genuine nightmare."

"You were Nikki's personal assistant. Now that she's gone there's no need for you to stick around, you know."

Mona nodded. "I was just coming to that realization myself. But how will I pay my rent?"

"Why don't you tell Bobby that you need to give up your apartment and move in with him temporarily until you can find another job?"

"I'm on board with the finding another job part, but what if he says no about me moving in?"

"Then he doesn't deserve you. Trust me, you won't have any trouble finding someone who does."

She colored slightly. "You really mean that?"

"I do. I'm a healthy red-blooded guy. I know about these things." I glanced at Lisa's closed door. "I thought I'd pay my respects."

"Good luck with that. She hasn't spoken to anyone."

I knocked on her door anyway.

"Go away!" she cried out. "Stop bothering me, will you?"

"It's Hoagy, Lisa!" I called through the door.

"Hoagy . . . ? Okay, you can come in. But only if Lulu's with you."

"It so happens that she is."

We found Lisa sitting on her workroom floor cutting a pattern with a pair of scissors. She was still playing with her Nikki doll. What a strange, childlike person she was. Messy, too. Hair disheveled, work-stained *bleu de travail* rumpled and filthy. Her pale, pudgy bare feet were dirty and covered with scratches, and she smelled of sweaty physical exertion. All of which I found quite odd for someone who rarely left her room.

Lulu moseyed over and bopped her on the shoulder with her nose. Lisa smiled at her and petted her.

"I'll be leaving soon, Lisa. Just came upstairs to pack. I wanted to tell you how sorry I am about Nikki, but also how glad I am that I had a chance to get to know you."

Lisa didn't respond for a moment. She seemed somewhere else. Somewhere far, far away. Then she shook herself and said, "No one is ever glad to know me."

"I am."

She looked up at me in confusion. "Why?"

"You're talented and interesting. I don't meet many people who are."

"Right." Lisa nodded. "They just think they are, but they're actually conventional, dull, and a total waste of skin." She resumed cutting her pattern, humming tunelessly under her breath now.

"What's that you're working on?"

"I have no idea yet."

"And how are you doing?"

She continued humming to herself. There was something haunting about the way she sat there, cutting and humming. "Doing? What do you mean?"

"I mean, will you be okay without Nikki?"

She gazed around at her workroom. "She was my only reason for being."

"You'll find another reason."

"What reason?"

"Someone else to design for. I guarantee you there will be major stars inundating you with phone calls."

"But they won't be my baby sister. They'll never be my baby sister."

"Nikki meant that much to you?"

"She was the only person I've ever loved. It's always been *us*, going all the way back to—to . . ." She trailed off into silence.

"All the way back to when, Lisa?"

"Trancas," she whispered at me.

"Right. Your dad told me you spent a lot of summers out there when you were kids. That you loved it out there."

She shook her head slowly at me. "Trancas is the bumpy road to hell."

"Why do you say that? Did something happen there?"

She didn't answer me.

"What happened in Trancas, Lisa?"

She still didn't answer me. Just went back to humming. She was somewhere far, far away again. And all done talking to me. I'd get nothing more from her, aside from the genuinely spooky vibes she was giving off. I glanced over at Lulu, who looked profoundly unsettled. She was getting those same spooky vibes, too.

I climbed to my feet, bent over, and kissed Lisa on the forehead.

She recoiled in horror, her eyes wide with fright until she squinted at me and recognized who I was. Then she relaxed and returned to cutting her pattern, humming.

I refilled my toilet kit, and washed and dried Lulu's bowls and stowed them in their doctor's bag. Put my dress clothes back into their garment bag. I was opening my suitcase on the bed when the phone on my nightstand rang. I picked it up and said, "This is Hoagy."

"Darling, please tell me that you're okay." Merilee's voice was strained with emotion.

"I'm fine, Merilee. And I'm sorry to bother you but—"

"You're not. Bothering me, that is. We're on a much-needed break. I've been in conference for two solid hours with Rob and his brain trust—Marty, Andy, and Liz. We heard the news about Nikki, of course. It's horrible. I'm so, so sorry. You liked her. You were looking forward to working with her. Please tell me what I can do to help."

"I hate to ask, because you told me your life is already super complicated right now, but the homicide detective who's in charge of the case, Lieutenant Emil Lamp, wants me to—"

"Sorry, did you just say *Emil*?"

"I did."

"I wonder if he was named after Sergeant Emil Klinger in *North by Northwest*. Possibly his parents were big Hitchcock fans."

"I'll be sure to ask him."

"Oh, dear. I apologize, darling. This is what happens to me when I sit in an office with movie people and shpritz for hours. You were saying . . . ?"

"I know him from the Sonny Day case. He's asked me to stick around town for a day or two. Seems to value my insights."

"As well he should."

"And I can't stay here at the *Being Nikki* house. Or I should say I can but I don't want to."

"Of course not. You and Lulu are moving in with me. I'll call the concierge at the Four Seasons and have him cancel your reservation for tonight's redeye flight to New York and give you a key card to my suite. Come on over whenever you're ready to get out of there."

"Are you sure about this?"

"Positive."

"Thank you, Merilee. I appreciate it." Lulu let out a whimper. "*We* appreciate it."

"Hoagy . . . ?

"Yes, Merilee?"

"Did you honestly think I'd say no?"

"I had hoped you wouldn't."

"I'm not free this evening, sorry to say. I'm having a working dinner at Spago with Rob and the others. But make yourself at home. Order room service."

"As it happens, I'm having with dinner Lieutenant Lamp."

"You mean *Emil*?"

"You really like that name, don't you?"

She fell silent for a moment. "It must be dismal up at that house."

"It's not a lot of laughs."

"I'm sorry, darling."

"So am I."

Chuy's was a little neighborhood Mexican place on Sawtelle and National where Chuy's mother made the soft corn tortillas by hand over an open hearth and served them to you fresh off the griddle—hot, fragrant, and golden around the edges—accompanied by bowls of guacamole and salsa.

By the time I'd stowed my bags in the trunk of Lisa's BMW and fled the *Being Nikki* house to meet Lamp there I had to fight my way through a crush of TV news crews and newspaper photographers who were being held back behind a barrier on Bowmont. Five news choppers were now circling overhead.

It wasn't quite six when I arrived at Chuy's but it was already starting to fill up. He didn't take reservations. On Saturday nights people were lined up on on the sidewalk halfway down the block.

Lamp and I both ordered the chiles rellenos, which were the best in the city. Lulu wanted two fish tacos, minus the tacos, and circled three times under the table before she curled up on my feet to wait for them. I drank down a half bottle of Dos Equis practically in one gulp. Lamp had a Coke, sucking on the ice cubes as he sat there across the table from me with his notepad and pen close at hand, jacket off, sleeves rolled up. On his right wrist he wore a bracelet of turquoise and silver, vaguely Zuni in design, on his left a bulky digital watch with a black plastic band.

"Good to see you again, Hoagy. Sure wish it was under happier circumstances."

"I get the feeling we're not destined to meet under happy circumstances. How's your mom?

"Great. She's taking a jewelry class. Made this bracelet for me."

"Very nice. Zuni, isn't it?"

"Gosh, I don't know. I'll have to ask her."

"I couldn't help noticing that you've started shaving now. Is she letting you date girls yet?"

Lamp grinned at me. "Always with the jokes." Then he turned serious. "Actually, it's not easy to be in a relationship when you work homicide. You put in long, crazy hours and they can be plenty grisly hours. I did date a kindergarten teacher for a few weeks last summer, but she couldn't handle what I do. A lot of us end up dating ER nurses, who work crazy shifts themselves and aren't totally grossed out by what we encounter on the job." He took a sip of his Coke before he opened his notepad and said, "What have you got for me? And please, God, make it good."

"Don't know how good it is, but I do have something . . ." I'd put a khaki shirt on over my long-sleeved Izod shirt. I unbuttoned one of the chest pockets and unfolded the typewritten message that read:

IF YOU WRITE THIS BOOK YOU WILL DIE

"I found this in my bed last night," I said, handing it to him. Then I removed the page of directions to Pasadena from my other chest pocket and handed that to him. "Nikki's assistant, Mona, typed these directions for me yesterday on her IBM Selectric. The threat wasn't typed on the same typewriter."

He compared them closely, frowning. "Who'd want to scare you off? And, more importantly, why?"

"The who is somebody who was aware of the existence of the project, which limits it to a very small group. It was a tightly held trade secret. That means Nikki's immediate family and a tiny handful of others—Mona, George, and

George's lover, Rory, the pool boy. He knew why I was out here. As to the why, my gut feeling is that this will turn out to be a family thing."

"As in . . . ?"

"As in someone was afraid Nikki might spill some damaging dirt, which seems unlikely because the book was intended to be a hip, spicy romance novel, not a tell-all memoir about the skeletons in the Dymtryk family closet. But possibly someone in the family has an awful secret to hide and was afraid Nikki might toss it my way and sneak it into her novel."

"Do you think she would have?"

"I honestly have no idea."

"Is anyone at the top of your list?"

I mulled it over as I munched on a soft tortilla laden with guacamole. My mind went straight to Enid, she of the darkest of dark souls, who possibly wasn't as pious and pure as she pretended to be. Maybe Nikki had some dirt on her. Dirt that she'd have loved nothing more than to reveal. But how on earth could Enid have teleported herself from Pasadena and slid that note into my bed? "Not really, Lieutenant. Both Jack and Rita no doubt had numerous affairs before they split up. And it's a slam dunk that Jack's been involved in his share of shady legal maneuvers. We're talking about show biz, after all. Speaking of which, are you familiar with a messenger service called Daylite Courier?"

Lamp made a face. "Sure am. I'm also familiar with their reputation for the extra goodies that they deliver in those pouches of theirs."

"Why hasn't the LAPD put them out of business?"

"Connections in high places. Never forget that the president of Panorama Studios, Max Diamond, who's the single most powerful man in the city of Los Angeles, was a Detroit hoodlum sent out here in the late forties by Meyer Lansky to settle some union troubles. The man who Max reported to was Bugsy Siegel. Max is crooked. The entertainment industry is crooked. And this whole city is crooked. It's not La-La Land, Hoagy. That's nothing but a sunny illusion, same as the movies are. But it's not as if I'm telling you anything you don't already know, am I?"

"That would be a no."

He peered across the table at me. "So why this interest in Daylite Courier?"

"Because I think Jack Dymtryk is Daylite's lawyer."

"Wouldn't surprise me one bit. Are you suggesting that Nikki was planning to blow the whistle on some of his shady dealings?"

"I'm suggesting it's possible, although I would have no idea why she would. But I do know that Nikki was a lot smarter than the public realized." I drained my Dos Equis and moved on. "It's also possible she knew something about Rita's soon-to-be ex-husband, George, that he would rather not have seen in print. But seeing as how the guy came out of the closet on *Being Nikki* it's hard to imagine how she could have further sabotaged his broadcasting career. Rory may have something shady in his past, but he doesn't strike me as someone who'd hide a threatening note in my bed. Especially a typewritten one. Honestly? That damned note puzzles me. I showed it to Nikki this morning."

"So she saw it?"

"She did. Figured her mom got high on pills and was reliving an episode of her old TV spy series. She thought it was funny."

"Doesn't seem so funny now, does it?" Lamp said quietly.

"No, it doesn't."

"May I hold on to this?" Lamp asked.

"Of course."

"And I'll get a warrant to search the house for any and all typewriters. Also all the typewriters in Jack's office, if it comes to that," he said as our waiter arrived and set huge plates of chiles rellenos, beans, and rice before us, then slid Lulu's fish tacos under the table.

I asked him for another Dos Equis, Lamp wanted another Coke. And then we both dove in. The chiles rellenos were even more delicious than I'd remembered. Also, for some reason, murder makes me hungry. No idea why. I prefer not to regard it as a flaw in my character. "What have you got so far, Lieutenant?"

"Forensics found no fingerprints on the sledgehammer. It was wiped clean. So was the latch to the backyard toolshed. They found no traces of muddy shoe prints on the pavement surrounding the pool or on the brick path to the backyard. Everything was tidy and bone dry."

"So they turned up bupkes."

"In a word, yes. But I do have the coroner's preliminary autopsy report."

"That was quick."

"When it's a high-profile celebrity like Nikki Dymtryk, he moves faster than a speeding bullet. It's by no means a complete autopsy. He doesn't have any results on her blood chemistry yet, as in any drugs she might have had in her system. And he was just getting ready to run a pregnancy test on her."

"What leads you to believe she was pregnant?"

"Nothing, but you never know what you're going to find until you find it."

"That's a good line. Can I steal it?"

"It's yours."

Lamp studied his notes. "Time of death was approximately one thirty P.M. She was hit with tremendous force on the upper rear of her skull. Bone fragments penetrated the subdural brain tissue, which caused massive clotting. She was still alive for a second or two when she hit the water. He found thirty milliliters of pool water in her lungs. But that's equivalent to two tablespoons, as in almost nothing. She by no means drowned."

"Any idea how strong or tall her attacker was?"

"Height's impossible to tell. We have no way of knowing if she was standing up straight when she was struck or crouching by the side of the pool to test the water temperature. As to strength, anyone who can swing a five-pound sledge with force could have done it."

"A woman?"

"A fit, good-sized woman, sure. Have somebody in mind?"

"Plenty of somebodys, with the possible exception of Rita, who can barely get up out of a chair, let alone have crushed her daughter's skull. There's her Aunt Enid, who thought that Nikki was the devil's spawn. And Mona looks plenty fit herself. She was Nikki's best friend in high school. Also a year older and had a car. Used to drive them to wild, boozy UCLA frat parties when Nikki was only fifteen. Also took Nikki to get both of her abortions."

Lamp's eyes widened. "She had two abortions?"

"She did. Told me so herself. And there's no way Mona didn't resent Nikki's fame and fortune, even though she denies it. Then there's Pam Hamilton, who works out every day and could have made up that whole story about finding Nikki floating in the pool."

"Why would she do that?"

"Maybe she was afraid Nikki would spill something about her."

"*Is* there something to spill about her?"

"No idea, but Pam's a big TV star. She'd stand to lose a lot if her reputation took a hit. Might be worth it to have someone sniff around."

"Agreed. There's also Nikki's sister, Lisa," Lamp said. "If we're still talking about women, that is. I wouldn't exactly call her fit but she's got plenty of heft. Can we be sure she hasn't been boiling inside ever since they were kids because she was the short, lumpy one and Nikki was so tall and beautiful?"

"That's a good question, Lieutenant."

"Thank you, I try."

"I spoke with Lisa before I left the house. Supposedly, she rarely leaves her room yet she was all sweaty and disheveled and her bare feet were filthy and scratched up. Maybe she slipped out of the house unnoticed, ran down the street barefoot, and smashed her sister's skull in—even though she told me that Nikki was her whole world and she'll be totally lost without her. Furthermore, there's something decidedly peculiar about Lisa."

"Peculiar as in . . . ?"

"An eerie, haunted quality that I can't quite place. Nikki told me Lisa's never been in a serious relationship. She was pretty sure that Lisa's still a virgin."

"So you think she's a person of interest."

"I think I wouldn't rule her out."

Lamp flipped through his notes as he continued to eat. "The blow to the skull was the only mark the coroner found on Nikki's body. No scratches or bruises, no evidence of sexual assault. There was no else's blood or skin under her fingernails. Appears as if her assailant simply nailed her on the head from behind as she was getting to ready to dive into the pool."

"Hmm . . ."

Lamp peered at me "Hmm . . . what?"

"That doesn't work for me. The sledge was taken from the toolshed, correct?"

"Jack said there had been a five-pound sledgehammer in the toolshed and that it's not in there anymore. Therefore, we're operating under the hypothetical assumption that it's the same one."

"Did Nikki go into the house before she swam?"

"Pam said Nikki had a spare key, but that there was no indication she or anyone else had been in the house."

"Have you found the key at the scene?"

"No, we haven't."

"I suppose it's possible she went in the house to use the bathroom before she took her swim, but would she actually need to do that? Her own house was a mere three-minute walk away. Nope, it still doesn't work for me."

"Gosh darn it, *what* doesn't?"

"How could someone follow Nikki into the backyard, grab the sledge from out of the shed without her noticing, sneak up behind her, and whack her over the head in the same amount of time that it took her to toss her beach towel on a lounge chair and dive in? It doesn't play."

Lamp furrowed his brow. "You're right, darn it. It doesn't. Unless the sledgehammer had already been removed from the shed and was, say, leaning against the back fence so that her killer simply had to grab it and sneak up behind her."

"That would mean Nikki's killer anticipated she'd be leaving her house to swim there and had set up everything ahead of time. Again, I don't buy it."

He worked on his dinner in silence for a moment. "What *do* you buy?"

"That Nikki and her killer had a conversation of some kind before she got whacked. I have no trouble believing that Nikki could carry on a calm, reasonable chat with someone who had just removed that sledgehammer from the toolshed and was standing there wielding it. She was supremely self-confident. And if this whole business had to do with her spilling a secret in her book then, again, we're dealing with that same small circle of people, mostly family. Therefore, she'd feel certain that he or she had no actual intention of using it and was merely trying to throw a scare into her. I can also buy that Nikki believed that she'd defused the situation. Had no reason to fear her killer. And so she turned away, started to dive in, and that's when she got her skull crushed in."

"That makes some sense." Lamp sipped his Coke. "Unless, that is, we're going about this all wrong. I'm going to have a conversation with Mona in the morning."

"Meaning you like her for it?"

"Meaning I want to widen out our search. Find out if she remembers the names of the two UCLA frat boys who knocked up Nikki."

"How on earth does that factor in?"

"Possibly something has arisen that would cause one of them to want to have her eliminated."

"Such as . . . ?"

"Such as he's now an up-and-coming lawyer in his thirties who could be planning to run for the LA City Council or a seat in the US Congress. If that's the case, a potential opponent might hire a private detective to dig up some dirt on him. *This* kind of dirt. Or maybe he's planning to marry a very wealthy girl from a distinguished family and her father has hired someone to run a background check on him. There are plenty of reasons why an ambitious guy with a wild frat-boy past would want to tie up any loose ends."

"Is that what you think Nikki was? A loose end?"

"I have to consider every possibility, Hoagy."

"You're right. It makes perfect sense. But how does it tie in with that note in my bed?"

"Maybe it doesn't. Maybe Nikki was right when she told you her mom was tranked to the gills and reliving a plot from her TV glory days. Believe me, this doesn't mean I'm ruling out someone who was close to her. In fact, I sent a man up to the house a while ago to tactfully find out everyone's whereabouts early this afternoon."

"Twenty seconds."

"Excuse me?"

"That's how long it took Enid to tell your man that her great-great-grandfather was the chief justice of the Pennsylvania Supreme Court."

"How on earth did you—?"

"She was in Pasadena volunteering at her church's clothing drive, or so she claims. Kenny was at the Record Plant on the Strip meeting with a British rocker named Nigel Hamer and Nigel's manager. George was at his TV station editing a Hollywood nostalgia piece on June Allyson. Rita was at the beauty parlor, where she got doused with a perfume sample that made Lulu sneeze. Which reminds me—Lulu smelled something on Mona's Nikes. She may turn out to be quite a valuable asset as a crime dog. Did you know that basset hounds are the second-highest rated scent hounds in all of dogdom? Only bloodhounds top them. What I mean to say is that she's more than just another pretty face."

"That's real interesting, Hoagy. Can we go back to what she smelled on Mona's Nikes?"

"Tuna fish, supposedly. Mona told me she spilled some on them when she was making lunch. But who knows if that's true? And that's not all Lulu smelled while we were in that house of horrors. She was keenly interested in something on the cuffs of Kenny's trousers. Enid said that he'd gotten a mayonnaise stain on them and that the dry cleaner had to use a solvent to remove it. But, get this, Enid didn't like it when Lulu started sniffing *her* gabardine trousers. She not so subtly crossed her legs and bonked Lulu on the nose."

"Meaning . . . ?"

"Meaning maybe there was something on *them* that she didn't want Lulu to get a good whiff of. Let's not forget that Enid thought that Nikki was a satanic tramp."

"I haven't forgotten."

"She especially disapproved of Nikki having slept with a black rap musician. Told me it was just like jumping into bed with an alligator."

Lamp's eyes narrowed at me. "She's a racist?"

"I'd say that's a safe conclusion to draw. Also an anti-Semite."

"What are you basing that on?"

"When she and Kenny first moved out here, they looked at houses on the West Side near Jack's Beverly Hills office. But she told me she didn't feel comfortable because there were too many 'show-business types,' which is code for J-E-W-S. So they ended up in Pasadena, where you'll find very few 'show-business types.' I don't like Enid."

"Yeah, I'm getting that. Talk to me some more about Jack. Do you trust him?"

"Are you kidding me? The man gets paid by the hour to lie. But he's been very nice to me. I like the guy. I like his brother Kenny, too, even though they're totally different. Jack's a womanizer who runs with the Hollywood crowd. Kenny's politically conservative and deeply religious." I cleaned my plate with the last of a soft tortilla and sat back, sipping my beer. "Did Rory turn up yet?"

Lamp rolled his eyes. "No, and he's beginning to piss me off."

"Lieutenant, I had no idea you were capable of becoming pissed off."

"It doesn't happen often, but it happens. We believe we can account for his whereabouts at the time of Nikki's murder. He was working on a faulty garage-door opener for a lady on Bowmont."

"Was it Julie Christie?"

"Why, does she live on Bowmont?"

"Don't mind me. It's been a long day."

"But he still hasn't come home. One of my men would have contacted me by now if he had." Lamp glanced at his watch. "It's past seven o'clock. His truck and motorcycle are at the house, but he's not. And he's got me wondering why."

"I assume you've had men combing the neighborhood for him."

"You assume right. All day long people kept telling them, 'Oh, he was here ten minutes ago. You just missed him.' I don't know why we can't find him."

"Based on what little I know about him he could be tucked into bed with a rich, naughty housewife who has a taste for scuzzy guys and isn't answering her doorbell."

"Could be," Lamp conceded.

"Or a tasty young Guatemalan housekeeper. Or a Filipino houseboy or—"

"Okay, you made your point. Have you got anything else?"

"You were talking before about widening out. Nikki famously left behind a string of dumped boyfriends and pissed-off girlfriends and wives. Is it possible her killer could be one of them?"

"Absolutely. We also have to consider the possibility of a whack-job celebrity stalker who has been patiently watching her and waiting for an opportunity to strike. We've got a team at Parker Center right now working the pissed-off exes angle. They ran a check on Lil' Bi'tch, the rapper who shot up Nikki's Porsche. She's still back home in Atlanta. The Atlanta PD paid a call on her. She's now married to a UPS driver, has two kids and weighs in at at least two hundred pounds. I'm guessing no one calls her Lil' anymore." He grinned at me, looking all of nineteen.

"As far as whack-job celebrity stalkers go, there could definitely be some loser out there who has been obsessed with Nikki ever since he saw her butt in *Playboy*. We have no indication yet that anyone has been watching or following Nikki—but that doesn't mean they haven't been. We're checking with the postal carrier to see if he's noticed the same car parked on Hazen the past few days. Hardly anyone parks there, so he'd notice. Nikki hadn't complained about anyone following her or sending her threatening letters. Jack assured me he would have contacted us right away if she had. And Mona hasn't been fielding any creepy phone calls. The house's phones are not only unlisted but they change the numbers every few months." He finished cleaning his plate and sat back, tilting his head at me slightly. "So tell me more about Miss Nash."

"What makes you think there's more to tell?"

"I'm a trained detective, Hoagy, remember?"

"Fair enough. She tracked me down last evening through my literary agent in New York and I went to see her at her suite at the Four Seasons after I had dinner with Pam and Jack."

Lamp raised his eyebrows. "And . . . ?"

"She wanted to alert me before it hits Liz Smith's column that she's divorcing her husband, that fabulously successful British playwright Zach somebody. She's pretty upset about it."

"Not necessarily bad news for you and Lulu though," Lamp said.

Lulu whimpered from under the table.

"We couldn't agree more. In fact, we all went to Pink's for lunch today, as I believe I already told you."

"You left out the Pink's part."

"I apologize. And after you gave me your 'Don't Leave Town' edict—"

"Gosh darn it, Hoagy. That was a request, not an edict."

"I called her and she's making sure that the concierge has a key card to her suite ready and waiting for me."

"So you and Lulu are staying over with her tonight?"

"That's the general idea," I said as Lulu let out a gleeful whoop.

Lamp beamed at me. "Gee, that's great, Hoagy."

"I have a steep hill to climb, but it's a positive development. I sure have experienced a wild swing of emotions in these past twenty-four hours."

"What'll you do for work now that Nikki's romance novel has turned to dust?"

"No idea. But if there's one thing I learned back when I hit rock bottom it's that obsessing about what comes next is hazardous to my health."

He studied me carefully from across the table. "But you're doing okay?"

"Yeah, I'm okay. Thanks for asking."

Our waiter hurried toward us now with a nervous look on his face. In a low, urgent voice he said, "Lieutenant, we have a phone call for you. You can take it in the kitchen."

Lamp's jaw tightened as he got to his feet, notepad and pen in hand, and darted off.

I took care of our check and finished my beer. I had plenty of time. Lamp was gone ten minutes. When he came back, he swiftly rolled down his shirtsleeves and put his tan suit jacket back on, a look of intense concentration on his face. "Sorry, Hoagy, but I have to cut out on you. I'm riding tail on a high-speed chase."

"Did you just say a high-speed chase?"

"I did."

"Does this have anything to do with Nikki's murder?"

"It does."

"Then we're coming with you," I said as Lulu and I followed him out of the dining room toward the front door.

"Not a chance. This is official police business." His cruiser was parked out front. He unlocked it and glared at me as I grabbed hold of his passenger-door handle and wouldn't let go. "No way, Hoagy. Forget it."

"Don't try to talk me out of it, Lieutenant. You're the one who told me to stick around town, remember?"

Lamp heaved an exasperated sigh. "Okay, fine. Jump in."

We jumped in, Lulu on the seat between us with her tail thumping. She'd never been in a police car before. I'd never seen her so thrilled. Lamp lowered his window, slapped his red rooftop bubble on, then raised his window and took off, high beams on, siren blaring. He got onto the San Diego Freeway heading north and floored it, weaving his way expertly through the sluggish evening traffic at eighty-five miles per hour, his hands gripping the wheel in the ten-and-two position as he raced his way north of Sunset and climbed into the hills toward the San Fernando Valley. I lowered my window halfway so Lulu could stick her head out but she didn't budge. Just sat there between us, her eyes gleaming.

I studied Lamp for a moment before I said, "So . . . ?"

"So we had officers stationed at a barricade at Bowmont and also at the Cherokee-Coldwater intersection. Rory Krieger managed to rabbit on us anyway. He knows the territory. Must have jumped every gate and fence in the neighborhood so that he could make his way one block farther up Coldwater to Sherwood Forest Lane, where he hitched a ride to the Valley from a young guy who dropped him off at the Hughes supermarket on Coldwater and Ventura. He got out there, found an old lady who was putting her groceries in the trunk of her blue Acura, shoved her to the ground, grabbed her keys, and took off. But it's not Rory's lucky night. Two officers in a black-and-white were right across the street pulling out of the parking lot of the Sportsmen's Lodge, where someone had just had their room broken into, and they witnessed the whole thing. When Rory came screeching out of the parking lot in the blue Acura, they took right off after him, siren blaring, and called it in. He got on the Ventura Freeway and headed north, doing a solid ninety miles per hour. A high-speed chase is now in progress. He has at least six cruisers on his tail."

As we crested at Mulholland and began our descent into the Valley, we could make out the lights of a cluster of police and TV news choppers way off in the distance.

"Jeepers, he's already gotten as far as Hidden Hills," Lamp said. "He'll be in Thousand Oaks before we know it. I'm told it's being carried live on local TV. People sitting at home in their lounge chairs love watching high-speed chases."

"He can't get away, Lieutenant. What on earth is he thinking?"

"He's not thinking. You've heard the expression 'fight-or-flight mode'? He's in flight mode. A state of crazed panic."

"Not to belabor the obvious, but I gather we should take this to mean that he's Nikki's killer?"

"Sure as heck looks that way." Lamp got off the San Diego Freeway and onto the Ventura Freeway, commandeered the left lane with his bubble light, siren, and high beams, and zoomed through the evening traffic at that same steady eighty-five miles per hour. Lulu continued to sit there between us, her eyes still gleaming eagerly. "When Rory kept pulling his disappearing act on us this afternoon, I tasked a team at Parker Center to contact Fresno and start digging into his past. They got all kinds of juicy background intel from the Fresno PD, most of it off the record. For starters, his name in Fresno wasn't Rory Krieger. According to his driver's license it was Robert Douglas Sahm. As far as we know, it still is, since Rory lives rent-free at the *Being Nikki* house and, according to George, pays cash for everything. Gets paid in cash, too. Has no bank account, no credit cards. It was George who bought those motorcycles."

"You mean there is no such person as Rory Krieger?"

"That's exactly what I mean. And it gets better. Turns out he's not originally from Fresno. He'd only been living there for a few months, working as a custodian at a 7-Eleven, when he left for our fair city three years ago. And it seems he left under a cloud."

"What sort of a cloud?"

"Knocked up a counter girl who worked the same shift as he did—a high school girl whose dad has a cousin who's an assistant DA. The assistant DA told him to clear his belongings out of his rented room, get on a bus, and go far, far away or he'd find himself working on a road crew in an orange jumpsuit. That's how the man who we know as Rory ended up here."

"Wait, wait, there's something that doesn't add up. *Being Nikki* was a huge reality TV sensation. Wouldn't someone from Fresno have recognized him when he popped up as Rory the pool boy and tipped off the tabloids? They would have eaten that story up."

"You make a good point, Hoagy," he said, his eyes never leaving the road as he flew past the evening traffic, siren blaring, focused and amazingly calm.

"Thank you. I try."

"No one in Fresno contacted the tabloids because when he lived there he weighed thirty pounds more, wore his hair in a buzz cut, and was clean-shaven. And, wait, this gets even better. The Fresno assistant DA, an obvious numbskull, didn't run a criminal background check on Robert Douglas Sahm or fingerprint him. The Fresno PD, which is manned by more numbskulls, just shot us a copy of his California driver's license, which they never bothered to run. We did, and guess what? It's a forged license. There's no such person as Robert Douglas Sahm either. However, chubby, clean-shaven Robert Douglas Sahm is a dead ringer for *bing-bing-bing* John Thomas Vaughan from Odessa, Texas, where he was convicted in 1980 for felony assault and battery and was sentenced to five to seven years. He got paroled after three, jumped parole, and fled Texas for California."

"Which would mean he's a fugitive from justice."

"Indeed, he is. He most likely hitchhiked his way to Fresno. Washed dishes at small-town diners in exchange for meals and a bunk. He's a career lowlife. Knows how to work the underground. When he hit Fresno, he got himself that forged California driver's license with a brand-new name and Social Security number. Rented a room, went to work at 7-Eleven, and lived on the down low until he couldn't keep his hands off that high school girl. The Odessa, Texas, PD has shot us his prints. We've sent some forensic guys up to the *Being Nikki* house to dust his room. If they're a match, and I have no doubt they will be, then we've got our man."

I mulled it over as Lamp continued to race his way through the traffic, his bubble flashing, siren blaring. When the traffic started to get slower ahead of us—even though we were still several miles from the police and news choppers circling overhead with their powerful lights shining down on the freeway—Lamp swerved into the emergency breakdown lane and continued to tear his way along.

Until a deafening explosion up ahead of us suddenly shook the ground and sent a fireball high into the air. Lulu immediately dove to the floor at my feet, trembling. Loud noises terrify her. The traffic ahead of us immediately came to a dead stop.

Lamp slowed to a creep but kept on going in the breakdown lane until he got as close as he dared to the horrific flaming wreckage that blocked every northbound lane of the freeway. The black-and-whites that had been on the tail of the blue Acura had formed a barricade across the lanes several hundred yards away to keep everyone safely back as one fire truck after another came roaring up the off-ramp that was just past the scene of the massive flaming pileup.

It appeared as if the man who we knew as Rory Krieger had smashed into the back of a Bekins moving van and set off the explosion. Both vehicles were engulfed in poisonous-smelling gas-fueled flames. So were three other cars that had had the misfortune of being adjacent to the collision. Five vehicles in all were on fire. The firefighters jumped out of their trucks and went to work as fast as they could, hosing them down with huge amounts of foam.

215

"Stay here," Lamp ordered me. He got out and joined the officers who were standing beside their black-and-whites.

A pair of ambulances had parked in the exit lane for the off-ramp and EMT workers were attending to the Bekins drivers, who'd managed to escape from their truck before it exploded. They were both injured but conscious. A dented and scraped Trans Am that seemed to have been involved in the wreck was also parked there. Its driver, a young guy, was leaning against it speaking with the people who I assumed were the drivers of the three flaming cars, all of whom appeared to have escaped unharmed but were clustered together in fear. They were young and old, male and female. Some had been carrying passengers, two of them little kids. I spotted seven people in all.

The only person whom I didn't spot was Rory.

A half dozen tow trucks started to amass in the middle of the freeway beyond the pileup, readying to pull the vehicles off the road when it was safe. One of them was big enough to tow the Bekins van.

Lulu climbed into my lap, trembling. I reassured her that we were okay as I watched the whole scene unfold under the illumination of the chopper lights, feeling stunned and slightly disoriented. It was as if I'd been watching an elaborately choreographed action sequence for a Bruce Willis film and all these people were actors and the director up in one of the choppers had called "Action!" and the cameras were still rolling.

But this was no movie.

Lamp remained there for several minutes, speaking to three different officers in uniform. Then he returned and got back in, shaking his head. "According to the drivers who he'd sped past seconds earlier, doing at least ninety, the fool tried to swerve around a slowpoke, lost control of the Acura, sideswiped that dented Trans Am over there, spun out and before he could regain control smashed head-on into the Bekins truck, which was doing a sedate sixty-five. I'm told it's not a pretty sight inside of what's left of the Acura. Rory's not only crispy but was beheaded. The Bekins drivers suffered some back and neck injuries but should be okay. The others are just shaken up."

"As in scared shitless."

"That's certainly one way of putting it. It'll be hours before they clear all this off the road. Freeway's going to be backed up half of the night."

He called it in to the homicide division on his two-way radio and got numerous rapid-fire responses I couldn't understand a word of. I guess it's an acquired skill, because they seemed to be carrying on an actual conversation. When he was done, he said "Ten-four" just like

Broderick Crawford used to on *Highway Patrol*. Started up his cruiser, edged it across the freeway alongside of the police barricade toward the exit lane, and made his way to the off-ramp, bubble light and high beams on so that we didn't plow headfirst into an emergency responder coming up the ramp. He made a left onto a surface street and then another that was the freeway underpass. Then he got on the freeway again, heading back toward the West Side. The traffic was so clogged with rubberneckers that he had to turn on his siren and high beams again for a couple of miles until we were clear of it. But the northbound traffic was at a total standstill for miles and miles. The police were trying to reroute drivers to off-ramps onto surface streets but it was an overwhelming task. Lamp was right. It would take half of the night before normal flow resumed.

"I assume someone will pay a visit to the *Being Nikki* house to inform George in person," I said, my voice sounding unusually hoarse as we made our way back toward Chuy's, where we'd left Lisa's BMW.

"Already have," Lamp answered tightly.

"How did he take it?"

"Ultracalmly, I'm told. That George is one cool customer."

"Yeah, I wouldn't say he exudes human warmth. We had a long chat by the pool late last night."

"What's your read on him?"

"He's a kid from Van Nuys who has a taste for the good life and should in no way be confused with a rocket scientist. He never wanted to be a TV news anchorman. His true ambition in life was to be the next Lee Majors."

"He wanted to be an actor?"

"And still does. He swore to me he was genuinely crazy about Rita at first but as soon as he met Rory sparks flew and he dumped her for our crispy critter back there. My guess? He'll shrug this off and find himself someone new and much classier than Rory in no time."

"It would be hard to find anyone less classy."

"And George is a bona fide tabloid celebrity. He'll get invited to parties. Latch onto an agent who can get him auditions. He'll do fine." We'd made it back to the San Diego Freeway interchange by now and started our climb to Mulholland and the eventual downslope that would return us to the West Side. "May I ask you a rudely impertinent question, Lieutenant?"

"Heck, you can ask me anything."

"Is it remotely possible that Rory *wasn't* Nikki's killer? That he fled because he knew that as soon as you ran a routine investigation on him he'd get sent back to prison in Texas?"

Lamp considered his response for a moment. "Based on what we now know about him he was a violent, amoral lowlife. You yourself told me that before he took up with George he made a crude pass at Nikki, who smacked him in the face. A guy like that doesn't take well to humiliation. I guarantee you he made a promise to himself that he'd get even with her one day. Today was the day."

"But he didn't sexually assault her. Didn't so much as yank off her bikini. Doesn't that strike you as odd?"

Lamp glanced over at me. "You don't believe he's our man. Is that what you're telling me?"

"I told you before that my gut feeling was Nikki's murder would turn out to be a family affair."

"It's true, you did," Lamp conceded. "But my gut's not infallible. Is yours?"

"Yes, it is. If there's one thing I've learned during my somewhat checkered career, it's that if I've written a scene that feels wrong then it *is* wrong. I trust in my gut—and my gut's telling me that Rory didn't kill her."

He looked at me doubtfully. "Despite everything that's just happened?"

"Despite everything that's just happened."

He shook his neat blond head. "Afraid I can't go along with you. He had a history of felony assault. He had motive, opportunity . . . and when we arrived at the murder scene, he panicked and fled. It's textbook stuff, Hoagy."

His two-way radio squawked at him from the dash-board. He picked it up, said, "This is Lamp," and launched into another conversation that I didn't understand a single word of. After he'd said "Ten-four," he put the radio back on its dashboard clip. We'd crested at Mulholland by now and would soon hit Sunset Boulevard. "John Thomas Vaughan's prints match Rory's prints in his bedroom. Same man. It's confirmed, not that I had any doubt. And the coroner reported in a while ago. Just wanted us to know that Nikki wasn't pregnant at the time of her death, in case that proved relevant."

We fell into silence as Lamp cruised south in the direc-tion of National Boulevard.

Until I said, "Since you're convinced that you've closed the case do you need for me to stick around tomorrow?"

"If you wouldn't mind. There may be some loose ends. Unless you really need to get back."

"No, I don't mind staying another day. I'm still not satisfied."

"You've made that abundantly clear. Do you have any-thing to go on besides your infallible writer's gut?"

"Nothing worth mentioning. You've already got plenty on your plate, and a crazy night ahead of you."

"That's for darned sure." He got off at National and steered us back to Chuy's, which was still doing a brisk dinner business. He pulled up beside Lisa's BMW and patted Lulu affectionately. "Hoagy, I sure am sorry you got caught in the middle of another poop storm. Does that happen to you a lot?"

"Didn't used to. Before I signed on to do the Sonny Day memoir I'd settled into the sedate, hand-to-mouth literary life of someone who was once considered an elite novelist."

"You still are an elite novelist."

"That's kind of you to say. No, this is all new for me. I've never been in a high-speed police chase before, let alone witnessed a flaming five-vehicle pileup. Neither has Lulu. Aside from the explosion she really seemed to enjoy herself. In fact, this past hour is as excited as I've ever seen her." She let out a woof, her tail thumping eagerly. "Maybe she should become a police dog."

"I'm afraid we have a height requirement."

"Sorry, girl," I said, scrunching her ears as she let out a sour grunt. "If you need me for anything, Lieutenant, you can reach me at the Four Seasons. I'm glad to be out of the *Being Nikki* house. That place gives me creeps. So do the people. The whole setup reminds me way too much of Big Daddy's speech from *Cat on a Hot Tin Roof.*"

He frowned at me. "Can you remind me what he said?"

"I can. He said, 'What's that smell in this room? Didn't you notice it, Brick? Didn't you notice a powerful and obnoxious odor of mendacity in this room? There ain't nothin' more powerful than the odor of mendacity. You can smell it. It smells like death.' "

Lamp let out a low whistle. "That's some speech."

"Yeah, Tennessee Williams could write a little."

It was nearly ten when I pulled into the Four Seasons next to that stupid statue of the man who never moves, hopped out, and got my bags out of Lisa's trunk. A valet parker took the car. A bellhop snatched up my bags and led us inside to the front desk, where the concierge was right there ready with a key card to Merilee's suite. Miss Nash had not returned from dinner yet, he informed me discreetly.

The bellhop rode up to the tenth floor in the elevator with my bags and opened the door with the key card. I tipped him and sent him on his way. Put down Lulu's bowls in the bathroom and gave her some 9Lives mackerel and water. Hung my garment bag in the closet, deposited my toilet kit in the bathroom, and left the rest of my things in my suitcase for now.

The clothes that I was wearing smelled of that noxious flaming wreckage on the Ventura Freeway. I stripped them off and put on the second of the two complimentary robes that the hotel provided. Then I turned on the TV in the suite's living room, found CNN, and watched a replay of the news-chopper footage of the high-speed police chase that Rory Krieger, live-in pool boy from the reality TV hit *Being Nikki*, had set in motion when he'd carjacked a blue Acura from the parking lot of a Hughes supermarket. The chopper's camera actually caught the blue Acura side-swiping the Trans Am, swerving, and spinning out. But CNN tastefully cut away just before it smashed head-on at full speed into the back of the Bekins truck and exploded. Evidently, that was deemed a bit too graphic for viewers at home to see up close and personal. Instead, they cut to an aerial shot of the fiery explosion. As they ran the footage from several different angles, a news anchor provided the newly updated details about the fingerprints in Rory Krieger's bedroom matching those of one John Thomas Vaughan, an escaped parolee from Odessa, Texas, who'd been convicted of felony assault and battery.

The TV viewers were left with no doubt about who'd murdered Nikki. None.

I reached for the phone. By now it would be 2:00 A.M. in New York City but the Silver Fox would be wide-awake. She pored over manuscripts in bed deep into the night, a glass of bourbon and a pack of Newports close at hand.

She answered on the first ring. "This is Alberta."

"It's Hoagy, Fox."

"I am so relieved to hear from you, dear boy. I've been following that insane high-speed chase and fiery collision. Before you say another word please tell me that you and Lulu are both okay."

"We're fine and dandy."

"Well, I'm glad to hear that. But what an awful turn of events. Sylvia James from Guilford House is so distraught that she's called me four times. She was *positive* Nikki was going to be a major franchise author for her, especially with you at the controls. She may have been right, too. But now we'll never know, will we?"

"No, we will not."

"I'm sorry I roped you into this. I can't begin to tell you how awful I feel."

"No need. You had no way of knowing what would happen. Besides, I actually liked Nikki. And I think the book would have been fun to write."

"If that's the case, you could still write it under a pseudonym. I can't promise to sell it as anything more than a paperback original, but it'll keep you busy and there might be healthy residuals on the back end."

"No, don't think so. I'll feel as if I'm cashing in on what happened to her. It'll leave a bad taste in my mouth."

"I understand perfectly. And I'll make some calls when I get to the office in the morning. If I hear of anything that sounds promising, I'll let you know. When are you flying back?"

"Soon. Merilee's in town, as you're well aware, and has been kind enough to let me bunk in her suite at the Four Seasons with her. I'm just getting settled in."

"I'm glad she managed to track you down. When she phoned me yesterday, she sounded so upset that you hadn't returned her calls. Poor thing had no idea you were out in LA yourself. Not that it's any of my business, but now that she's kicked Zach's butt back to London this is an excellent opportunity for you to win her back."

"How do you know about Zach? Liz Smith hasn't broken the story yet."

"Merilee told me about it herself on the phone, silly boy."

"She did? What did she say?"

"That it had been a stupid rebound marriage and that she felt like an idiot. She phoned me again this morning to tell me you'd visited her last night and been incredibly nice. In fact, she said she'd forgotten what a kind man you are."

"That's me, all right."

"It's a suite she's staying in, you said?"

"Yes, Alberta, it's a suite. And it's about four times the size of my crappy fifth-floor apartment on West Ninety-Third Street, and those are all the details you're going to get out of me."

"Not only kind but discreet, which I must say is annoying the hell out of me right now."

"Good night, Alberta."

"Good night, dear boy. Give my best to Merilee. And Lulu, too, of course."

"Of course."

I hung up and sat there a moment, exhausted but miles away from sleepy. My mind was racing. Plus I could still smell the smoke from the explosion. It hadn't just been on my clothes. It was in my hair, on my skin, inside my nose. I decided to avail myself of the hotel's four-star accommodations and treat myself to a bubble bath in the giant tub. I dumped out some bath crystals they'd provided and began filling the tub with steaming hot water. Grabbed an ice-cold Heineken from the minibar and closed myself in the bathroom with my four-legged partner, who'd inhaled that same smoke, has always been a sinus sufferer, and would benefit greatly from some quality time with me in a bathroom filled with fragrant steam, even if it did mean that her mouth breathing would give off the aroma of the Fulton Fish Market. I put down a nice, thick towel for her to curl up on, took off my robe, and climbed into the tub as it filled, the water almost too hot to take but not quite. When the bubbles were just about up to my nose, I shut off the water and lay back, sipping my cold beer and feeling my tensed muscles relax.

But my mind did not stop racing.

Merilee arrived home just after I'd settled in. She called out my name.

"We're taking a bath!"

She joined us in there, closing the door swiftly behind her so that the steam wouldn't escape, and stood there looking every inch a movie star in a black silk dress that clung to every curve and a pair of stiletto heels, her waist-length golden hair brushed out and gleaming. "Well, aren't the two of you adorable?" she said, kneeling so that she could stroke Lulu, who whimpered at her softly.

"She's had quite an evening. We both have. You've heard the news?"

"Are you kidding? It's the only thing anyone in Spago was talking about. So Nikki's pool boy killed her?"

"That's what the police think. I was having an early dinner with Lieutenant Lamp when he got the news about the high-speed car chase. Lulu and I went along for the ride."

Merilee's eyes widened. "You weren't in any danger, were you?"

"No, we were trailing miles behind. Well out of harm's way from the explosion, though Lamp did get out and talk to the officers at the scene."

"What a ghastly ordeal."

"It wasn't pretty. When I got here, I realized I smelled of foul smoke so I decided a steaming hot bubble bath would be a good idea. I hope you don't mind."

"Of course not, darling. Besides, sweetness loves her steam, don't you?" she cooed as she continued to stroke Lulu.

"Water's piping hot and there's plenty of room if you'd care to join me."

She smiled at me. "I was hoping you'd say that."

"How was dinner?" I asked as she stepped out of her shoes, tied her hair up in a bun, and began to undress.

"I had a wonderful veal chop. And I'm not at all tipsy. We only drank two bottles of wine among the five of us. That's a sober, hard-working bunch."

"You're welcome to some of my beer. Or I should say your beer."

"That's very generous of you." She stood before me naked, looking as breathtakingly gorgeous as she had the very first time I'd seen her without any clothes on. The only difference between ten years ago and now was that a personal trainer had designed a customized daily workout regimen for her. I know this because I read about it in *Sports Illustrated*. "But I'm fine."

"Yes, you certainly are."

She eyed me in amusement. "You haven't forgotten how to flirt, have you?" She climbed gracefully in at the other end of the giant tub so that she was facing me. Settled herself slowly into the hot bubble bath, lay back with a contented sigh, and rested her feet on my shoulders just like she used to back in our sunshine days. I held her loosely by the ankles and kissed her toes slowly, one by one by one. She has ten if you're keeping count at home.

"Oh, my . . ." she purred. "No one has done that in a *long* time."

"Are you telling me that not only is Zach a wimp but that he ignored your toes? That's shameful."

"A minute ago you said, 'That's what the police think.'"

"Sorry?"

"When I said that Nikki's pool boy smashed her head in."

"It's true, I did."

"Somehow, I get the feeling you don't agree."

"Let's just say I have my doubts."

"And are you going to do anything about those doubts?"

"Who, me? I'm just a writer, freshly unemployed. And that's enough about me. Seeing as how Castle Rock is paying for this spa treatment how is *Random Harvest* coming along?"

"It seems very promising. The only key person who has any misgivings is, well, me."

"*You?*" I looked at her in surprise. "Does Rob know that?"

"Hasn't a clue. I've been nothing but enthusiastic, which I do very well."

"Why the misgivings?"

"Because Greer Garson was *so* marvelous as Paula. I don't know how I can do it any better than she did. If someone has already played a role as well as it can be played—defined it—what's the point?"

"You didn't hesitate to play Tracy Lord in that Broadway revival of *The Philadelphia Story*, even though Kate Hepburn defined Tracy, on Broadway and on screen. But you brought a fresh approach to it. How is this any different?"

Merilee reached for my beer and took a sip. "Because I don't have that fresh approach. I don't know how to bring anything new to Paula."

"Rob hasn't been able to help you?"

She shook her head.

"Maybe Jeremy Irons will when the two of you have a chance to sit down together in New York and read some scenes together. Maybe what you need is to play off *his* Smithy, not Ronald Coleman's."

She considered this. "Tell me something, will you? How you did you get to be so smart?"

"I spent a lot of time with you some years back. If you decide not to do it, then I think you should play Maggie in *Cat on a Hot Tin Roof*. When's the last time it was revived on Broadway?"

"Um, seventy-four. Liz Ashley played her."

"Who played Big Daddy?"

Merilee snorted. "You'll never guess."

"Come on, tell me."

"Fred Gwynne."

"Fred Gwynne as in Herman Munster Fred Gwynne?"

"The same. He was, and is, a fine stage actor despite the fact that he got roped into starring in that ridiculous sitcom."

Lulu let out a sour grunt from her towel.

"What did I say?"

"It so happens that *The Munsters* is one of her favorite shows."

"What made you think of *Cat on a Hot Tin Roof*?"

"Lieutenant Lamp and I were talking about it. I mentioned that there was something creepy and wrong about the *Being Nikki* house and the whole family. The words 'odor of mendacity' happened to come up."

"Emil sounds like a most unusual homicide detective."

"He is. Big fan of my novel, too," I said, stifling a yawn.

"Getting sleepy?"

"I guess I'm finally starting to relax. It's been a long, emotional day. It started with Nikki waking me up at dawn with coffee in bed. She's no longer alive. Rory's no longer alive. And now here I am taking a late-night bubble bath with the great love of my life."

She batted her eyelashes at me. "Are you referring to *me*, darling?"

"I don't see anyone else in this tub."

"Shall we rinse off and dive into the feathers?"

"You've had worse ideas, Miss Nash."

"Seeing as how this has been such a long, emotionally draining day for you I promise I'll be gentle."

"No need. Murder makes me eight different kinds of ravenous."

"You're a most unusual man, Mr. Hoag."

"Are you just realizing that?"

CHAPTER SEVEN

I had the best night's sleep I'd had in years in that king-sized bed with Merilee snuggled in my arms and Lulu sprawled next to us, snoring contentedly.

Fog rolled in during the night and the morning was chilly and gray. Merilee ordered orange juice, coffee, and croissants from room service while I fetched her complimentary copy of the *Los Angeles Times* from the floor just outside the door. The *Times* had given over most of the front page to the high-speed chase on the Ventura Freeway that had resulted in the fiery death of the Dymtryks' pool boy, Rory Krieger, aka Robert Douglas Sahm, aka John Thomas Vaughan—including how he'd been on less than cordial terms with Nikki, who'd spurned his advances. Although the *Times* didn't literally come out and say so, it seemed obvious from their coverage that Rory had been Nikki's murderer.

But the LAPD homicide detective in charge of the case, Detective Lieutenant Emil Lamp, was extremely careful in his assessment. "We're still collecting evidence and consider the Nikki Dymtryk killing an open case," Lamp stated. "All we know for certain right now is that John Thomas Vaughan was wanted in Texas for a parole violation and that his fingerprints match those of Rory Krieger that were found in the Dymtryk home."

Nikki's father, the powerful entertainment lawyer Jack Dymtryk, wasn't nearly so cautious. "We're relieved that Nikki's killer met with a form of swift justice on that freeway, and grateful that no one else was seriously injured. But the pain and horror of losing our beloved Nikki will never, ever go away."

IF YOU WRITE THIS BOOK YOU WILL DIE

Me? I kept thinking about that neatly typewritten warning that I'd found in my bed the night I arrived. I continued to doubt that the former John Thomas Vaughan of Odessa, Texas, had typed it and put it there. Why would he care if I ghosted a steamy romance novel for Nikki? No sense. It made no sense.

I put on my old blue turtleneck, torn jeans, and Chuck Taylors and took Lulu for a swift morning constitutional on Burton Way. By the time we returned our coffee and croissants had arrived. Merilee got busy pouring the coffee while I opened a can of 9Lives mackerel for Lulu in the bathroom and set it down for her. Lulu had a good appetite that morning. Actually, I've never known Lulu not to have a good appetite. When she had cleaned her bowl, she climbed up on the bed, sprawled out, and let out a huge yawn. She always needs a nap after breakfast. It's hard work being Lulu. I sipped my coffee, which was piping hot and most welcome, tore off a chunk of croissant, and munched on it. Merilee was standing before the French doors to the terrace in her terry-cloth robe, drinking her coffee and gazing out at the fog-shrouded view of downtown Los Angeles, when the phone rang at nine thirty.

She answered it. "Why, good morning to you, too, Rob. Heavens no, you didn't wake me. What's up?" Merilee listened in silence as he talked and talked and talked, her eyes widening in surprise before she said, "Are you kidding me? I'd absolutely love to! Yes, I do have my passport with me. Never travel without it. And not to worry, back in the days when I worked the old Keith-Orpheum circuit

I could pack my trunk so fast that my fellow troupers called me Ten Minute Merilee . . . Okay, I'll be downstairs waiting for your limo at ten thirty. No, no, I'm totally up for it, I swear. Just a bit bowled over. Okay, right, see you soon!" She hung up the phone and stared at it, stunned. "That was Rob."

"So I gathered."

"He got so excited talking about *Random Harvest* at dinner last night that he's decided he can't wait for Jeremy to come to New York in two weeks, so he called him first thing this morning and told him that we're leaving for London on today's noon flight. Which means I have almost *no* time to shower, dress, and pack." She darted for the closet, pulling out her suitcases and opening them on the bed next to Lulu, who stared at them suspiciously. "Gawd, I'm glad I have my passport. I don't know what I'd do if . . ." She trailed off, gazing at me fretfully. "I hate that I have to rush off and leave you this way, darling. I was hoping we'd be able to spend more time together. I'm so sorry."

"Don't be," I said, my chest aching. Breathing in and out was a challenge. "We've spent a magical couple of days together. It's been like something out of a dream. But for people like us, work always comes first. And Paula is a major, major role. Besides, I need to get back to New York, sit down with Alberta, and figure out what's next for me."

She kissed me lightly on the mouth, her green eyes shining at me. "Thank you for being so understanding."

Lulu let out a whimper.

"I'm afraid one of us may not be."

Merilee stroked her gently. "Aw, sweetness, please don't make this any harder. I'll see you again soon, I promise."

But Lulu was not mollified. She parked her face glumly in between her front paws and refused to look at Merilee. There's nothing glummer than a glum basset hound who won't look at you.

"The concierge still has your ticket info, darling. He can get the two of you on a flight tonight. Just call him before I check out."

"Will do. I have an errand to run today. I can stow my things in the trunk of Lisa's car." I watched her pull her clothes from the closet and fold them at warp speed. She truly was the speediest packer I'd ever seen. "Not that it's any of my business, but will you reconnect with Zach while you're over there?"

"Not a chance. I never want to see that putz again."

"Merilee Gilbert Nash! They didn't teach you that kind of language at Miss Porter's School. You've been hanging around with an unsavory crowd."

She let out a delicious laugh, her green eyes shining at me. "I'm glad we've had this chance to get back to being two people who are still fond of each other."

"Likewise."

"It's also so gratifying for me to see you taking charge of your life again. You almost destroyed yourself, you know. And took me with you."

"I do know. And I'll never be able to forgive myself."

"Yes, you will. You were in a terrible place. You'd lost touch with your voice. But now you're getting it back. I can see it in your eyes. I see the real you again. I'll call you when I get back to New York. We have a dinner date, don't forget. The Blue Mill. Liver, bacon, and onions. Extra mashed potatoes."

"I'd like that, Merilee. It'll be just like our sunshine days."

"Our sunshine days." She smiled wistfully as she continued to fly around the room, yanking things from the dresser drawers, until she came to a sudden stop. "I think I'll jump in the shower and get dressed before I finish packing."

"Go right ahead." I reached for the phone to call the concierge. "It'll only take me a minute to shave and dress. And I barely unpacked last night."

Merilee stood there with her green eyes shining at me. "Hoagy . . . ?"

"Yes, Merilee?"

"My toes missed you."

If you consult a road map or travel guide, it'll tell you that Malibu is a mere twenty-two miles up Pacific Coast Highway from the Santa Monica Pier, which makes it sound like a hop, skip, and a jump away. Nothing could be further from the truth. Just for starters, your point of origin is not likely to be the Santa Monica Pier. Or anywhere even remotely close to PCH. The Four Seasons in Beverly Hills is considered relatively close to the beach, yet it still took me thirty minutes to make it through Brentwood and Pacific Palisades to PCH by way of Sunset. Merilee had already gone rushing off to the airport with Rob by the time I left the hotel, my chest still aching. The morning fog was lifting and the sun had started to break through, so I put the BMW's top down before I took off. As I drew nearer to the beach, I found myself back in dense morning fog and the temperature had dropped back down into the fifties. I pulled over, put the top back up, put my flight jacket on and turned on the heat. Lulu, who was curled up in the passenger seat, was grateful for the heat, though still peeved that our bags were in the trunk instead of in her mommy's suite. Make that former suite.

You'd think the absence of sunshine would mean that the traffic on PCH would be light, since a foggy, chilly February weekday morning doesn't exactly cry out beach day. Not so. The highway was jammed with slow-moving Malibu-bound traffic. It took me another forty minutes to make it there. If my starting point had been, say, the *Being Nikki* house, then I would have easily been looking at a ninety-minute drive. That was why many of the show-biz elite kept both a place in town and a Malibu house for weekend getaways, much the same way wealthy New Yorkers had an apartment in the city and a place in the Hamptons.

Jack Dymtryk hadn't exaggerated. The old-timey image of Malibu as the carefree, ramshackle, sun-and-fun world of Gidget, the Big Kahuna, and "Surfin' Safari" was no longer a reality. Malibu was now a super-glitzy colony of multimillion-dollar waterfront mansions, fancy restaurants, clubs, and gourmet shops. Sleepy little Pepperdine University was growing like crazy into the foothills. But people still had to buy gasoline, so when I spotted a Union 76 station, I pulled over alongside of the phone booth, hopped out, and checked the phone book for Dymtryk, Jack.

"Trancas is the bumpy road to hell . . ."

He was listed in there, sure enough, as was his address on PCH. I jumped back in the car. As I kept on going, the traffic began to thin out a bit. His place was another ten miles north of Malibu. Jack had told me Trancas was practically deserted back when he'd bought it, since it was farther away from the city, had less cachet than Malibu, and nowhere to buy groceries. But as I drew nearer I discovered that it, too, was becoming home to showy beachfront mansions. As it turned out, I hadn't really needed an address to locate his whitewashed wood-frame shack. It wasn't hard to find at all. It was the last one standing, like a monument to his youth.

I made a left turn into Jack's driveway and parked. There was no garage. No mailbox either. He probably had a PO box in Malibu. I could see and smell the ocean from his driveway, and hear the waves crashing on the beach. The fog was starting to lift. Soon the sun would burn through it.

"Trancas is the bumpy road to hell . . ."

The shack was set far back from the beach on a bluff with a protective dune in front. There was no door facing the highway. Just shuttered bedroom windows. Lulu and I walked around to the beach side, where there were wooden steps that led up to a broad redwood deck, a set of sliding glass doors, and a kitchen door that appeared to serve as the front door. There was a picnic table on the deck where I imagined Jack and Pam ate most of their meals. Down on the beach there was a fire pit where the family used to make s'mores back when the girls were young. The nearest house was more than a hundred yards away. It was remote and private—nothing but the beach and an amazing panoramic view of the blue Pacific. Heaven. And yet, Jack's shack had a neglected feel to it, as if he and Pam didn't actually make it out here very often. Or maybe that was just the mood I was in. As I gazed around, Lulu took the opportunity to mosey down to the water's edge and sniff with keen interest at the remains of whatever denizens of the deep had washed up there and died. I just hoped she didn't roll around in whatever she found, which happened to be one of her top three favorite activities in the whole world, right up there with eating and sleeping. We all need a hobby.

"Trancas is the bumpy road to hell . . ."

I couldn't shake those spooky last words that Lisa had said to me seated on the floor of her workroom, humming to herself. Or the eerie tone in her voice when she'd said them. They had to mean something. What, I didn't know, but I wasn't flying home to New York until I'd had a look around.

I called out to Lulu to join me. She did, tracking wet, sandy paw prints onto the deck. The sliding glass doors were locked. The kitchen door was locked. It had glass panes. It would be easy enough to break one, reach in, and unlock the door. But I was hoping to avoid committing a crime. There was a window over the kitchen sink that I could have climbed in if it had been left unlatched—which was, unfortunately, not the case. I looked down at Lulu. Lulu was looking up at me. Before I resorted to breaking and entering I decided to try going old-school. There were a half dozen abalone shells piled by the kitchen door. I sorted through them in search of a spare key. No spare key. There was a flowerpot on the picnic table with nothing growing in it. I grabbed it and turned it upside down. Nope.

There was a rubber doormat at the kitchen door. The kind that's made out of old tires. Lulu was nudging at it with one of her front paws and making snuffling noises. I picked it up and, bingo, there was the spare key. Jack had probably been keeping it there since the sixties and saw no reason to change with the times. Besides, Trancas wasn't exactly a high-crime area—except for when a formerly famous author and his basset hound were attempting illegal entry.

The kitchen smelled damp. The house had been closed up for a while and was no stranger to fog. The power was on. I could hear the refrigerator running. I opened it. Not much in there. A six-pack of Coors, a carton of eggs, a loaf of Oroweat bread, butter. In the door there was mustard, mayonnaise, a bottle of Tabasco sauce, and . . . a jar of anchovies. It was definitely Lulu's lucky day. I gave her one, which lifted her grumpy spirits. Okay, I just lied. It took two anchovies to lift her grumpy spirits. The freezer had nothing in it except for ice-cube trays and a bottle of vodka. The refrigerator's contents definitely lacked the female touch. So did the cupboards, which were bare except for a few cans of soup, and pork and beans. This wasn't Jack and Pam's getaway. It was Jack's. If they came out here together, they no doubt ate out at those fancy restaurants in Malibu.

I wandered.

Passed through a doorway into the living room with those sliding glass doors that faced the ocean. There was no rug, just a whitewashed wood floor with the paint worn to bare wood in spots by sandy bare feet. Anchoring the middle of the room, on sawhorses, were two Hobie surfboards, the creation of Hobie Alter, whose fiberglass surfboard was the definitive Malibu board of Jack's youth. One of them was an almost colorless pale yellow vintage board—his high school board, no doubt—which had spent who knows how many thousands of hours in the water. It had its share of dings, but was well waxed and well kept. Clearly, he loved that board. His second board, which was much newer, was bright green and at least a foot longer.

There was a canvas-covered sofa, some director's chairs, big pillows heaped on the floor. A fireplace with a stack of wood and driftwood kindling, although it didn't smell as if a fire had been made in there for a long time. There was an old black-and-white TV with rabbit ears. There was a bookcase crammed with just the sort of steamy paperbacks he'd told me Nikki had loved to read when she was out here. With just a quick glance, I spotted *Valley of the Dolls* by Jacqueline Susann, *The Other Side of Midnight* by Sidney Sheldon, and *The Carpetbaggers* by Harold Robbins. Nothing but the best.

I wandered.

There was a hall closet filled with bed linens, bath towels, and big, colorful beach towels. There was a bathroom with a stall shower. The medicine chest held the usual basics—toothbrushes, toothpaste, dental floss for those who choose to spend their lives sticking wet string in their mouths. There were first-aid supplies, combs, brushes, and a wide array of suntan lotions. No prescription meds.

I wandered.

There were three bedrooms. One large, two small. When I say large, I don't mean spacious. None of the rooms in the shack was spacious. The master bedroom was maybe twelve by fourteen feet. I flicked on the ceiling light. The queen-sized bed had a spread on it but no sheets or pillowcases. The décor was Early Spartan. No art hanging from the walls. No curtains. Just plain wooden shutters. There was a beat-up dresser with three drawers. A closet. A few things were hanging in the closet. A purple muumuu type of thing that I assumed was Pam's, unless Jack liked to cross-dress when he came out here. Two pairs of old jeans that I did assume were Jack's. On the closet floor there were flip-flops and sandals. In the dresser I found an assortment of T-shirts, sweatshirts, men's and women's bathing suits. Not a vast quantity. Just enough for a spontaneous weekend getaway.

I wandered.

The two smaller bedrooms were the girls' rooms. It wasn't hard to tell which one was Lisa's. When I flicked on the light, I found childhood sketchpad drawings thumbtacked all over the walls. Drawings of starfish, girls in bikinis, boys in surfer shorts. All were quite primitive and showed no hint of the gifted fashion designer she was destined to become. Her room had a single bed in it with a spread thrown over it, no sheets or pillowcases. The air smelled stale, as if no one had opened a window in there in years. There was nothing in the closet aside from a few empty hangers. Lulu sniffed dutifully around, nose to the floor, but found nothing of interest.

I flicked on the light in Nikki's bedroom, which was not much different than Lisa's. Same size and shape. Same stale smell. A single bed with a spread thrown over it, no sheets or pillowcases. In lieu of drawings tacked to her walls Nikki had a dozen or more *Tiger Beat* crush photos of Simon Le Bon, the lead singer of Duran Duran. I stood there looking around and wondered why Jack hadn't taken down his daughters' preteen wall adornments. Maybe it made him smile. Clearly, neither Nikki nor Lisa had been out here for a long, long time, or they for damned sure would have yanked them down.

I opened the door to Nikki's closet. Again, I found nothing but empty hangers. I was starting to close it when Lulu found something on the closet floor that interested her. She snorted and then let out a low whoop.

"What have you got, girl?"

When she whooped again, I opened the window shutters to let in more light and knelt to take a closer look at where the whitewashed floorboards butted together. I discovered a one-eighth-inch space between them where the wood and paint had been chipped away so minutely that I hadn't noticed it.

"Lulu, you are becoming an ace crime dog. Just earned yourself another anchovy."

I pulled my penknife out of my pocket, inserted the blade in the space between the floorboards, and gave my wrist a gentle twist.

A one-foot section of the floorboard lifted out.

It was a secret hiding place.

Not much of a secret hiding place as secret hiding places go. Just a two-inch space between the floorboard and subflooring. But it was all the space that Nikki had needed. There was a letter-sized envelope in there and a small object in a chamois bag that was cinched at the top. I started to reach for them but thought better of it. Went back to the bathroom and found a pair of tweezers, then dug around in the kitchen drawers for a couple of paper napkins.

As Lulu crouched next to me with keen interest, I used the tweezers to lift the small chamois sack from its hiding place under the floor, set it on Nikki's dresser, and uncinch the sack. Then I used them to grab hold of what was inside, feeling my pulse quicken as I slowly lifted out . . . a pearl necklace. Genuine pearls judging by the luster they gave off. Dipped synthetic pearls possess no such luster. They also tend to be uniformly sized and shaped. They're beads, after all. These were not beads. They were the real deal, and worth a lot of money. Carefully, I returned the necklace to the sack. Then I used the napkins to gingerly remove the envelope by its corners and set it on the dresser next to the sack. I was pleased to discover it wasn't sealed. Holding it open with a napkin I tweezed out a sheet of lined paper that was yellowing with age. I unfolded it gently with the napkins, afraid the tweezers might rip the paper. It was notebook paper, the kind that students use in a three-ring binder. On it was a short, handwritten note:

> *I will never stop loving you, but we both know this can't go on. I'm sorry. Your One and Only, now and forever*

I stood there and stared at it.

"My secret . . ."

Nikki had told me there had only been one true love in her life, back when she was fourteen. She would not tell me who he was. She was quite adamant about it, in fact, for a young woman whose each and every sexual exploit had been tabloid fodder. So it must have been a boy she'd known out here. Except that I was not looking at a boy's handwriting. The words had been written by a more mature hand. A firm, strong hand. A college-aged guy at least. A hunky summer lifeguard, maybe? A Pepperdine student who was taking a summer-school class? Or possibly a handsome young assistant professor who was teaching one? But would someone that young be able to afford these pearls? Yes, if he came from a family with money. Then again, was it possible he was someone considerably older? Why had Nikki taken such great care to hide the note and the pearl necklace away under her closet floor in Trancas for all these years?

"My secret . . ."

Fourteen. Within a year she and Mona would be going to wild and crazy UCLA frat parties. But this was before that. Her first love. Her only love, to hear Nikki tell it. What was it that Enid had said to me? That Nikki *changed* when she was thirteen. Became insolent and disobedient. No longer a nice girl. Not that I could imagine Nikki had ever qualified as Enid's idea of a nice girl. Not like Lisa, who would sit quietly by herself all day drawing pictures.

I was afraid to refold the delicate paper so I left the note open on top of her dresser next to the pearl necklace. I also left the floorboard hiding place open, but closed the closet door to keep Lulu out of there.

The phone was a wall phone in the kitchen. I used it to call Lamp's office. He wasn't in, but I left word that I needed to speak to him, that it was urgent, and rattled off the phone number where I could be reached.

Lulu had followed me in there, parked herself in front of the fridge, and was staring at it.

"Oh, right. I forgot. A deal's a deal, girl."

I gave her the anchovy I'd promised her, then washed the oil from my fingers, dried them with a paper towel, and stood there staring out the kitchen window at the beautiful blue Pacific.

Lamp called me back ten minutes later.

"Hey, Hoagy," he chirped. "What's going on?"

"I'm at Jack Dymtryk's house in Trancas."

"What in the holy heck are you doing out there?"

"How long will it take you to get here?"

"Why would I want to do that?"

"Because there's something here I think you need to see."

"Hoagy, the case is closed. We've got Nikki's murderer."

"What you've got are the burnt remains of a headless pool boy. You don't have Nikki's murderer."

"Do you actually have some concrete evidence for me to go on?"

"I repeat, how long will it take you to get here?"

"More than an hour. I'm on Hazen Drive buttoning things up at the murder scene."

"What about if you use your bubble and siren?"

"Okay, maybe less than an hour. But what have you got for me?"

"You'll see it when you get here. The sun's burned through the fog. It's a nice day to take a drive on PCH. Have you eaten lunch yet?"

"No . . ."

"I'll get us lunch at one of those gourmet delis in Malibu. How's that for a deal?"

He sighed defeatedly. "I want you to know that the only reason I'm even considering this is that we have a history together, and I admire your insights. But if this is some kind of wild goose chase . . ."

"It's not, Lieutenant. Believe me."

"Fine. Tell me where I'm going."

I gave him the address. "You can't miss it. It's an old white shack. And Lisa's black BMW will be parked out front. I'll see you in less than an hour. Trust me, you won't be sorry. Actually, you will be. Sorry, that is. I know I am. But I'm afraid that part can't be helped."

I drove back to Malibu and found a promising-looking upscale deli where I got two lobster salad sandwiches on fresh-baked foot-long baguettes, two bottles of San Pellegrino water, and a container of lobster salad for Her Earness. Then I returned to Jack's place, put Lamp's lunch in the refrigerator, sat down at the picnic table with mine, opened Lulu's container for her, and the two of us dove in. She enjoyed the lobster salad thoroughly. I thought my sandwich was pretty good myself. The fresh sea air and panoramic view of the sun sparkling on the water didn't hurt. As I sat there munching away, a jogger ran by and waved at me. I waved back at him. He was the only person I saw.

I became aware of Lamp's siren when it was still miles away. He flicked it off once he cleared Malibu and pulled into Jack's driveway a few minutes later. I climbed down the steps and walked around front to meet him.

He did not look fresh-faced or boyish at all today. He looked hollow-eyed and exhausted. His tan suit was rumpled, and I swore I could see some faint blond stubble on his chin. He must have worked straight through the night. "Before you say a single word, Hoagy, I need to know whether you broke into this house. And don't lie to me."

"Have I ever lied to you?"

"Yes. You told me a Boston Red Sox scout was so impressed by your javelin prowess when you were on the Harvard track team that the Sox gave you a tryout as a pitcher."

"I was just testing you to see how gullible you were."

"Oh." He gazed out at the waves, then back at me. "You didn't answer my question. Did you break in?"

"No, I found a spare key under the mat outside the kitchen door. Actually, I didn't find it. Lulu did. And that's not all she found. Come on inside."

"I can't. Any evidence I discover once I cross that threshold will be inadmissible. I don't have a search warrant for the house."

"So does that mean you want me to bring it outside to you?"

"Hoagy, why are you doing this to me?"

"Everyone has to be good at something." On his pained expression I said, "Lieutenant, are you telling me you came all the way out here and you're *not* going to look at what I found?"

Lamp let a defeated sigh. "Aw, heck, I'll figure out a way to finesse it later if I have to. Show me what you've got." He followed me up the steps to the deck. I opened the kitchen door and headed inside. He hesitated at the threshold before he joined me and stood in the living room doorway, staring in surprise at Jack's surfboards parked there on their sawhorses. "This isn't what I was expecting at all. I figured it would be real fancy."

"Jack's a sentimental guy. He's worth millions yet he yearns for his 'Surfin' Safari' days, as he calls them, when all he had was his VW bus, his board, and ten dollars in his pocket. That's his old high school Hobie board right there, the smaller one. And I can guarantee you he still prefers riding it to that shiny new one. He's had this house for a long time and is very proud of the fact that it's practically the last of the old surf shacks. One bathroom. Three small bedrooms. Simple furnishings. He's kept it exactly the way it was." I led him across the room to the hallway. "That's the master bedroom over there. The girls' rooms are right here. The one on the right is Lisa's. He's kept her childhood artwork up on the walls, as you can see. And this is Nikki's old room, as you might guess from her idea of artwork."

He stood there in the doorway, gazing rather blankly at the photos of Simon Le Bon that were plastered everywhere. Lulu headed straight for the closet and pawed at the closed door.

"Nikki had a hiding place in there under a floorboard. Lulu found it. Have a look."

Lamp walked slowly into the room, donning a pair of latex gloves before he opened the closet door and examined the shallow hiding space between the floor-board and the plywood subflooring. "What did she have hidden in there?"

I turned him by the shoulders and pointed him in the direction of her dresser, where I'd left the farewell note and chamois sack. I removed the pearl necklace from the sack with the tweezers.

He read the note first, slowly and carefully, before he murmured, "'*Your One and Only, now and forever.*'"

"Remember I told you that when Nikki was fifteen she used to slip out of the house late at night to go to UCLA frat parties with Mona?"

"I remember. I also remember the part about the two abortions. So . . . ?"

"So I asked her if that was when she first started having sex. She said no, she'd had her first experience when she was fourteen. When I asked her if it was a boy from school, she got real quiet and said, '*My secret.*' Just that, nothing more. And I couldn't get another word out of her about him."

Lamp stared down at the note. "Hmm . . ."

"Hmm . . . what?"

"That's not a teenage boy's handwriting."

"I agree. My initial thinking was maybe he was a Malibu lifeguard. Or a Pepperdine summer-school student. Possibly a handsome young professor."

"That would play." Now Lamp examined the necklace. "What do you make of those pearls?"

"You mean aside from the fact that they're genuine?"

"How can you tell?"

"Because they're irregularly shaped. And see that luster they give off when the light hits them? Synthetic pearls don't do that. Synthetic pearls are also uniform in shape because they're nothing more than dipped beads."

"So this necklace is valuable."

"Very."

"Are we talking thousands?"

"Most definitely. My guess? Nikki didn't dare wear it because Rita would have recognized the pearls as genuine and demanded to know who gave the necklace to her. But she also couldn't just toss it, so she hid it here—because he's 'My secret.'"

Lamp thought this over before he said, "You said your *initial* thought was maybe *'Your One and Only, now and forever'* was a lifeguard or someone hooked up with Pepperdine. You've come up with another idea?"

I used the tweezers to return the pearls to their sack and said, "Let's leave this stuff here for now and talk outside. When you've got an ocean view staring you in the face, it's a sin not to stare back at it. Besides, I bought you lunch."

I fetched his sandwich and San Pellegrino from the refrigerator and we sat down at the picnic table facing the water. He unwrapped the foot-long baguette and took a bite. "Wow, is this *lobster* salad? It's really good."

"I almost swallowed mine in three bites."

"How much do I owe you?"

"My treat."

"No, that's not fair. You picked up the dinner tab last night."

"Actually, Jack Dymtryk did. He paid me a fat ten-thousand-dollar bonus to fly out here just in time to be around when his beloved daughter got her skull caved in."

He ate his sandwich thoughtfully, pausing to sip his San Pellegrino, before he said, "So what changed your mind about who the guy might have been?"

"It was Lisa, in her own strange way. I stopped by her room yesterday to pay my respects. She was sitting there on the floor acting really strange. Spooky and other-worldly, humming to herself."

"Think she was stoned?"

"Doesn't do drugs. Doesn't drink. Doesn't party. But she said something that sounded so odd to me that I thought I'd check it out. And now, well, now it seems more than odd."

"What did she say?"

"She said, '*Trancas is the bumpy road to hell.*'"

He nodded his head as he ate. "Plenty odd all right. Cryptic or something."

"Or something."

"Do you think she knows who *'Your One and Only, now and forever'* is?"

"I do. But she'll never tell us."

"Why not?"

"Because Nikki didn't want anyone to know."

"My secret . . ."

Lamp swallowed the last bite of his sandwich. "I'm afraid I'm still not tracking you, Hoagy. The note, the pearls, what Lisa said about this place . . . what does all of it have to do with her sister's murder?"

"Because it means I was right."

"When?"

"When I said that these sorts of cases usually end up being a family matter."

He started to take a gulp of his San Pellegrino then froze, his eyes widening. "Time out. You're not going where I think you're going, are you?"

"That all depends on where you think I'm going."

"You know exactly where I think you're going. No way. Not possible."

"Beg to differ. Everything's possible. May I ask you something, Lieutenant?"

"Would it matter if I said no?"

"Have your people checked out all of the family members' alibis for yesterday at the time of Nikki's murder?"

"We never got a chance to. Chief Gates's position is that the Nikki Dymtryk case is closed."

"Do you agree with him?"

"It's not my place to agree or disagree. He's my boss, and he expressed tremendous urgency to close it. A beautiful young celebrity got her head bashed in with a sledgehammer by her pool boy, a violent felon from Texas who engaged the department in a high-speed chase that resulted in a five-car fireball that killed him in a highly grisly fashion. Not the sort of thing that fits with Southern California's sunny, carefree image. Chief Gates places a high priority on protecting that image."

"So you don't actually know if someone's alibi didn't pan out, do you?"

"Well, no," he admitted.

"Just out of curiosity, if Nikki's case is closed then what were you doing at the murder scene when I phoned you?"

"Making sure that our forensics people didn't leave any traces of their presence behind. Pam Hamilton is quite traumatized by what happened."

"In other words, you were going the extra mile. Being a good guy. Would you consider going that extra mile for me? Doing me a personal favor? Check out those alibis."

"Hoagy, where are you going with this?"

"Absolutely nowhere I want to be going. Will you do it?"

He peered across the picnic table at me. "There are times when I don't understand you. Your mind works in ways that mine doesn't."

"You should consider yourself very grateful for that. Will you do it?"

"Aw, heck, okay. But only because I consider you a friend. An annoying friend, but a friend nonetheless."

"Thank you, Lieutenant. I appreciate that. The phone's on the wall in the kitchen. Lulu and I will take a nice, long walk on the beach. Wave me down if you turn up anything interesting."

He wadded up his sandwich wrapper and went inside. Lulu and I went down to the water's edge, where the sand was wet and firm, and walked. I checked Grandfather's Benrus. We walked for thirty minutes, passing a number of million-dollar beach houses. Hardly any of them seemed occupied except for one where an elderly man and woman were seated on beach chairs playing chess. They waved to me. I waved back, enjoying the fresh sea air and sunshine. Lulu enjoyed sniffing at the shells and various forms of former aquatic life she found—although she happily refrained from rolling around in any of it. After thirty minutes I stopped, turned around, and started back toward Jack's shack.

I was nearly there when Lamp came down to the water's edge and waved me down.

I hurried toward him and called out, "What have you got?"

He started back toward the house. "We have to go," he said, sounding very stern and official. "I put that closet floorboard back in place. I have the love letter and pearls in an evidence bag in my car. We need to lock up and take our trash with us. Leave the place exactly the way we found it."

"Whatever you say, Lieutenant." I bagged up our sandwich wrappers, water bottles, and Lulu's empty salad container. Checked to make sure all the lights were out. Locked the kitchen door and slid the key back under the mat.

"I'll follow you there," Lamp said as he strode toward his cruiser. "You know where we're going."

"Okay, but I should warn you that it's a long drive. Do you need to pee before we leave?"

"I'm good," he said curtly.

"Then let's ride." I deposited the bag of trash behind the driver's seat of Lisa's BMW, then opened the passenger door and Lulu hopped in, depositing a great deal of beach sand on the floor before she curled up on her seat. I started up the engine.

Lamp started to climb into his cruiser, then stopped. "Hoagy, how did you know?"

"Gut feeling, like I told you last night."

"I have to confess something . . ."

"What is it?"

"My gut hurts right now."

"Do you think mine doesn't?"

After inhaling that fresh, clean ocean air in Trancas, the smog in Pasadena was so thick it made me cough when I took my first breath of it. It was also fifteen degrees warmer here. I took off my flight jacket and tossed it in the back seat. I would have taken off my blue turtleneck sweater, too, except that it's not considered acceptable to pay a social call on Hillcrest Avenue wearing a tattered Sex Pistols T-shirt. Lamp had taken his tan suit jacket off while he was driving. When he got out of his cruiser, he put it on, ever the courteous professional. He shut his car door and joined Lulu and me there in the driveway, looking tense and serious. He'd tucked the clear plastic evidence bag inside a manila envelope.

"Not too shabby for a plumber's kid, is it?" I said as I took in the awe-inspiring grandeur of the historic house once again.

"Very nice." Lamp barely seemed to notice the place as he strode to the front door and rang the bell.

No one answered, despite the fact that both Ken's Volvo and Enid's Saab were sitting in the driveway.

He rang it a second time.

Again, no one answered.

It was so quiet here that I could hear the faint *snip-snip-snip* of pruners coming from the garden around back. We followed the sound and found Enid working on the rosebushes that enclosed the patio. She stood there, tall and severe, wearing garden gloves that snapped at the wrist, a long-sleeved khaki blouse, pale green pants, and an oversized straw hat. *Snip-snip-snip.*

Enid worked with such determined concentration on her face that she didn't notice us until Lulu ambled over to say hi, startling her momentarily before she allowed herself a faint smile. "Why, hello there, Lulu." Then she turned and looked at me standing there with Lieutenant Lamp and his manila envelope, her eyes narrowing ever so slightly. "Good afternoon, gentlemen. It's turned out to be a rather warm one, hasn't it?"

"Yes, it has," I said. "We rang the bell but no one answered. Then we heard you pruning. Hope you don't mind us barging our way back here."

"Not at all." Enid took off her hat and fanned herself with it, her face slightly flushed from the heat and the work she'd been doing. "Mother always welcomed friends and neighbors dropping by our garden unannounced. We didn't believe in gates and fences. It's not like that out here, I've noticed. People aren't nearly as neighborly. To what do we owe this honor, Lieutenant?"

"I called your husband's office. They said he was working at home today."

"Yes, Kenny is . . . heartsick." Enid's voice was heavy with sadness. "He didn't want to deal with all those long faces and consoling words. Everyone means well, of course, but it truly isn't helpful or comforting. Jack didn't go in either. Probably won't for several days. He has the added burden of the media hounding him, what with being the girl's father and all."

"Nikki," I said. "Her name was Nikki."

She gave me a cold stare before she turned back to Lamp. "Kenny's working in his study. He was probably on the phone when you rang the bell and didn't hear it. Is there anything I can help you with?"

"Just trying to close out my paperwork," Lamp said. "I need a few family background details and didn't want to disturb Jack, so I thought I'd go over them with Kenny. If he won't mind, that is."

"That's very thoughtful of you. I'm certain he won't mind. Do come inside. May I offer you gentlemen some iced tea?"

We both politely declined.

Enid unsnapped her gloves and left them and the pruners on the patio table along with her hat before starting her way toward the kitchen. "I hope you gentlemen don't mind coming in the back way. Mother didn't believe in formality." She led us through the kitchen and down the cool, dimly lit oak hallway toward Kenny's study, Lulu's nails clacking on the floor. His door was closed. "I'll see if he's free." She tapped on it and went inside. I heard a murmur of voices. She emerged a moment later and said, "He'll be happy to see you. Please go in."

Kenny's paneled study was as imposing as I remembered, with floor-to-ceiling shelves crammed with books and a vast Arts and Crafts oak desk. The shutters over the windows were closed. The only light in the room came from his desk lamp and a table lamp in the corner, both Dirk van Erps. He sat there hugely behind the desk in a swivel chair wearing a white oxford button-down shirt and striped tie, despite the fact that he was working at home and could have worn gym clothes if he'd chosen to. He'd been writing a brief of some kind on a long yellow legal pad—although it was Jack who was the lawyer, not he. When we walked in, he set down his gold Mark Cross pen and sat back in his chair, his big hands flat on the blotter before him.

Enid excused herself, closing the door softly behind her.

"I thought this whole awful business was over and done with," he said, sounding very somber, very down. Heartsick, Enid had called it. "But if there's anything I can do to help I'm anxious to oblige, naturally. Please, sit."

We sat in the two matching Arts and Crafts oak chairs that faced the desk, Lamp clutching the manila envelope in his lap. Lulu stretched out by the door and let out that weary groan of hers that sounds like a basketball deflating.

"How may I help you?" Kenny asked.

"Mr. Dymtryk, my men made some follow-up calls today that they didn't have a chance to make yesterday and it seems your alibi doesn't hold up," Lamp began, wasting no time on small talk. "You weren't at the Record Plant at a two o'clock meeting with a British rocker named Nigel Hamer. Nigel's manager said they waited there for an hour but that you never showed, never called, nothing."

Kenny puffed out his cheeks, exhaling slowly. "It's true, I didn't show up. Would you like to know why? Because I'm sick of rock musicians. I'm sick of actors. I'm sick of show business. I'm sick of this city full of crazy, out-of-control children masquerading as adults."

"If you weren't at the Record Plant, then where were you?"

"I drove by our old house in Santa Monica. It's been fixed up. Looks real nice. Then I stopped at a McDonald's and ordered two Big Macs, a large order of fries, and a chocolate shake from the drive-through window, sat there in my car in the parking lot, and stuffed my face."

"Why did you lie to one of my officers?"

"Because I was in no mood to talk about it," Kenny responded gloomily. "I don't mean to be contrary, Lieutenant, but why does any of this matter now?"

"It matters," I said, "because I made a drive out to Jack's beach house in Trancas this morning." On someone's cough I quickly added, "Along with Lulu, of course."

Kenny frowned across the desk at me. "What on earth for?"

"Because Jack speaks of it so glowingly. He urged me to check it out if I had the time. He sure is fond of that place."

Kenny nodded his head. "As well he should be. It's one of the last of the old shacks left. That whole area has been taken over by show-biz millionaires who've torn them down and built one gaudy mansion after another. But it was wonderful there back when the kids were young. We used to have a great time."

"I can well imagine. Being a nosy writer, I was desperate to take a peek inside. Lulu found the spare key under the kitchen doormat and we had a quick look around. I didn't think Jack would mind. It's a genuine old-time beach shack, all right. Jack's surfboards are parked right there in the living room. I poked around for a minute. It was like time travelling. Lisa's childhood drawings are still tacked to the walls in her room. And I gather Nikki had a schoolgirl crush on Simon Le Bon, because there were photos of him plastered all over her room."

Kenny smiled faintly. "I remember. Although I forget the name of his band."

"Duran Duran. They're eminently forgettable. While I was in Nikki's room Lulu started prowling around, nose to the floor, snuffling and snorting. She found a narrow gap between the floorboards in Nikki's closet and raised a real ruckus. When a basset hound raises a ruckus, you pretty much have to pay attention. I pried open the gap with my penknife and found a shallow hiding place between the floorboards and the subflooring. When I discovered what was in there, I called Lieutenant Lamp."

Lamp removed the plastic evidence bag from the manila folder and placed it on the desk before him. Put his latex gloves back on and opened the bag, carefully removing the good-bye letter from Nikki's "*One and Only, now and forever*" and sliding it across the desk toward Kenny.

Kenny read it over, slowly and carefully, his face revealing nothing.

Then Lamp opened the chamois pouch and placed the pearl necklace on Kenny's desk blotter. "Mr. Dymtryk, we believe that these are genuine pearls, which is to say they're quite valuable."

He squinted at them. "I'm no expert on jewelry. Enid would know. Shall I ask her to have a look?"

"Not necessary," Lamp said.

I said, "Early yesterday morning, Nikki and I had a good, long talk about her book. I suggested we make it a spicy story about an aspiring young actress and all the hoops she has to jump through to get ahead. Nikki loved that idea, as long as I didn't make her character out to be some kind of an innocent babe in the woods, which Nikki most definitely was not. Did you know that when she was fifteen she and her friend Mona used to sneak out late at night and go to wild UCLA frat parties, get blind drunk, and have sex with guys who they didn't even know?"

"Why, no," he said with a shake of his head. "No, I didn't."

"I asked Nikki if that was when she first became sexually active—at age fifteen. She said no, that she started having sex when she was fourteen. When I asked her if it was with a boy from school, she suddenly turned very

271

serious and said '*My secret.*' When I pressed her on who her first boyfriend was, she just said those same two words again, '*My secret.*' Which I must say I found rather peculiar coming from someone whose teen sexual exploits were so outrageous that she became a national tabloid phenomenon. Yet when it came to the identity of this boy, she just kept saying, '*My secret.*' And that's when I remembered something that Jack had said to me . . ."

Kenny stared at me from across the desk. "Which was that?"

"That you and Enid were nice enough to house sit in Trancas whenever he and Rita were able to get away on a vacation. This was back when Nikki and Lisa were teenagers and Junior was still a little boy. Enid mentioned to me how quiet and well behaved a girl Lisa was, but that Nikki's personality underwent a radical transformation when she was thirteen. She became insolent, foulmouthed, and disobedient. Would come and go as she pleased. Take off down the beach after dark with a gang of other kids and smoke pot. Come home whenever she felt like it. Or not. Enid found her so impossible to deal with that she would invent excuses to head back to Pasadena with Junior for a few days and leave you out there by yourself with the girls. She felt bad about sticking you with the responsibility but that you seemed to take it in stride. Plus Nikki wasn't nearly as nasty toward you as she was to her."

I realized it suddenly seemed quieter in Kenny's office, the reason being that Kenny was barely breathing.

Lamp said, "When Hoagy showed me this note that Nikki had hidden away, I felt certain it hadn't been written by a young boy. That's the handwriting of a mature man."

Kenny studied it again. "Could be. You'd know such things. I don't. My business is financial planning. Where are you going with this, Lieutenant?"

"You know exactly where I'm going," Lamp said bluntly.

Kenny sat there across his desk from us in heavy silence for a long moment before he said, "You're right, I do. As it happens, when you showed up here just now, I was in the process of completing my confession. It's about ten pages long. I simply . . . I can't live with the lie that Rory killed Nikki, even if the bastard was a convicted felon and lowlife. He didn't smash her skull in with that sledgehammer. I did."

"Before you say another word," Lamp said, "I'd advise you to seek legal counsel. Pick up the phone and call your brother. He can put you together with a good criminal defense attorney."

Kenny shook his head. "There's no point in that. I did it, and now it's eating me alive. That's why I've been putting my confession down on paper."

"That confession, as you call it, is just a piece of paper that won't stand up in court," Lamp said. "Proper procedures have to be followed. They exist for your own protection. Who's to say I didn't coerce you to write this so-called confession? Again, I strongly advise you to retain an attorney before you say anything more."

"You're wasting your breath, Lieutenant. I'm miles beyond caring what happens to me. My only concern now is Enid and Junior. I wasn't thinking about them back then in Trancas. I'd always thought of myself as a good Christian," Kenny said in a calm, detached voice. "But Nikki had an uncanny capacity for bringing out the evil beast that lives inside me. She did it to me that summer in Trancas when she turned fourteen. And she did it to me again yesterday. I—I can't explain my behavior."

"Why don't you give it a try?" Lamp said to him.

"I guess . . . I guess it's a form of madness. What I did with Nikki in Trancas was certainly madness. My only excuse for what happened back then was that Enid had had a difficult time giving birth to Junior and after that she rejected my sexual advances. She even insisted we start sleeping in separate bedrooms.

"That summer I was a healthy young man in my thirties who was sexually starved beyond belief. It was just like you said, Hoagy. Nikki gave Enid such a hard time that she'd flee home to Pasadena with Junior and leave me alone with the girls. Lisa was so quiet and well behaved I barely knew she was there. But Nikki drove me out of my mind flaunting that incredible body of hers on the beach in those skimpy bikinis, day after day. And so I, well, I—"

"Crossed the line you're not supposed to cross?" I said.

He nodded reluctantly, swallowing. "In my own pathetic defense, I can only say that she looked exactly the same at age fourteen as she did last week. She was not a child. She was a beautiful, desirable young woman. Also sexually precocious, although still a virgin. I was her first. I was fully aware that I was committing statutory rape, even if what we did together was totally consensual. I never, ever raped her. She wanted me just as much as I wanted her. We were crazy about each other. I knew it was wrong, but I was powerless to stop myself. I was also acutely aware that it was incestuous. So I always made sure I wore a condom, because I fervently believe that abortion is a sin."

"Okay, wait," I said. "I'm having a little trouble wrapping my mind around your religious beliefs. You were cool with having sex with your own fourteen-year-old niece yet you consider abortion to be a sin?"

"You're being very rude to me right now," Kenny said indignantly.

"I apologize. It's strictly because I'm finding it so hard to stop myself from diving across this desk and strangling you with my bare hands."

Kenny reddened angrily. "I'd like to see you try."

"Hoagy, settle down or leave the room," Lamp said to me sternly.

"Sorry, Lieutenant. I'll behave myself." I glared across the desk at Kenny, who glared right back at me.

Lamp said, "Mr. Dymtryk, did Lisa have any idea what was going on between you and Nikki that summer?"

"Trancas is the bumpy road to hell."

"No, never," he answered with total certainty. "Lisa always went to bed early. Nikki and I would wait until she turned out her light. Then we'd grab a blanket and go to a secluded spot we'd found down the beach. 'Our spot,' she called it."

"Weren't you concerned that Nikki lacked the emotional maturity to keep quiet about it? That she'd tell Enid what was going on?"

"I wasn't the least bit concerned. We were in love. It was our secret."

"My secret . . ."

"You say you were in love," Lamp said. "And yet you broke it off. Why?"

"I had to. The summer was coming to an end. Jack and Rita were due back from Europe in a few days. School was starting soon. Besides, it was sheer madness. It couldn't go on."

"Why did you give her that pearl necklace?"

"As a remembrance of the love that we'd shared. I wanted her to know I truly cared."

"Did Nikki hate you for breaking it off?"

"She wept. Couldn't believe that it had to be over. But she didn't hate me. In fact, she told me yesterday that she never stopped loving me."

"Which is why she kept your note and the pearls," Lamp said.

"And in response to your insulting remark about my religious beliefs, Hoagy, I've prayed for forgiveness every single day for what happened that summer. I knew that what I did was wrong. God tested me, and I failed the test."

"Nikki achieved great notoriety for her sex life not long after that," I said. "She got it on with rockers, rappers, ballplayers, actors. Hell, she'd screw anyone to get attention. Was is it *your* attention she wanted?"

Kenny frowned at me. "I don't understand what you're asking me."

"Do you blame yourself for Nikki turning out the way that she did?"

"Oh, I see. No, not at all. Why would I? Nikki lived her life she way she wanted to. She was an unleashed force of nature."

I gazed across the desk at him, wondering if he genuinely absolved himself of any responsibility for Nikki being Nikki, or if he was totally bullshitting me. "Yet you were terrified that you'd end up as a thinly disguised character in her romance novel, weren't you? That's why you slipped the note into my bed warning me that if I wrote Nikki's book I would die. You put it there when you darted inside the house to use the bathroom after you drove me there from the airport. Muttered some apologetic remark to Rita about how your prostate wasn't what it used to be. Did you honestly think a note like that would send me scurrying back to New York with my tail between my legs?"

"I'd read that you suffered from panic attacks when you were unable to follow up on the success of your first novel. That being the case, I thought it might convince you to reconsider."

"You were wrong. Not to mention ill-informed. There's a world of difference between suffering from panic attacks and being a fraidycat. Besides, even if I had gone home, Jack would have found someone to replace me."

"But not someone who's as gifted a writer as you are."

"Well, I can't disagree with you there."

Lamp said, "Mr. Dymtryk, you said Nikki told you yesterday that she never stopped loving you. Did this conversation take place at Jack and Pam's pool?"

"Yes, it did, Lieutenant. She phoned Jack yesterday morning to tell him that she'd had a terrific conversation with Hoagy and was really looking forward to working with him. Jack came bursting into my office to tell me. He was tremendously excited. He'd been having such a hard time finding a writer that Nikki approved of. I pretended I was excited, too. But I became worried sick the more Jack told me."

"Which was what?"

"That not only did Nikki think Hoagy really 'got' her but that he wanted her romance novel to be about how an aspiring young actress is preyed upon by older men in order to make it in Hollywood. Which confirmed my own worst fears, let me tell you. I phoned her right away and said I'd like to have a talk with her about her book. She said, 'So talk.' I said that I'd rather do it in person. She said, 'So come on up.' She was heading to Jack and Pam's to take a swim and suggested I meet her there. Just as I arrived she came strolling along barefoot from the top of the hill, free as a bird, a beach towel wrapped around her like a shawl because all she had on was a thong bikini. I pulled into the driveway, parked, and got out."

"As far as we've been able to determine, none of the neighbors saw you."

"And I didn't see any of them. I followed Nikki around back to the pool and said, 'What are going to put in this book of yours?' '*I'm* not putting anything in it,' she said. 'It's Hoagy who'll be writing it.' I said, 'Yes, but you have all sorts of naughty stories to tell him. The kind of stories that make these books into big best sellers, especially if your readers think the lead character is based on you, which they will.' She shrugged at me and said, 'I don't know what you want from me, Uncle Kenny.' And I said, 'You know exactly what I want. I want you to promise me that there won't be anything in it about *us*.' She batted her blue eyes at me and said, 'Why not?' I said, 'Because you'll ruin me. Enid will divorce me. And Junior will grow up thinking that his dad was . . . that I once . . .' And she said, 'That you had an affair with your own niece when she was fourteen? You should have thought of that before, Uncle Kenny. I still love you, you know. I've never stopped loving you, except for the times when I totally hate you. But if you don't stop bothering me I *will* tell Hoagy to make a really, really big deal about how my character was deflowered when she was fourteen by her devoutly religious uncle, a big-time Hollywood money manager.'" Kenny trailed off, his chest rising and falling.

"What did you do next?" Lamp pressed him.

"I went so far as to plead with her. She seemed to enjoy watching me squirm. And that made me angry. So I said, 'I don't want to stop you from writing about us, but I will if you make me.' Nikki, in that mocking way of hers, said, 'Stop me how?' I opened the toolshed, glanced around in there, and grabbed the five-pound sledgehammer. Showed it to her and said, 'I don't want to hurt you, Nikki, but I will if you refuse to be reasonable.' She didn't take me seriously. Just laughed at me. Then she turned to dive into the pool and that's when I hit her. I guess I had a lot of pent-up rage inside me. Guilt. Self-loathing. Whatever you want to call it. I truly loved that girl. But I also hated the weakness that she'd brought out in me, so I hit her harder than I'd imagined I would. Crushed her skull like it was a cantaloupe and into the water she went with a splash." He glanced at me. "Chlorine. It was chlorine from the pool water that Lulu smelled on the cuffs of my pants, not cleaning solvent. I wiped my fingerprints off the sledge-hammer and toolshed handle with my handkerchief and took off. I—I had to get away. My niece was floating dead in the pool with blood oozing out of her head," he said, his voice rising with urgency. "So I hurried out to the car and drove away. Again, no one saw me."

"Where did you go?" I asked him.

"To a McDonald's in Westwood. I ordered two more Big Macs, another large order of fries, and a chocolate shake from the drive-through window. Sat there in my car gorging myself and listening to all-news radio and thinking the same thing over and over again."

"Which was what?" Lamp asked.

"That she'd brought out the evil beast in me in Trancas all those years ago, and now she'd brought it out again. But I told myself that I *had* to do what I did. I couldn't let her tell the whole world about what had happened between us. Couldn't let her drag Enid and Junior through the mud because I'd committed an unspeakable act that summer. It would destroy them. When the story broke on my car radio about Nikki's body being found, I called home from a phone booth in the McDonald's parking lot and left Enid a message on our machine." He paused for a moment, gazing down at his big hands. "I'm sorry that Rory got caught in the middle of it. That dumb slob is dead because of me. Dead because God is punishing me. That's why I've decided to put it all down on paper. Clear my conscience, or at least try. I know that I never, ever will."

"Did Enid ever suspect anything about you and Nikki?" Lamp asked.

"Enid would never believe such a thing was even possible."

"So this is going to devastate her, isn't it?"

"Not necessarily. She has a very low opinion of men. Thinks we're craven beasts with our knuckles dragging on the ground. This will do nothing to disabuse her of that notion. It's Junior who will be crushed. He's always looked up to me. Now what'll he think? I imagine that once the dust settles they'll get as far from Southern California as they can and make a new life for themselves. She'll go back to using her maiden name." He reached for his pen and added one more sentence to the confession he'd been writing when we walked in. "I'm going to sign and date this now. You fellows can write that you've witnessed it and add your signatures to that effect. Then it's all yours, Lieutenant."

"All right," Lamp said. Even though Kenny's so-called confession in no way qualified as legally binding, if it would get him out of that chair, out the door, and into the back seat of his cruiser in handcuffs then Lamp was willing to play along. So he signed and dated it where Kenny had written, "Witnessed by."

Kenny thanked him and passed the pad to me. I also signed and dated it. Then he carefully tore the perforated pages from the legal pad, ten or twelve pages in all, opened the top drawer of his desk, fished around for a paper clip to bind them together and handed his confession across the desk to Lamp.

Lamp took it from him. "I'll have to ask you to come with us now."

"Of course. I'll be happy to. Relieved, actually," Kenny said before he reached inside the desk drawer again, pulled out a Beretta 9mm, and in one swift movement pressed it above his right ear and blew his brains out.

Lulu let out a whimper and approached my chair, nosing my fingers as I stared at what once been a man named Kenny Dymtryk. I stroked her gently and said, "It's okay, girl. We're okay."

Enid came running at the sound of the shot, threw open the door, and saw him there slumped over in his chair, gun in hand, his eyes wide open, blood and brain matter pouring down his neck and drip, drip, dripping onto the polished oak floor. She didn't move. Didn't speak. Didn't blink.

"You shouldn't be in here, Mrs. Dymtryk," Lamp said in as calm a voice as he could muster.

"Yes, I should," she said. "I don't believe in turning a blind eye to anything. What's that document you're holding, Lieutenant?"

"Your husband's confession letter. It was he who killed Nikki."

"Did he confess as to why?"

"Yes, he did, and I'm afraid it will be very hurtful to you."

"Don't let that concern you. I'm accustomed to pain."

"I need to make some phone calls, ma'am. Is there a phone in another room that I can use?"

"There's one in the kitchen."

"When does Junior get home?" I asked her.

"Not for another two hours. He has basketball practice."

"Good," Lamp said. "Then he won't have to see this."

"Yes, he's better off not seeing it," Enid said quietly. "I don't want this to be his memory of the last time that he saw his father."

CHAPTER EIGHT

"Uncle Kenny was a total LIAR!" Lisa exploded at me as she stood at her drawing table before an array of fabric swatches, all of which looked to be the exact same shade of orange, but apparently weren't. She'd ditched her filthy *bleu de travail* for a baggy black smock and equally baggy pair of white house-painter's pants. "Aunt Enid knew everything that he did to Nikki. She's *always* known!"

"And why do you say that?"

"Why do I say it?" Lisa gazed out the window at her hilltop view of the San Fernando Valley before her eyes returned to me. "Because I know plenty of things myself, that's why."

I'd brought her BMW home at Lamp's urging. He would be stuck in Pasadena dealing with the forensics team and coroner for hours, he'd told me when he led Lulu and me toward the front door. Enid was seated in the parlor with her hands folded in her lap, lost in her thoughts and prayers as numerous large men began tromping in and out of her historic home.

I tried to think of something to say to her but couldn't come up with anything that didn't sound feeble and mealy mouthed, so instead I asked her about something that had been bothering me. "Why wouldn't you let Lulu sniff your trousers when you were sitting on the sofa next to Kenny?"

She gazed up at me blankly for a long moment before she said, "I'm sorry, what . . . ?"

"When we were up at the house after Nikki's murder. You bopped Lulu on the nose with your leg. Hard."

Enid exhaled slowly. "Oh, that. They were light tan trousers and Lulu's nose was very wet and had been God knows where. I was afraid she might stain them. I abhor stains. Always have."

"I understand. Thank you."

And with that Enid retreated back into her thoughts and prayers.

"I'll catch up with you on Hazen when I'm done here," Lamp said to me as we stood in the driveway next to Lisa's car. "Give you a lift to the airport, okay?"

"Okay," I said quietly. Lulu stood with her head against my leg. She hadn't strayed more than three inches from me since Kenny had shot himself.

"I finally got through to Jack on the phone and told him what's happened," Lamp informed me. "He and Pam are in seclusion at the Beverly Wilshire and had ordered the front desk to block all calls. It took some serious convincing that I was a genuine homicide detective and not a tabloid reporter."

"How did he sound?"

"Shattered. In total disbelief."

"I take it that means you shared the contents of Kenny's confession with him."

"I did. He asked me to be as discreet as humanly possible with the media. I assured him I would be. You'll probably run into him up at the house. When I offered to inform Rita about it, Jack said he'd prefer to tell her himself—which was fine by me. Not my favorite part of the job."

"Do you actually have a favorite part of your job?"

"Hoagy, at this particular moment I can't think of one."

And now I stood with Lisa in her workroom, Lulu continuing to stay close to me. We were alone on the second floor. Mona had cleaned out her office and left last night.

"Care to talk about them, Lisa?"

"Talk about *what*?"

"The plenty of things that you know about."

"Just for starters," she said to me, her jaw clenching and unclenching, "I know that Uncle Kenny tried to molest *me* two summers before he scored with Nikki, when *I* was the one who was fourteen."

I drew in my breath, but stayed silent. She was talking, I was listening.

"Nikki was barely twelve then," Lisa went on. "I wasn't nearly as eye-popping in a bikini as she was, although I was a lot thinner than I am now. But looks really didn't seem to matter to Uncle Kenny. All that mattered was that my parents were in Hawaii for two weeks, my Aunt Enid and Junior were visiting her mother in Pennsylvania, and he had me all to himself one night on the beach. Nikki had gone to bed after the three of us made a fire in the pit and gorged ourselves on s'mores. He and I sat there on the sand, gazing up at the stars, listening to the surf. We talked about how much we loved the peacefulness of the beach. I genuinely liked him. He was nice to me. Never talked down to me like I was a stupid girl. And then he . . . he suddenly *fell* on me like a giant tree, dug his knees between my legs and his hands were all over me and he was kissing me and—and breathing really hard. It all happened so fast that it took me a moment to realize that he was about to *rape* me."

"What did you do?"

"Fought him," she recalled in a determined voice. "I kicked him. I punched him. None of which stopped him. He was so big and strong, and I wasn't. But when he tried to tear my bathing suit off, I bit him on the hand. Hard. I mean, I sank my teeth into him deep enough to draw blood. He let out an angry cry of pain before he went running into the house to stop the bleeding. I ran inside and locked myself in my room, sobbing and gasping. All that slamming around woke Nikki up. She called to me through the wall to ask if everything was okay. I said everything was fine and told her to go back to sleep."

"What did Kenny say to you the next day?"

"Not a word. It was as if it had never happened. I could almost have believed I'd imagined it—if he didn't have that bandage around his hand."

"Did Nikki ask him about it?"

"She did. He told her he'd gone for a walk on the beach at dawn and encountered someone with a rambunctious young Golden Retriever that had bit him. It had its rabies tags and everything, and the owner was incredibly apologetic. He said it was no big deal."

"Did you say anything to your Aunt Enid about it when she got back from Pennsylvania?"

"You bet I did," Lisa recalled angrily.

"And . . . ?"

"Enid accused me of making up stories. I said, 'Oh, yeah? Did I make up *these*?' And I showed her the bruises all over the inside of my thighs from his knees. She got real angry at me and said, 'Just because you slipped on the rocks when you were climbing around and bruised yourself is no reason to tell vicious lies about your uncle. I want you to stop this at once.'" Lisa let out a sigh of disgust. "Aunt Enid knew perfectly well that I wouldn't make up a story like that. But she refused to believe that the man she loved, the father of her son, had tried to rape his own fourteen-year-old niece. She wouldn't listen to another word about it. And that was the end of it, aside from the part that I've never, ever been the same person since then."

"How do you mean?"

Lisa lowered her eyes to the swatches on her worktable. "I used to like boys. I was friends with boys at school. I thought I'd start having boyfriends soon. Eventually, if I was lucky, fall in love with someone, get married, have kids, all the things that I thought of as what a normal . . ." She trailed off, swallowing. "But after that I couldn't stand to be touched by a guy. I still can't. The mere thought of it makes me shudder all over. So I keep gorging myself on candy bars just to make sure I'm as undesirable as possible. I'm a twenty-six-year-old virgin because of what Uncle Kenny did to me that night. I have men friends from Otis who I'm cool with, but that's strictly because they're gay." She studied me. "But you're not, are you?"

"No, I'm not."

"That's strange, because you don't terrify me. You're nice."

"Thank you. For what it's worth, I think you're nice, too."

"Uncle Kenny wasn't. He was evil, because he wasn't done. He was just waiting for another chance. And he got it two summers later when Mom and Dad went to France. He was much more calculating with Nikki. Worked his way up to it, slowly and carefully. He had plenty of time because Enid was staying more and more in Pasadena with Junior. She couldn't stand to be around Nikki, who'd become *Nikki*."

"As in . . . ?"

"Wild, headstrong. Plus she was super bitchy to Enid. They hated each other so much that Enid had to get away from her, which played right into Kenny's hands. He flattered Nikki. Went for walks on the beach with her. Waited patiently until he was convinced she'd be receptive to his advances."

"Which, I take it, she was."

"Totally. It wasn't long before I was in bed late one night and heard them come sneaking into the house, giggling and shushing each other. I got out of bed and asked her where she'd been. She stood there in her bedroom doorway all sweaty, her lips bruised and swollen, a silly grin on her face. She just laughed at me like I was clueless and said, 'Go back to bed.' The two of them carried on all summer. He *awakened* Nikki sexually. She wanted him day and night. Would plop down in his lap when he was sitting on a lounge chair, wriggle around and get him all hot. He'd suddenly say he had to drive to Malibu to pick up something at the hardware store, and Nikki would say, 'I'll go with you.' Which was not like her at all. Run an errand with her boring old uncle? No way. But off they'd go together and they'd be gone for, like, two hours. I figured they'd probably found some deserted canyon road where'd they'd pull over and have sex in the back seat of his car."

"How did they act when Enid would come back out?"

"She'll totally deny it, but Enid was positive that something was up between them. One day, the two of them were horsing around in the kitchen, giving each other playful little shoves. Enid stood there real stiffly on the deck watching them, and said to me, 'Why do I feel as if I'm in the way here?'"

"She *said* that to you?"

"She did. My uncle was a sexual predator, Hoagy. He belonged in jail. Instead, he and Nikki continued to get it on all summer. And Enid continued to come up with excuses for staying in Pasadena. She didn't want to believe that her beloved husband was fucking his own niece. Until he wasn't anymore, that is. When our folks came home from France, Kenny dumped her. He didn't have the nerve to tell her to her face. Just left her a note and a pearl necklace."

"So you know about the pearls."

"Of course I know. She sat there on her bed with that necklace in her hands and wept and wept. I honestly think she believed that she and Uncle Kenny were in love. It was truly sadistic what he did to her. She was *fourteen*."

"What about your parents? Did you say anything to them about it?"

"No, strictly because Nikki begged me not to. She was my kid sister, and I loved her, so I kept my mouth shut. I'd never said anything to them about what he'd done to me either. I didn't want to talk about it. It just brought it all back and made me want to throw up. Besides, there was no point. Uncle Kenny was my dad's straight-arrow kid brother. He would have flatly denied it, my dad would have believed him, and that would have been the end of it." Lisa opened her candy-bar jar, grabbed a Snickers bar, tore the wrapper off, and took a bite out of it. "I don't come from a normal family, in case you haven't figured that out."

"There are no normal families. That's a fantasy manufactured by Mr. Walt Disney. Lisa, I'm curious about something. When I visited you in here after Nikki's murder, you were all disheveled and sweaty. Your feet were dirty and scratched up. How come?"

"I totally freaked out when I heard what had happened to Nikki. Had to get out of here. Just had to. So I ran out into the backyard and down the hill into the wild-sage brush until I was far enough away from the house that I could scream at the top of my lungs and no one would hear me."

"Kenny managed your business affairs," I said, glancing over at the rack of clothing she'd designed for Nikki. "You worked together even though you despised him. How did you . . . ?"

"I worked for Nikki, not Uncle Kenny," she said heatedly.

"What will you do with yourself now that she's gone?"

"Keep designing. It's the only thing I know how to do. Maybe a name designer will take me on."

"*You're* a name designer."

"Nikki was the name, not me."

"I'm going back to New York today—which reminds me, here are your car keys." As I set them on the worktable, I reached for a piece of paper and a red pencil. "I'm going to give you my phone number there. Also my address. Call me, write me. I want to know how you're doing."

Lisa watched me scribble down my contact info and tack it to her cork wall. "Why do you want to know how I'm doing?"

"Because I like you. And if you ever have any business that brings you to New York I'll take you to dinner, okay?"

"Okay. I mean, if you want. But you have to promise me something."

"What is it?"

"That you won't ever tell anyone what I just told you about why I'm the way I am. Any of it. Not one word."

"Okay, I promise."

Lulu ambled over and nudged her leg. Lisa smiled down at her, patted her. "Bye, sweetie. I'm going to miss you."

"Lisa, why did Nikki keep Kenny's letter and pearl necklace under the floorboard of her closet in Trancas?"

"They really meant something to her, I guess. He *was* her first, after all. Plus she knew if she brought the necklace home Mom would find it. Mom always used to go through our drawers."

"So is that why you said that to me last night?"

She frowned. "Said what?"

"You said, *'Trancas is the bumpy road to hell.'* That's the reason why I went out there this morning."

Lisa's eyes widened at me in surprise. "Did I?"

"Yes."

"That's strange." Her gaze returned to the window and her hilltop view of the Valley. "I don't remember saying that."

Jack and Pam had arrived by the time I returned downstairs. They were seated on the living-room sofa with Rita, who was clutching a glass of Scotch in both hands and looking emotionally wrung out and very drunk. Those Eurasian eyes that her plastic surgeon had left her with seemed to go in and out of focus. George, her so-called husband, was sitting alone out by the pool in a lounge chair with his arms crossed in front of his chest.

When Jack saw me approaching, he sprang to his feet, threw his arms around me, and cried, "He was my baby brother, Hoagy. And Nikki was my baby girl. I was supposed to look out for her. I failed her. I failed them both."

"No, you didn't, Jack," I said. "It's not your fault."

"He's right, darling," Pam said soothingly as Lulu climbed up onto the sofa and curled up in her lap. Lulu had a major crush on Pam, who stroked her gently. "Don't blame yourself."

Jack released his hold on me, tears streaming down his face. "How did I let this happen, Rita? How did I not know what he did to our little girl? *How?*"

Rita took a belt of her Scotch. "Because he fooled you, that's how! You thought he was a decent man. He wasn't. He was a *monster!* Nikki was a good kid before he got his beefy, disgusting hands on her. Smart-mouthed and wild, sure, but no different than most of these rich, spoiled girls around here. *He* started her down the road to becoming Nikki the tabloid slut. Nikki who had sex with rap-music stars. Nikki who posed naked with oil all over her—"

"He was my baby brother," Jack protested, wiping his eyes. "We grew up in the same bedroom. And now he's gone."

"Because he was too much of a coward to stand trial!" Rita took another belt of her Scotch, glaring at her ex-husband. "Are you honestly telling me you never knew about what he did to her?"

"Never! How *dare* you even suggest that?" Jack demanded.

It suddenly hit me that if I had to listen to one more second of their squabbling I was going to lose it, so I went outside to talk to George. Lulu stayed put with Pam. After the horrifying scene she'd witnessed in Kenny's study, some extra cuddling was definitely called for.

George was still stretched out in that lounge chair with his arms crossed, lost in thought.

"How are you holding up?" I asked him.

He turned his big, blocky head to look at me as I sat down in the lounge chair next to him. "I'm okay," he answered in that deep-chested anchorman's voice of his. "Thanks for asking. No one else has. I didn't know a thing about Rory's past, I swear. Why he left Fresno or Texas or any of it. And I still call him Rory, even if that wasn't his real name. I'm waiting for the LAPD to release his body so that I can arrange a proper burial. Apparently, there's still some question about whether his remains ought to be sent back to Texas. Depends on whether he still has family in the state, which it seems no one in authority there wants to bother finding out. It's frustrating. I'd like to be done with it. I need to pack up and start looking for a new place to live."

"Understandable."

"But I still have my job at the station. I like working there, and everyone's been real nice and supportive." George fell silent for a moment. "I'll be okay."

"Sure you will."

I heard a car pull into the driveway. A moment later the doorbell rang. Then I heard voices. One of them was Jack's. The other belonged to Lieutenant Lamp, who was giving his solemn condolences as I made my way back inside.

"Ah, there you are," he said to me. "Ready to head to the airport?"

"You've got an awful lot on your plate, Lieutenant. I can catch a cab."

"Nonsense. I'm giving you and Lulu a lift."

"Okay, you talked us into it."

Jack's brow furrowed. "You're heading back to New York so soon?" He'd lost a daughter and his brother in the past twenty-four hours. Even the likes of the first major new literary voice of the 1980s skipping town seemed to pain him.

"There's no project, Jack, so there's no reason for me to be here. But thank you for the opportunity. Nikki and I had a chance to spend some quality time together and I'm grateful I got to know her. She was a special person."

"Special," he repeated faintly. "I enjoyed your company, Hoagy."

Pam smiled at me from the sofa. "So did I. And *you* are a doll," she said to Lulu, who was still snuggled comfortably in her lap. "I just may have to get a Lulu of my own now."

"You can try," I said. "There are plenty of bassets out there. But there's only one Lulu."

"Mr. Dmytryk . . ." Lamp adopted a more official voice. "I wanted to tell you in person that the department feels there's no need for any link to be drawn between the contents of your brother's written confession and Nikki's murder. In fact, his confession will never be made public. As far as the LAPD is concerned, the man who we knew as Rory Krieger was responsible for her death. He'd been convicted in Texas of a violent felony. He fled the scene of the crime yesterday and engaged the department in a horrific high-speed chase. The man was clearly no good. Kenny, on the other hand, was a respected member of a prominent entertainment-industry family. So the department's preference is to simply let it be."

"Are you trying to tell us that you're going to let him get away with her murder?" Rita demanded furiously.

"I wouldn't put it that way, ma'am. He *is* dead, after all. A form of justice was served. Perhaps not the form you would have chosen, but what's to be gained by pursuing it any further—other than dragging your whole family through a painful ordeal?"

Jack considered this, nodding his head slightly. "What reason will you give the media for Kenny's suicide?"

"Enid will confirm that he'd been suffering from depression recently. He even failed to show up for an important business meeting with a major rock star the day of Nikki's death. His grief over her murder was, apparently, just too much for him to handle."

Jack ran his hand over his hair. "Thank you for your consideration, Lieutenant. I can see why you're entrusted with the job that you hold."

"Just doing what they pay me to do," Lamp said, glancing at me. "Ready to hit the road?"

Lulu gave Pam a good-bye lick on the nose, climbed down from the sofa, and ambled her way toward the front door as I shook hands with Jack.

"I hope our paths cross again," he said to me. "I'll take you surfing."

"I'd like that."

Lamp and I carried my bags out the front door, deposited them in the back seat of his cruiser, and got in. Lulu sat between us, her tail thumping. He started his engine and eased down the driveway. As we neared the gate, it swung open and we headed down Hazen, slowing as we drove past Pam and Jack's house. There were three black-and-whites stationed there to keep the show-biz ghouls away. Not that they actually could. They could merely try to maintain order as one car after another arrived at the house where Nikki had had her skull smashed in. Already, the bouquets of flowers, framed photographs, and other tokens of love and devotion were starting to form a mountainous shrine in the driveway. Some fans were taking pictures of each other standing in front of the house. Others were hugging each other and crying.

"I'll never understand these people," Lamp said as we drove by. "They show up every time I work a celebrity death. Are they nutso or what?"

"Or what. They lead empty lives. People like Nikki help to fill them. She wasn't a flesh-and-blood loved one. Just someone who they saw on TV. But their sense of loss is no less real to them. We live in a genuinely sick society, in case you haven't noticed."

"Oh, I have, believe me."

I glanced over at him as he drove past the Julie Christie *Shampoo* house on Bowmont. "So tell it to me the way you didn't tell it to them. Is the department really going to bury what happened?"

Lamp made the sharp right onto Cherokee and went down the steep hill to Coldwater, where he hit a red light. When it turned green, he made a left and started his way toward Sunset. "That was a bit of a white lie. The department doesn't know squat about Kenny Dymtryk's confession letter. No one but the two of us and the family do. His confession is currently in my possession and will disappear into my safe-deposit box tomorrow. My conscience won't allow me to destroy it. But the gist of what I told them is true. Absolutely nothing good will come from the public finding out about what he did to Nikki. It'll be better for Enid and Junior, whose lives would be permanently stained. Better for Jack, Rita, and Lisa. Better all around. There are times when it's more important to protect the interests of the survivors than the victims. So I say let the public believe that the man who we called Rory Krieger smashed Nikki's skull in. Heck, if that high-speed chase didn't reek of guilt then I don't know what does. We've got three people dead. The circle is closed. I'm closing it. And I've spoken to the Texas AG's office, by the way. They have zero interest in expending resources to transport Rory's charred remains home to Texas. So he's all ours."

"George is willing to see to his burial. Anxious to, actually."

"Good to know. I'll have the coroner's office contact him."

After we made it down to Sunset, Lamp turned right and sped past the Bel Air gate and northern edge of the UCLA campus to the San Diego Freeway, where he got on, heading south. As in back toward LAX. As in home.

I studied him as he drove, his hands at the ten-and-two position. "You've changed since the last time we met. You used to be strictly by the book."

"I've discovered something since then, Hoagy. There is no book. Just a code that I can live and work by that doesn't keep me awake at night wondering if I should hand in my shield and get a real-estate license."

"You're growing up, Lieutenant. I'm kind of proud of you."

"Are you busting my chops?"

"No, I'm perfectly serious. You're no longer a Boy Scout."

"Have to disagree with you there. I'm still a Boy Scout. If I weren't, I'd sell that pearl necklace and put the money toward buying myself a nice piece of beachfront land down in Ensenada. I'm simply doing what I think is best for everyone concerned." He shot a quick look at me. "What about you?"

"What about me?"

"Have you told me everything you know?"

"I've told you everything I can."

"What in the holy heck does that mean?"

"It means I was told something in the strictest confidence that has no direct bearing on this case or your handling of it."

"Now you're getting cagy with me."

"I don't mean to. I just made a promise, that's all."

"To whom?"

"That would be telling."

We rode in silence for a while as he steered us through the sluggish traffic toward the airport. I stared out my window, thinking I'd spent more than half of my waking hours since I'd arrived in Los Angeles on one freeway or another.

"Just out of curiosity, Lieutenant, what *will* you do with Nikki's pearl necklace and Kenny's love letter?"

"I've been giving that a lot of thought."

"I'll bet you have. And . . . ?"

"I'm going to drive up to Trancas right after I drop you at LAX and return them to that hiding place in the floor of Nikki's closet where she'd put them—until Lulu found them." He patted her on the head and got a low whoop in return. "It's what Nikki would have wanted, don't you think?"

"I do. Seems like the decent thing to do."

"The *decent* thing to do," he said with a slight edge in his voice. "There are so many Kenny Dymtryks out there who think of themselves as *decent* family men. And yet, time and again on this job, I've found out it's a total sham. Every single person on this case told me Kenny was the 'good' brother growing up. A jock who busted ass so he could get into Dartmouth on an academic scholarship. He didn't chase girls. Didn't get high. It was Jack who was the party animal and surf bum. But it was Kenny—solid, steady, *decent* Kenny—who ended up totally losing control of himself. That's the part I can't wrap my mind around. Have you got any words of wisdom for me?"

"Well, just for starters, Kenny never watched *Rocky and Bullwinkle* when he was growing up, which should have told me something from the get-go if I'd been paying closer attention."

"Like what?"

"That he grew up with an absence of comic lunacy in his life. Why, I'll bet he didn't even read a single issue of *Cracked* magazine."

"That's it? That's all you've got for me?"

"No, there's more, although I doubt they're words of wisdom. But if he hadn't clamped down so hard on himself, had cut loose like Jack did, then I don't think this would have happened. I've always believed that it's the people who repress their wild urges when they're young—don't hitchhike through Europe for a year with no idea where their next ride will take them—that are the ones who erupt like volcanoes when they reach middle age. Someday I ought to write a book about it."

"Hey, maybe that's the germ of your second novel."

And, strangely enough, it turned out that it was. But I would wander around lost in the woods for another four years before I realized it.

Lamp got off the freeway when we reached LAX and circled his way around the huge airport until he arrived at my terminal and pulled up at the curb. "It was good to see you again, Hoagy." He gave me a firm, dry handshake. "Maybe next time it will be under happier circumstances."

"You don't really believe that, do you?"

He let out a laugh. "I guess not. Lulu, I sure am going to miss you," he confessed, patting her.

She climbed up on his chest and licked his face. She was very fond of Lamp. Her life was never dull when he was around.

We got out and I fetched my bags from the back seat. Then I waved good-bye and he drove off.

Our flight to JFK would begin boarding in three hours. I handed over my return tickets and suitcase, got our boarding passes, and then found the Commodore Club, or whatever the hell that particular airline called it. I was still a member from my sunshine days when I was constantly flying around the country to appear on TV talk shows or give guest lectures at major universities. My publisher had paid for the membership and forgotten to terminate it, so my key card still worked when I stuck it in the slot next to the door, which swung open and ushered us into carpeted, elegantly lit luxury.

I ordered a Macallan at the bar, and a shrimp cocktail for Lulu, and sat there enjoying the solitude and silence—which lasted a solid thirty seconds before a hushed voice came over the intercom and asked for Mr. Stewart Hoag to please come to the reception desk. Right away, I was filled with dread that Jack had tracked me down through Lamp and that I was about to get pulled back into the Dymtryk family horror show.

"I'm Stewart Hoag," I said to the young woman at the reception desk.

"I have a call for you, sir," she said with bland politeness. "You can take it at that desk in the corner over by the window."

I thanked her and sat down at the desk in the corner over by the window, picked it up, and said, "This is Stewart Hoag."

Briefly, I heard nothing but silence, then a bit of fuzz on the line before Merilee said, "Thank God I found you, darling. The concierge at the Four Seasons told me which airline you were on and I hoped and prayed you still had your key card. I so desperately needed to hear your voice."

"It's good to hear your voice, too, Merilee," I said as Lulu ambled over and let out a low whoop, plenty happy to hear her mommy's voice herself.

"Is that my sweetness I'm hearing?"

"None other. How's London?"

"We'll get to that in a minute, mister. Rob's office called him with the news about Kenny Dymtryk blowing his brains out."

"Oh, that."

"Yes, that. Please tell me you weren't there when he did it."

"I wish that I could, Merilee."

"It must have been awful."

"It wasn't pretty."

"I should never have left you there," she said fretfully.

"Don't be silly. You couldn't have done anything to stop it."

"But I'd be there for you now. You're all alone."

"No, I'm not. I have Lulu. Mind you, she's had a tough couple of days herself."

"Why on earth did he do it, Hoagy? Nikki's killer had already died in that horrendous car crash. It doesn't make any sense."

"You're right, it doesn't. No sense at all."

Merilee fell silent for a moment. "There's more to this that you aren't telling me, isn't there?"

"Yes."

"Do tell."

"Can't. I promised I wouldn't say a word to anyone."

"Not even me?"

"Not even you. I'm sworn to secrecy. Now tell me about Jeremy Irons. How are the readings going?"

"Amazingly well. He's not playing Smithy the way Ronald Coleman did at all. He's behaving more . . ."

"More like Billy Crystal?"

"How did I know you were going to say that?"

"Face it, you would have been disappointed if I hadn't."

"Jeremy is highly emotional about Smithy's amnesia and stammer. He's *angry*, in that understated British way. It creates a whole new dynamic for me to play off. Plus he's such a talented actor. We're both incredibly excited. And so is Rob."

"That's wonderful. I'm glad. How long will you be there?"

"Just another day or so. Then he'll join us in New York in a couple of weeks as we'd originally planned. It's nearly three A.M. here. We've done nothing but work since we landed and I'm totally exhausted, but I needed to hear your voice before I could get to sleep. So I'm going to hang up now, darling. I was so sorry I had to leave you. I was enjoying us being *us* again. I . . . wasn't expecting that to happen."

"Nor was I, believe me."

"I suppose it was something we both needed."

"I sure did. For a brief window in time you made me feel like my old self again. I can't begin to tell you how much that meant to me. You'll call me when you get back to New York?"

"That's a promise. And I haven't forgotten that I still owe you that dinner at the Blue Mill."

"Extra mashed potatoes?"

"Extra mashed potatoes."

"Get some sleep, Merilee."

"Yes, I think I'll be able to sleep now. Have a safe flight home, darling."

"You, too. Sleep tight."

I hung up the phone and sat there for a moment, my chest feeling heavy. Lulu whimpered at my feet. I told her to shut up. She shut up.

CHAPTER NINE

I did warn you from the start that I was about to share the most sordid show-business experience I've ever encountered in my career as a celebrity ghostwriter. I also told you that I've kept it to myself because I promised someone that I would. That someone, as you now know, was Lisa Dymtryk.

Lisa didn't write or call me after I got back home to New York. I hadn't expected that she would. Hadn't expected I'd hear from her ever again. So I was genuinely surprised when a letter from her showed up at my crummy old, unheated fifth-floor walk-up on West Ninety-Third Street almost exactly five years later—on January 17, 1994, for

those of you who are into the precision thing. Her handwriting on the envelope, which was postmarked Montecito, California, had an artist's flourish to it. And she'd
used a fountain pen.

A lot had happened in my life during those five years.
Merilee and I were making a go of it again. Lulu and I
were back living in the sixteenth-floor luxury pre-war
building on Central Park West that we'd once called home.
Mind you, I'd kept my old place in case everything turned
to shit again. But so far we were getting along great. The
remake of *Random Harvest* was a huge critical and com-
mercial success. Merilee brought so much freshness to the
role of Paula that she was nominated for her third Best
Actress Oscar. She didn't win, but she already has one on
her mantle to go along with her two Tonys. How many
trophies does a person need?

As for me, I was at long last making huge strides on
my second novel, *A Sweet Season of Madness*. When I gave
Alberta the first 250 pages to read, she pronounced them
"thrilling" and promptly sold my manuscript-in-progress
to a top publisher for major bucks. I was waking up early
every day now, my fingers tingling, and writing my ass
off in the guest bedroom that Merilee had converted into
an office for me. I had absolutely no idea how many pages
were still left to write, because I had absolutely no idea

from one day to the next where the story was going. It was simply flowing through me and telling me where it wanted to go.

That's the joy of writing. It's what I live for.

I hadn't thought about the Dymtryk family for a long time, I realized, as I carried Lisa's letter up the five flights of stairs to my apartment, Lulu huffing and puffing alongside me, and unlocked the door. When I opened the door, I discovered, to my complete lack of surprise, that it wasn't much warmer in there than it had been outside, so I kept my shearling coat on as I gave Lulu an anchovy and slit Lisa's envelope open with Grandfather's silver letter opener. Then I sat down in my one good chair to read what she had to say, Lulu curling up in my lap for warmth.

> *Dear Hoagy—You told me to write you if I ever had anything to say. I know it's been a long time, but I finally do have something to say.*
>
> *By the time you read this letter I'll be dead.*
>
> *Hoagy, I just can't stand the pain anymore. Uncle Kenny didn't just kill Nikki and himself. He killed me, too. I've been dead inside since that night he attacked me when I was fourteen. God, how I wish I could be as strong a person as Nikki was, but I'm not. I've been frightened and lost since the day she*

died. I got all sorts of amazing offers to work with famous designers, but I turned them all down. Without Nikki to design for I lost my desire to do the one thing I loved to do. My friends from Otis keep trying to urge me on. But it's no use. I'm empty.

You understand what I mean, don't you? You're the one person I can think of who would. I remember you wrote a celebrated first novel when you were young, then had no idea for a second novel and self-destructed. When you and I met, you were in the process of trying to rebuild yourself. I admired your courage. I wish I had that kind of courage, same as I wish I had Nikki's strength. But I don't.

Can I tell you something? When I met you, I desperately wanted to be normal when it comes to men. You were so smart and funny. Good-looking, too. I thought it would have been so cool to spend time with you, if only I was normal. But I'm not normal and I never will be. Not after what Uncle Kenny tried to do to me. I still can't stand to be touched. I'm now a thirty-one-year-old virgin, in case you're keeping track at home.

Speaking of homes, we sold the house on Hazen not long after Uncle Kenny murdered Nikki and shot himself. The family's business empire was dismantled and the assets were distributed to each of us. I came away with many millions, most of which I donated to Otis, which gave me my training and is always in need of money. I kept a couple of million to live on and also bought myself a small, Spanish-style cottage from the 1920s high up in the hills of Montecito, near Santa Barbara. I think it was once the caretaker's cottage of a giant estate that a movie mogul built back in the silent-film days. I have a wonderful view of the ocean. Mostly, I sit in my garden, gaze out at the ocean, and wish that I was someone else. I have no friends here. No one to talk to. I had a stray cat for a while but she wandered off and never came back.

My mom is trying yet again to dry out at a very exclusive clinic for rich alcoholics not far from here in the Santa Ynez Valley. She isn't allowed to have visitors, which is just as well because I have no desire to visit her. My dad, as you probably read, divorced Pam and married an actress in her twenties named Cricket who he thinks is going to be a big star. Being honest, I don't think he's ever gotten over losing Nikki and Uncle Kenny. He seems pathetic and lost, kind of like a shell of the man who he used to be. Pam sold the house where Nikki died and bought a place in Brentwood. Her prime-time soap opera, Mill Valley, *is now in its eighth season and still going strong. And she's engaged to a successful sitcom producer named Mel who couldn't be more different from my dad. He's short, bald, roly-poly, and very funny. I seem to remember that her dad was a comedy writer. I guess Mel makes her feel safe. I'm happy for her. My Aunt Enid sold that huge mansion in Pasadena and she and Junior moved somewhere back east. I have no idea where. Don't know. Don't care.*

Hoagy, I've never forgotten how nice you were to me when you were staying with us. You treated me like a normal person instead of a weirdo. I still remember the way you let me just charge right into your room and go rummaging through your wardrobe. You gave me all sorts of amazing suggestions for how to dress Nikki for her book tour. You even told me that when Nikki was autographing books she should use a Waterman fountain pen. That's what I'm using right now. Can you tell?

Just to make sure that this letter gets to you I'm going to put it out for the postman to pick up tomorrow morning. Then I'm going to sit here in the backyard, gaze out at the ocean, and watch my very last sunset before I swallow an entire bottle of Seconal and wash it down with a pint of Cuervo

Gold, which was Nikki's favorite tequila. Not to worry. The gardener will come tomorrow morning and find my body before it becomes a rotting corpse. I've left instructions that I want to be cremated. No funeral or anything. So not to worry about any of that.

I guess in my own weird way I fell in love with you, which is why I wanted to write and say good-bye. I'm not writing anyone else. Just you. I wish you nothing but the best with Merilee and with your next novel. I'm positive you'll write another one, and I know it'll be great. I'm sorry I won't be around to read it. Please give Lulu a good-bye tug on the ears for me, will you? She's a sweetie.

    —*Love, Lisa*

PS. You don't have to keep anything I said to you a secret anymore. I don't care who knows what really happened.

I did tell you that my failed attempt to help Nikki Dym-tryk become a best-selling author of hip, spicy romance novels had cost four people their lives. It took five years but it was Lisa who ended up being the fourth victim.

And, because she gave me permission, I'm now able to share the whole, horrible truth of those days I spent in Los Angeles back in February of 1989. Horrible except for those wonderful hours I spent with Merilee in her suite at the Four Seasons.

In case you're wondering, Merilee made good on that promise to buy me dinner at the Blue Mill when she got back to New York from London. Liver, onions and bacon with extra mashed potatoes. And slowly, ever so slowly, we found our way back to each other. Me, I'm still convinced that the two of us would never have gotten back together again if we both hadn't been out in LA on business when Nikki was murdered by her Uncle Kenny, her first great love. *"My secret . . ."* It's a strange and unsettling thing to think about—that something so wonderful could come out of something so awful. But I genuinely believe that our love for each was rekindled by Nikki's death, and for that I will always be indebted to Nikki, even though I know it's a debt I can never, ever repay.

All that I can do is tip my fedora and say, "Thanks, cuz."